AUNTIE POLDI AND THE HANDSOME ANTONIO

AUNTIE POLDI AND THE HANDSOME ANTONIO

MARIO GIORDANO

Translated by John Brownjohn

THORNDIKE PRESS

A part of Gale, a Cengage Company

LIBRARY OF CONGRESS CIP DATA ON FILE.
CATALOGUING IN PUBLICATION FOR THIS BOOK
IS AVAILABLE FROM THE LIBRARY OF CONGRESS

ISBN-13: 978-1-4328-8116-0 (hardcover alk. paper)

Published in 2020 by arrangement with Houghton Mifflin Harcourt
Publishing Company

Printed in Mexico
Print Number: 01   Print Year: 2020

With love and gratitude for my friends Julia, Niels, Agnieszka, Cornelia, HaJo, Verena, Andrea, Antonie, Neithardt, Kirsten, Sahar, Evgenjia, Jörg, and Martina. And, of course, for you, Otti.

And you, Poldi.

Namaste!

1

Tells of the perils of intercultural communication, of men, fish cleavers, engine size and Poldi's past. Poldi is in something of a tight spot, Handsome Antonio gets noisy, Poldi's nephew burns some rubber, and Montana gets jealous again. And all because of John.

Handsome Antonio was sick of messing around. He held a fish cleaver to my Auntie Poldi's throat — it resembled a machete and could easily have bisected a mature tuna — and repeated his question.

"Where. Is. It?"

Whereupon my Auntie Poldi repeated her reply. "I've no idea what you're talking about, so put that in your pipe and smoke it!"

Which exemplifies the misunderstandings that were clogging the situation like limescale in a tap. The first one, of course, was lack of communication, because Handsome Antonio put his questions in strongly accented Sicilian Italian, whereas Poldi answered him in immaculate Bavarian German. Misunderstanding number two was the fact that Poldi hadn't a clue where "it" was. Handsome Antonio had hitherto rejected her asseverations to that effect by brandishing his cleaver and yelling, with the result that Poldi had dug in her heels and switched to Bavarian. From her point of view, what aggravated this extremely limited form of communication was misunderstanding number three: the tear-proof duct tape with which Handsome Antonio had secured her to a chair by her wrists and ankles. But the greatest misunderstanding, from my point of view, was . . . me. Like the crucial detail in a spot-the-error picture, I was sitting beside my aunt, secured to a chair likewise and almost wetting myself with terror. Expecting to bite the dust at any moment, I visualised my death as an amusing GIF animation looping endlessly on the internet: the cleaver whistling down, my panic-stricken face, the blade lopping off my head (like a knife through butter), the fountain of blood and finally the Great Light and some weird, plinky-plunky music.

I shouldn't be sitting here, I told myself

— no, I certainly shouldn't be sitting here. Nor should my Auntie Poldi, of course, but in her case this series of misunderstandings could justifiably be regarded as an occupational hazard. I, on the other hand, was merely the chronicler of her escapades and investigations. I was the nerdy author of a half-baked family saga, the untalented nephew devoid of a girlfriend or profession. What was the point of slicing me in half? Needless to say, though, this cut no ice with Handsome Antonio. To him, we were both in the same boat.

The unproductive to and fro between my aunt and Handsome Antonio had bred a certain irascibility on both sides — one that was steadily eroding my hopes of a favourable outcome for the situation; they were in fact nearing zero. However, all of Antonio's threats seemed to trickle off my Auntie Poldi like beads of condensation off a freshly pulled tankard of beer. This was because, unlike me, she had the knack for switching to a belligerent mode that inoculated her against all kinds of everyday tribulations and fears of failure and the future. Admittedly, she could have looked better. Squinting sideways at her, I saw that her camouflage-pattern trouser suit was torn in several places. Her Nefertiti make-up was smudged after our strenuous crawl through the undergrowth, and a small graze was reddening on her forehead. She was still wearing her wig, but this had also suffered quite a bit on our trek; it was dishevelled and partially disintegrating. Although she didn't look her sixty years as a rule, your age tends to show when you're tied to a chair with your wig mussed up and your mascara smudged. That makes it hard to preserve a *bella figura.* I felt momentarily relieved that Vito Montana, the grumpy, chain-smoking, jealous commissario of police, Poldi's light of love and — according to her — a sexual force of nature, couldn't see her in that state, although Montana's presence would have signalled a welcome turn of events. Why? Because my Auntie Poldi and I were in a really tight spot.

"Go on, Poldi, tell him!" I hissed.

"I'm not telling him a thing, the jerk!"

Handsome Antonio now changed his interrogation tactic: he gave up on Poldi and applied the cleaver to my throat instead.

"Poldi!" I whimpered.

"Take it easy, my boy! If I tell him, he'll kill us anyway, you know that, don't you, so calm down, you hear? I know his sort. He's a typical *leone di cancello,* a textbook example of a paper tiger. Big mouth but no balls. Besides, Death hasn't turned up with his clipboard yet, so relax."

"Where. Is. It?"

"I'venoideaI'mjustthechauffeur!" I gasped in bad Italian.

"And a right wimp into the bargain!" said Poldi.

"Poldi, he's going to kill me!"

"Easy, sonny. Where there's a will, there's always a way."

I was nearing the end of my tether.

"Where is it?"

"I don't know," Poldi snapped, "and that's that. *Basta!*"

"I don't know either," I moaned. "I swear!"

"I'm going to kill both of you, starting with you!"

"No, I don't want to die, not yet!"

We were all yelling fit to bust: I squeaking in mortal terror, Poldi barking like a drill sergeant and Handsome Antonio bellowing like a maddened bull. He brandished the cleaver in my face and uttered obscene oaths involving genitalia, the Mother of God and unappetising sexual practices. And as he rampaged around in front of us, I saw something that finally robbed me of speech: my Auntie Poldi had taken on that look again. I refer to the slightly dreamy expression she assumed whenever she sighted a handsome traffic cop. Hard to grasp though I found it, she had taken a shine to Handsome Antonio.

Now it has to be said that Handsome Antonio was not undeserving of his sobriquet. He was an exceptionally handsome young man, even by Italian standards. The fine rib vest he wore with his jeans accentuated his muscular but not overly hairy chest, and his physiognomy, which would have captivated any Renaissance painter, could have been described as classical. His was a sensual face unblemished by any sign of mental acuity, and there was a hint of melancholy in his eyes whenever they weren't, as they were at this moment, blazing with histrionic rage. Even so, Handsome Antonio radiated a kind of — how shall I put it? — animal grace. More suited to the movies than the Mafia, he looked just the way I envisioned Barnaba, the hero of my half-baked family saga.

Animal grace notwithstanding, Antonio was still brandishing his cleaver in my face, and I was getting sick of it. I was sick of his ravings, sick of the hullabaloo, sick of anticipating sudden death and sick above all of my Auntie Poldi's salacious expression. It irked me that her mind dwelt on one thing

12

only — that she never passed up an opportunity to flirt. So Handsome Antonio was sick of messing around? *Benissimo,* so was I!

"That's enough!" I yelled. "*Basta!* Shut up! Pipe down, the two of you!"

Miraculously enough, silence fell at once.

Poldi stared at me in alarm. "What is it, my boy? Feeling all right?"

Struggling to regain my composure, I cobbled together my best Italian. "Look, let's find a solution to this problem that satisfies everyone, OK?"

"Like what?" Poldi said in German. "I'd be interested to know."

"Like some way of getting out of here alive."

"Don't get your knickers in a twist, sonny. Leave this to —"

"Shut up!" I turned to Handsome Antonio and, avoiding speaking in German so there would not be a fresh outburst, said in Italian, "On certain conditions, my aunt would be prepared to tell you where it is."

"Well, I'll be buggered. You've got a nerve!"

"Shut it, Poldi!"

"Hey, I'm still your aunt. I deserve some respect."

Handsome Antonio held the blade to my

13

throat again. "Fuck your conditions," he snarled. "Where is it?"

"It'll do you no good to kill us."

"I'll just kill you, then — very slowly. Your aunt'll spill the beans all right if I cut you into strips."

"You've seen what she's like. You honestly think that'd impress her?"

Handsome Antonio thought for a moment, a process that briefly crimped his harmonious features.

"Yes, I do."

"I ought to mention," I said, lowering my voice, "that she isn't quite, well, all there, know what I mean?"

"Whisperers are liars!" my aunt interjected loudly.

"She's gaga," I went on in an undertone. "Age, booze. I know her. She lives in cloud-cuckoo-land. Even if she told you something, you could never rely on it. It'd confuse her even more if you killed me. I'm the only one who can get her to talk."

"You're just her effing chauffeur."

"I'm her nephew and chronicler, chauffeur and booze destroyer, spiritual adviser and scapegoat, millstone and manager."

"Eh, what's that? Are you crazy?"

I did my best to ignore Poldi and look Antonio straight in the eye. "It's up to you,

14

Don Antonio."

Handsome Antonio's face clouded over again. He even knitted his brow in thought and paced up and down for a bit.

"Not bad, sonny, not bad at all," Poldi whispered in German. "You've obviously picked up some of my know-how. I told you, where there's a will, there's always a way."

"Oh, it's nothing," I said offhand.

But, secretly quite pleased with myself, I thought: *Yeah! Bingo! You cracked it! You're a cool dude, a wizard at empathetic negotiation.*

Handsome Antonio stared at us both with the huge blade dangling at his side. He was looking calm and relaxed.

"You're just messing me about," he said wearily. "You really don't know where it is." He pointed the cleaver at my aunt. "All right, shut your eyes."

And he took a big swing.

I always wake up at this point. It's like a bad film in which the protagonist has to overcome some trauma before he can save the world, his family, his dog and the United States — they always belong together somehow. We don't have to do all that, fortunately; we simply wake up from a nightmare and are happy to be still alive. Then I go down to the kitchen, drink a glass of water, take the first coffee of the day up to the roof terrace and feast my eyes on Etna and the sea. That has been my routine for the past few weeks. It's now the end of March, and I have to admit that in the interim, my dream gave my role in the above predicament a rather more heroic character than it actually possesses.

I've been living on my own at No. 29 Via Baronessa since the beginning of the month. I've cleaned the winter mildew from the corners and whitewashed the walls. I carry out minor repairs on the house, go shopping, water the plants, put out the rubbish, chat with Signora Anzalone from across the way and patronise Signor Bussacca's *tabacchi,* because I've recently taken up smoking. At nine every morning I consume a *granita mandorla-caffè* and a brioche in sad Signora Cocuzza's café bar. Sometimes I visit the aunts or hang out with my cousin Ciro. The rest of the time I write — or rather, spend the day typing a succession of sentences that I usually delete in the evening. I'm busy, in a manner of speaking.

But first things first.

In October last year, Poldi, who had become quite the amateur detective since she retired to Sicily from Germany, had just solved the Avola case. And that was when John appeared at the door like a ghost from the past. To be more precise, John Owenya, Poldi's Tanzanian husband.

My Auntie Poldi had told me very little about her Tanzania episode. As soon as it was mentioned she promptly changed the subject, and she could become quite grumpy if anyone harped on it. As a result, the wildest rumours circulated in the family. My cousin Marco persisted in claiming that Poldi had joined a Masai tribe and had only returned because of its teetotalism — a theory she never explicitly denied. My Aunt Luisa expressed the view that "Tanzania" was merely a code word for Poldi's spell in a rehab centre. Uncle Martino is still firmly convinced that Poldi was working for the CIA during that period and was on the point of uncovering the occult secret of the Knights Templar, a mission that would logically have brought her to Sicily, where the Templars had been based. I sometimes think Martino's theory came closest to the truth.

All that was known for a fact was that three years before her move to Sicily, Poldi had bought a house on the outskirts of Arusha, a Tanzanian town at the foot of Kilimanjaro. Masai country. Why Tanzania, nobody knew, but at that time even my Aunts Teresa, Caterina and Luisa had little contact with Poldi. She returned to Munich less than six months later, relieved of all her savings and so sick at heart that she had to get drunk every night — which, as everyone knows, has bad long-term effects on one's health. Poldi had always been fond of lifting her elbow, but I imagine that this was when she formed the plan to drink herself to death. The following year, both her parents died in quick succession, leaving her their small house in Augsburg. Poldi promptly sold it and used the proceeds to move to Sicily on her sixtieth birthday, intending to enhance her alcoholic suicide with a view of the sea.

We naturally suspected that there must be a man behind the Tanzania episode, and that it was there that Poldi's heart had been so thoroughly broken. We also surmised that she had probably been cheated out of her house there. When Poldi told me about it by degrees later on, however, the truth was even more outrageous than I could have imagined.

I hadn't been back to Sicily for over three months — an eternity, and I was still feeling miffed because her husband's sudden appearance had virtually uninvited me until further notice. John had moved into my attic room with the damp-stained walls and the stuffy, windowless bathroom. Poldi had merely told me to bide my time until she had "settled a few things." It was Aunt Teresa who had first told me about John, but even she had shrouded the precise circumstances of his visit in silence. It wasn't that the aunts uninvited me, but they no longer suggested that I fly to Sicily and look after Poldi for one week a month, and, well, I had my pride.

Feeling offended, I got my job back at the call centre and didn't write a single word of my family saga the whole time, though there were other reasons for that. Total silence prevailed for weeks. Not a single phone call — not even a text.

From November onwards, though, I was preoccupied with other things that kept me relatively busy and steered my thoughts in a quite different direction. I spent Christmas at my parents' place. January got off to a stormy start, unpleasant and really cold.

Early in February my Auntie Poldi called me in the middle of the night and genially invited me back as if nothing had happened. More precisely, she ordered me back to Sicily, having already booked my flight.

"And mind you don't forget your driving

licence, OK?"

"Are you feeling all right, Poldi?" I retorted rather sniffily. "You think I've got nothing better to do? You think you only have to call me when I haven't heard a word from you in three months — *three months?* You think I'll shout hurrah and hop on a plane at the drop of a hat? No way!"

"Meaning what?"

"Meaning forget it, Poldi. I'm busy!"

She collected me from Catania Airport the next day. No one can say I'm not consistent.

"God Almighty, you look terrible!" were her first words, and who wouldn't welcome such a greeting? "Been fighting?"

She was alluding to the plaster on my broken, swollen, green-blue nose.

I harrumphed sheepishly. "I'd sooner not talk about it, OK?"

"That novel of yours will never come to anything if you don't get over your eternal bashfulness, take it from me. My dear friend and mentor, Simone de Beauvoir, once told me that anyone with pretensions to being a novelist must drop their pants. Make a note of that."

"I've got my little secrets, that's all."

"For God's sake, drop your pants!"

I sighed. "All right, I'll make it short. Two

days ago I was buying a currant bun in a bakery when I spotted someone walking past out of the corner of my eye. We were at uni together —"

"A real hottie who always ignored you," Poldi broke in, "or a nice girl who kept giving you the eye and you were too uptight to speak to her?"

"Does that matter, Poldi? Anyway, I catch sight of her and think, hey, maybe she's got time for a coffee. So I grab my currant bun and dash out of the bakery. And — wham! — I run full tilt into this plate-glass door. It's suddenly there out of the blue, freshly washed but clean no longer, and all I can see is stars and my nose is bleeding like a stuck pig."

"And the hottie?"

I shrugged.

"Then it wasn't meant to happen. Still, it suits you somehow, the broken nose — it looks tough, and I know what I'm talking about."

"If you say so."

Poldi was in a hurry. She strode swiftly off to the car park, homed in on a red sports car and opened the driver's door.

I mean, a genuine sports convertible! An old Maserati Biturbo Spyder Cabrio from the eighties: six cylinders, 230 horsepower, with cream leather upholstery, an immaculate paint job and a white bonnet.

"Where did you get it?" I said delightedly.

"Don't ask. Did you remember your driving licence?"

"Yes, of course. Why?"

She tossed me the car keys. "Because."

This was something entirely new. Poldi isn't the passenger type, she prefers to be in the driving seat.

"Oh!" I exclaimed. "To what do I owe the honour?"

"I'll explain in due course," she said irritably, and squeezed, swearing, into the passenger seat.

She slammed a prehistoric cassette of eighties pop songs into the slot and turned the volume up full, and we were assaulted by "Africa," "Down Under," "It's Raining Men," "Eye of the Tiger," "Gloria" and "Like a Virgin." Poldi sang along with all of them. When we got to Spliff's idiotic "Carbonara," I eventually cracked and joined in.

Built in the year of my birth, that Maserati was a joke in terms of performance compared with the average sports car of today. But it had charisma. I enjoyed roaring round the orbital motorway in the direction of Torre Archirafi, the sound of the six-cylinder engine, the crash of the gears, the

22

bone-hard steering. I felt like a pop star in an eighties music video. All that irked me was Poldi, who alternated between flooring an imaginary brake pedal and urging me not to dawdle.

"Have you gone senile or something? Step on the gas, sonny! This car is like a racehorse — it wants to race! Race, not trot, understand? OK, so burn some rubber!"

She surprised me by instructing me to take the motorway exit at Acireale, not Giarre, and directed me onto the secondary road at the Bellavista Bar.

"I know the way," I grumbled.

"We aren't going to Torre," she said.

"Where, then?"

"Femminamorta."

My heart skipped a beat with excitement. At long last, I was going to be introduced to Poldi's secret paradise and to Valérie, Poldi's friend and Femminamorta's ethereal, preternaturally beautiful, utterly sexy chatelaine.

Poldi, who seemed to have read my mind, looked at me askance. "No need to grin in that goofy way. Valérie isn't there. She's visiting her family in France."

"So why are we going there?" I said, disappointed.

"Why? Because that's where I'm living

during the changeover."

"What do you mean, changeover? Is something wrong with the house?"

"Stop asking silly questions, I'll explain in due course. Now step on the gas, for God's sake."

And then came Femminamorta.

At kilometre eight we turned off the Provinciale onto the narrow approach road that led across the Piante Russo tree nursery. In the distance I could already glimpse the gateway flanked by two stone lions, and when I got out I found everything just as I'd always imagined it from Poldi's descriptions of the place: the old country house built of volcanic rock, its dilapidated walls lime-washed pink, the sun-bleached sundial, the ornamental eaves, the little bell over the entrance, the pines and palm trees, the enchanted garden. I grasped at once that it was a magical place where friendly spirits roamed and time stood still.

It was very chilly inside and smelt musty. The furniture and antiquarian library exhaled the dust of centuries. Poldi and I appeared to be alone in the house. She showed me a room on the ground floor, a former private chapel whose ceiling was adorned with frescos of saints and the Madonna. There was only one tiny window, the little

24

old bureau against the wall looked decrepit enough to collapse at the slightest touch, the bed creaked and groaned like someone with lumbago, the tiles in the adjoining bathroom were encrusted with at least half a century of lime deposit, and the place smelt even mustier than the living room next door. But I took to it at once. More than that, I sensed I would write some great stuff in there.

"Freshen up a bit and then we'll talk," Poldi decreed before going off to make some coffee.

I took my time. First I smoked a cigarette on the terrace. Waves were pounding lava cliffs in the distance and a cold east wind was driving masses of cloud and spindrift across the sea towards Etna. It was a bleak day. The Sicilian winter had chilled the house and nothing much would change before April. I stubbed out my cigarette but kept the butt in my hand rather than desecrate such a heavenly place.

And then I did something I really shouldn't have done, but something came over me — I simply couldn't resist it. I tiptoed through the house until I located Valérie's bedroom. I didn't root around in her things, I swear, but I wanted at least to take a peek at the place. It made a much lighter and airier impression than the chapel downstairs. The French window led to a stone balcony at the back of the house and afforded a fantastic view of Etna. Everything inside was white, including the painted furniture. There were piles of books and antique knick-knacks everywhere. The bed had been stripped, but lying on it was a pair of big sunglasses Valérie had obviously forgotten to pack. Standing in the doorway, I tried to imagine what she looked like. There were no photos of her anywhere, worse luck. I pictured her as being very petite, with big eyes, laughter lines, sensual lips, bobbed hair, tight jeans and a striped Breton fisherman's shirt. Or in a short, translucent wisp of a summer dress, all elfin and coquettish and as utterly sexy as a girl in one of those French movies with frustratingly unresolved endings — the ones in which the characters merely canoodle and quarrel and make no sense. But all at once I was gripped by a strange sensation, as if someone had come into the room and were eyeing me reproachfully. Feeling uneasy, I shut the door and went downstairs.

Poldi, who was waiting for me in the living room, seemed preoccupied. Beside her coffee stood a glass of grappa. She was looking wearier than usual, it struck me, but she only sipped her drink, which was uncharacteristic. She could easily sink a bottle of Prosecco and half a bottle of grappa a day, not to mention several *espressi* laced with brandy, some liqueur chocolates and a lunchtime beer or two. Quite an intake, in fact, and more than enough to have killed me. Uncle Martino had intimated on the phone that Poldi was going through a bad patch. It was clear that something had gone terribly wrong in recent weeks.

"You feeling OK, Poldi?"

"Don't I look it?"

"To be honest, no."

"Don't treat me like some daft old crone who has to be helped across the street."

I tried to change the subject. "Where's John?"

"Out," she said quietly. "He'll be back soon, but we'll be gone well before then."

"Mind telling me where to?"

"We have to go and find Handsome Antonio."

Whoever that was.

But she'd said "we." It was the first time my Auntie Poldi had actually said "we."

Nobody had known about Poldi's marriage to a Tanzanian man. Neither my other aunts nor Signora Cocuzza, with whom Poldi had recently shared many a spicy secret, nor Vito Montana.

So it was hardly surprising that Montana was dumbfounded when, one fine Sunday morning, Poldi's husband reappeared as if nothing had happened. I often picture various versions of this first encounter. These range from an ultra-cool black-and-white noir scene to the histrionics of a silent film to the emotional explosion of a neo-realist Italian social drama.

The probable scenario: Sunday morning, Poldi and Montana are cuddled up in bed like a couple of teenagers when someone rings the doorbell. *Ring, ring, ring!* It's almost incessant. Exasperated, Montana tumbles out of bed, wraps a towel around his slightly expanding waist, to which Poldi likes to cling during their nocturnal voyages across oceans of lust, and opens the front door. Confronting him is a tall, strapping black man. Mid-forties, alert expression, a head taller than Montana, pale chinos, white T-shirt, green puffa jacket. All very dapper.

Montana: "Yes?"

The man, in English that suggested an East African accent: "I'm looking for Poldi Oberreiter. She lives here, doesn't she?"

"And who are you?"

Montana had switched to commissario mode, not that the man facing him seemed at all impressed. He gets no further, because he hears a smothered exclamation behind him.

Poldi: "Well, I'll be buggered!"

Whereupon the stranger: "Poldi! Hey, Poldi! It's me!"

And Montana: "Will someone tell me what's going on here?"

Poldi has then to explain who the stranger is — namely, her husband John Owenya from Tanzania. And that is when things start to get difficult.

"My husband," she repeats quietly, avoiding Montana's eye. "Husband. Marriage certificate, ring, church — the works, know what I mean?"

Bewildered, she stares at the stranger as if he's a ghost, a revenant risen from the dead.

"Well I'm —"

"It really is me, Poldi." John comes closer and spreads his arms with a beaming smile, but Poldi promptly fends him off.

"Stop! Not another step!"

"What is all this?" growls Montana, who is becoming less and less enamoured of the situation.

Poldi strokes his cheek. "I was just about to tell you, *tesoro.* Get dressed and make us

29

some coffee, OK?" She turns to John. "No need to stand around, come in." She ushers him into the inner courtyard and points to a chair. "Sit down. Don't budge and don't touch anything."

"Poldi, I wouldn't have come, but —"

"Not a word. My house, my rules, or you can piss off again right now."

John raises his hands in surrender. "*Hamna shida.* Your house, your rules."

Poldi chivvies Montana into the bedroom to get dressed and disappears into the bathroom. Locking the door behind her, she flops down on the lavatory seat, buries her face in her hands and weeps.

Once she has recovered some of her composure, she quickly adjusts her wig and make-up, sprays herself liberally with scent and puts on her favourite caftan, the white one with the gold thread.

When she enters the courtyard, Montana and John are facing each other across the table in silence. Montana, who is filling two espresso cups with coffee from a little aluminium *caffettiera,* never takes his eyes off the newcomer. John seems unperturbed. His expression is serious, but not nervous. He holds Montana's gaze and nods his thanks for the coffee.

Montana naturally wants to fire a thousand questions at the new arrival, commissario fashion, but there's a minor problem: his English is poor, like that of most Italians of his generation, and the *bella figura* principle deters him from trying it out. So he chooses to rely on his celebrated "Montana look," which has been known to crack the toughest of tough nuts. Sadly, John seems impervious to it. Maybe he's a contract killer. Or worse . . . But Montana prefers not to speculate further.

Poldi joins them at the garden table, sweetens her coffee and looks Montana in the eye.

"As I said, Vito, this is John Owenya from Arusha, Tanzania. We got married four years ago. I loved him, but he broke my heart and stole my house. And it turned out he had another family on the side — a woman he had been with for a long time, but never married, and their kids. And now here he is, the bastard, sitting there as if nothing had ever happened. I've no idea what he wants, and I've no wish to know, because whatever he says will be a lie. Oh yes, and there's something else: he's a colleague of yours, a detective inspector with the Tanzanian Ministry of Home Affairs."

Montana sighs. It's just as he feared.

John clears his throat, but Poldi's raised

31

finger tells him to wait his turn. She continues to gaze intently at Montana and takes his hand, the big, shapely hand with the hirsute knuckles. She loves it for its combination of gentleness and strength.

"I'm just as much at a loss as you, Vito," she says. "I'll explain everything later, but first let's get this over with, OK?"

Montana shakes his head and gives a mirthless laugh. "You knock the stuffing out of me, Poldi!"

She kisses his hand and turns at last to John. My Auntie Poldi really is a model of composure.

"All right, I want to know why you're here and how you found me."

"*Hamna shida,* Poldi." John heaves a sigh of relief. "I need your help. Thomas has disappeared."

That, I imagine, was when it revived. The thrill of the chase. The moment when Poldi tasted blood.

"Why come looking for him in Sicily, of all places? Anyway, how did you find me?"

"I have ways of tracing people," John replies rather tetchily. "His mobile phone was logged in to a WLAN in Taormina a week ago. Nothing since then. I managed to trace the hotel he was staying at and checked his room. Thomas purported to be a Tanzanian financial investor. He paid a month's rent in advance but hasn't been seen for over a week, and yesterday, when I happened to see your picture in a newspaper, I thought —"

"You thought you'd drop in and break my heart again."

"Who is Thomas?" Montana interjects.

"His half-brother," says Poldi. "A nice enough fellow, but a bit unstable." She turns back to John. "So he disappeared?"

"Yes, from Arusha, two weeks ago. You know what he's like — he disappears from time to time, only to turn up again sooner or later. Rather the worse for wear, but OK otherwise. Like a stray cat. If you ask where he's been, he always says —"

"Don't worry," Poldi mimicked, "I just got lost in the bush."

John smiles. "Lost in the bush, yes, that's what he always said."

It doesn't escape Poldi that he's already using the past tense.

Montana starts to ask something, but Poldi gets there first. "Because in Tanzania, you never just get 'lost in the bush.' Why not? Because you don't go there on your own in the first place, and you don't get lost because you'll be torn to pieces by lions or hyenas, or, at best, die of thirst. The bush is a big, wild place. It's no fun, and you've no business there unless you're a game warden or a Masai and you really know your way around. Thomas is neither one nor the other — he's a big-city boy to his fingertips. Always looks cool and dapper in some swanky rented car. A likeable show-off who attaches a lot of importance to his *bella figura.* A guy like that never ventures into the bush."

Montana gets the picture. "In other words, a small-time criminal who does the occasional job."

"He really isn't such a bad lot," says Poldi. "But no, one doesn't always want to know exactly where he's been or what he's been up to."

Montana's frown deepens. None of this appeals to him: neither John Owenya's sudden appearance, nor Poldi's secretiveness, nor the sound of this man Thomas, nor the thrill of the chase reflected in Poldi's eyes. He is even less pleased by what John goes on to say.

"So we weren't too worried at first. Not until a week after his disappearance, when four guys with submachine guns pulled up outside our house and —"

"*My* house, you mean," Poldi cuts in sharply.

34

"I mean *our* house, Poldi. Your house and mine."

"No, you bugger, that's not what you mean! But get this straight once and for all: it's *my* house, just mine. Not yours. You took it away from me, John. You cheated me out of it."

John throws up his arms. "Do we have to thrash this out right now, Poldi?"

"No, but we *will,* believe you me. All right, these four guys — what did they want?"

"They were looking for Thomas."

"Kigumbe's people?"

John nods. "So four guys with submachine guns pulled up outside the house, jumped out of the car and asked for Thomas. All I gathered was that he'd made off with something that belonged to Kigumbe, who wanted it back at any price."

"Like what?"

John gives my aunt a searching look. "They didn't say. I suppose you wouldn't know?"

"Me?" asked Poldi. "Why should I?"

"You know why I'm asking."

"Yes, I know what you're getting at. But no, John, I've no idea what Thomas could have stolen from Kigumbe. If he did, though, it was the height of folly. Kigumbe wouldn't simply let someone rob him. If you ask me, Thomas is in deep shit."

John nods. "You can say that again."

"Who is this Kigumbe?" Montana interjects.

"A boss" is all Poldi says, but that's good enough for Montana. Everyone in Sicily knows what that means.

"I paid him a visit after that incident with his men," John goes on. "He asked after 'Mamma Poldi.' "

"Oh, how nice of him," Poldi says innocently. She mops her brow. "What did you tell him?"

"Only that you'd gone back to Munich and we hadn't been in touch since."

Poldi picks up the *caffettiera*. "More coffee, anyone?"

"Poldi?"

"Poldi!"

Poldi's two very different policemen might have been an echo. All at once, they sound unanimously suspicious of her, and she doesn't like that somehow.

"What? I honestly don't have a clue what Thomas may have stolen from Kigumbe. What else did the man say?"

"Only that it was something of rather sentimental value." John takes a sip of espresso. "And that it was probably worth ten million dollars on the open market."

2

Tells of picture postcards, Taormina and the tragedy of the Sicilian male. Poldi raises some dust, ruminates and has an idea. Montana gets sick of messing around, and John gets the guest room. After conferring with the padre and the sad signora, Poldi almost picks up a new scent.

"All right, tell me what it was," I demanded dutifully, just as Poldi meant me to, when she inserted a brief pause for effect in her story.

I didn't expect an answer, of course, for as Poldi always says, "Happiness is reality minus expectation." What's more, I'm not a complete fool.

"Why, how impatient you always are!" Poldi exclaimed — just as predictably. "I honestly don't know."

I didn't believe a word of it. "Ah, so it's a McGuffin."

37

"A what?"

"That's what Alfred Hitchcock called any object that drives the plot of a film or gives it momentum without being particularly relevant to the story."

"Oh, so we're back in wise guy mode again, are we? Fine, maybe you'd like to lecture me on the ways of the world — you men are fond of a bit of mansplaining, aren't you? Or maybe you'd like to read me some nice stuff you've written lately?"

"OK, OK," I sighed.

"So I can go on, pray?"

"*Forza,* Poldi!"

For a moment, silence reigned in No. 29 Via Baronessa. The sort of silence that takes possession of the world during a total eclipse. The sort of silence that falls when time stands still. When you realise that something has gone terribly wrong. When a child falls down a well or your brakes fail in the fast lane. When minus times minus no longer makes plus. When the sea retreats and you don't have much time before the tsunami comes racing towards you. The silence that precedes disaster.

"Ten million dollars doesn't sound like some sentimental souvenir you'd put on the mantelpiece," growled Montana, looking at

38

Poldi. "Why do I get the feeling you know more about this than you're saying?"

Poldi mopped her brow again. "I'd tell you if I knew. Besides, what matters is to find Thomas."

Montana knew my aunt well enough by now to know that she couldn't keep secrets to herself for long, and so, quite contrary to his nature and the instincts of a detective chief inspector, he refrained from pursuing the question. The furrows in his brow merely deepened.

"Do you have a photo of this half-brother of yours?"

"Yes, of course." John produced his mobile phone. He tapped a few keys and handed it to Montana.

Peering over Montana's shoulder, Poldi saw a good-looking black man in his early forties grinning cheerfully and rather cheekily at the camera.

"That's just how I remember him!" she exclaimed. "A real rogue — never without some daft idea in his head."

"Send it to me," said Montana, and he gave John his number.

"And to me," said Poldi.

"When did you say your brother disappeared?"

Poldi could see Montana assuming the

expression detectives always assume when taking scent. My aunt liked that. It was a sexy expression — it turned her on, one could say — but she also found it reassuring. Better the investigative mode, she told herself, than the jealousy mode.

"A week ago."

"And no sign of life since then?"

John shook his head. The two men exchanged a look that said they had long ago come to the same conclusion.

Montana eventually put it into words. "If this object is really worth so much, your brother could already be dead."

John nodded mournfully. "That's why I flew to Sicily at once. I found this in Thomas's hotel room . . ."

He felt in the pocket of his green puffa jacket, extracted something and handed it to Montana. Montana looked at it, turning it over and over in his hand, and then passed it to Poldi, who was fidgeting with curiosity.

Believe it or not, my Auntie Poldi inserted another pause at this point and sipped her grappa with relish.

I, for my part, played the cool, hunky, broken-nosed dude. I took a leisurely drink of water and sat back against the sofa cushions — meditatively, as if I had something of great importance to mull over. Life, for example, or world peace. Or the question of when I would finally get to meet Valérie and be able to impress her with my hunky new personality.

"Hey, you," snapped Poldi, "stop slouching and pay attention."

Ill-humouredly, she thrust a crumpled postcard into my hand. It was one of those cards that display a photo collage of assorted local sights in supersaturated colour. These included an eruption of Etna, the black elephant obelisk in the Piazza Duomo in Catania, a basket of lemons, some sinister-looking marionettes and a young couple in Sicilian costume. It was just the kind of postcard that would be stuck on the fridge at home when I was a boy.

The card did not bear an address, just a brief note in neat block capitals:

HANDSOME ANTONIO
393403469364

Without more ado, Montana got out his mobile phone and keyed in the number.

"Messaggio gratuito. Il numero selezionato è inesistente o momentaneamente non disponibile. La preghiamo di richiamare più tardi."

A friendly female voice reeled off this

41

recorded announcement in torrential Italian, and her news was both good and bad. The good: the information was free of charge. The bad: the number dialled did not exist or was temporarily unobtainable.

Montana rang off and immediately dialled another number.

"Pippo, it's me . . . Yes, I'm fine, you can cut out the soft soap . . . What? Yes, eating well and sends her best regards. Listen, you've got to check a mobile number for me. Probably a prepaid job, but I need all the traffic, locations, everything . . . Yes, Pippo, I know it's Sunday today. Look, don't mess me about, your pasta won't go cold. Call Dottore Castorina from the district attorney's office; he'll be grateful for a break from his family. Get his goddam authorisation and get me the info, OK? And call me back right away . . . What's that?" Montana rolled his eyes and sighed. "Yes, I will." He shut his phone and gave Poldi a look of irritation. "Assistente Zannotta sends his best regards."

"Oh, thanks for telling me," Poldi trilled. "How sweet of him."

"Very sweet, the mealy-mouthed bugger."

"Calm down, Vito. Take some deep breaths and then we'll be off."

"Off? Where to?"

"Taormina, of course. I'm sure you want to take a look at Thomas's hotel room."

As I've already said, my Auntie Poldi knows a thing or two about detective inspectors and the thrill of the chase.

I can picture the three of them speeding along the motorway to Taormina in Montana's Alfa. Montana grimly smoking behind the wheel, Poldi sitting beside him in a leopard-skin catsuit and, on the back seat, like an unloved foster child they would sooner have exchanged, John.

Not a word was uttered throughout the drive, but it didn't escape Poldi that Montana and John spent the whole time sizing each other up in the rear-view mirror. This aroused mixed emotions in her. After all, she was in love with one of them and had once been very much in love with the other. This presented a dire possibility: a risk that one love might be extinguished while the other reignited and she once more ended up with a broken heart. What choice did she have, though?

While the Mediterranean glittered on her right like an obsessively cheerful weather presenter, my Auntie Poldi wondered if she would ever be spared all the shit men inflicted on her. Poldi had been in love throughout her life. Even at primary school in Augsburg, she would have found life intolerable without some madcap Maxi or Hansi to fall for. She couldn't have endured her schooldays, her training, her job, her family and Augsburg, her holidays and weekends — indeed, her life in general — without being in love. For my Auntie Poldi love was a permanent condition, a kind of incurable malady no ointment or poultice could relieve. Sometimes it made her happy, sometimes not, but without that constant, sweet heartache she couldn't breathe, couldn't eat, couldn't go to sleep or get up. Booze was the only thing that helped, for my aunt drank in order to promote heartache, not banish it. She continued to drink until she could carry on and fall in love again. And if, on very dark days, she found she felt nothing at all, booze could nonetheless kindle a little fire in the place where there was room for a huge conflagration: her heart.

Men . . . Poldi loved men, there's no denying it. Her thoughts revolved incessantly around men. At the same time, she had always been a tough and belligerent demonstrator in favour of women's rights, and had never let guys dictate to her. It was only in matters of the heart that she always went soft. In that respect the Oberreiterish body behaved in accordance with its nature and destiny: the seeking of pure sexual pleasure. Her words, not mine.

At all events, Poldi was glad to be able to spend the trip cogitating in peace.

"Because you know," she explained on my first evening in Femminamorta, "once the initial shock had worn off — I mean, at the fact that my Johnny had popped up in front of me again like a jack-in-a-box — I realised that I was faced with a massive problem. You can guess what it was, can't you?"

"No. What?"

"God Almighty, how dense you are! That thing just now, what did you call it? The McGovern?"

"McGuffin."

"That's it, the Mac. I like that, the Mac. I really don't know what it is, but we'll sure as hell find out."

"Er . . ." I said suspiciously. "What's with the 'we'?"

"Stop interrupting. The thing is, if Kigumbe asked after me, he must have had a reason, right? Logically, that means I'm in the firing line. Why? Maybe because I know something I don't know I know, under-stand?"

"No, I don't."

"Why, it's as clear as daylight. I'm playing a key role in whatever it is, Vito and John cottoned on to that at once. I have to find out what this Mac is, because it will lead me straight to Thomas."

Taormina is a touristic petit four. A creamy, fragrant illusion composed of air and almond biscuit topped with pastel icing. A whispered promise of eternal spring and everlasting beauty. A sugary gem you could devour at a gulp, sighing voluptuously, but only nibble in awe of the patissier's art. Eternity is merely a backdrop, but for one sweet moment you're immersed in a Technicolor screen romance of the fifties, when kisses were still timid and men still faithful. When pomaded quiffs were trendy and girls were addressed as *signorina.* When *gelati* never melted and *limoncelli* weren't sticky. When gentlemen wore linen suits instead of three-quarter-length trousers and ladies wore floral petticoats instead of leggings, and when no one, but no one, had to go everywhere equipped with a survival rucksack containing energy biscuits, a laptop, charger and mineral water. An illusion, as I say, for the spirit of the times has affected the Corso Umberto too, wafting over stone steps, whirling through cypresses and luxuriant bougainvillea bushes, shaking orange trees, hibiscus and oleanders, and rattling shutters. The Taormina of my summer holidays, for example, was one big amusement arcade El Dorado where we fed our pocket money into slot machines, copped sugar rushes from cheap lemonades and could buy friendship bracelets, CDs, plastic toys and batik scarves on every street corner. Once a rip-off Mordor, Taormina is quite different today. Gone are the amusement arcades, and customers with loaded credit cards are awaited along the Corso by tasteful antique shops, craft shops, galleries, high-end boutiques, flagship stores, jewellers and gourmet cafés. But most of the tourists continue to be families with children, language students and young couples who aren't too ready to splash the cash — save possibly on friendship bracelets and cheap lemonade. At least the restaurants in the side streets offer genuine Sicilian cuisine, not just a limp *menu turistico* and *pizza al taglio.* And, thanks to my Auntie Poldi, the bars round about will even produce a gin and tonic or a Moscow mule.

So I'm fond of Taormina. The place no longer measures up to the glamour of former times, but a star does occasionally stray there for the film festival or a concert in the Teatro Greco, and the view of distant Etna across the middle of the amphitheatre's stage is truly spectacular. Taormina is at its most beautiful in the spring, but I also like it in winter, when the whole place comes to a standstill and a gigantic Christmas tree stands in the piazza — though the service in the bars of the Hotel Timeo or San Domenico Palace Hotel is no more attentive than usual. Unless, of course, I'm with my Auntie Poldi, in which case I'm addressed as *"Dottore!"* or *"Professore!"*

John's half-brother Thomas had not checked into either of those luxury establishments, but into the far less expensive Villa Nettuno, a pink-washed, family-run hotel notable only for its faded 1960s charm. The double room with the flagstone floor and the old furniture smelt of mothballs and looked unoccupied at first glance. The bed was undisturbed and no clothes were lying around, nor was there anything that might have indicated the presence of a hotel guest. Poldi peered into the bathroom. No toothbrush or toilet articles, the little packets of soap unopened.

"Where was that postcard?" Montana asked. He was standing in the middle of the room, just looking around.

John pointed to the bedside table.

"Nothing else?"

"No."

Montana thought for a moment. "Then you were probably meant to find it."

"I thought that too, but he could have made things easier for himself by simply leaving a message for me."

Without further comment, Montana proceeded to search the room systematically. The two waste bins were empty. He looked in the wardrobe, the chest of drawers, the bedside cupboard and the rickety desk, and glanced under the bed.

"You're wasting your time," said John. "I have looked everywhere already. I also questioned the chambermaid, but she said the bins were empty when she came to do the room."

Montana turned to Poldi. "Maybe you'd like to check, just to be on the safe side?"

"No need to be sarcastic, *tesoro.*" Assuming her most indignant expression, she handed her bag to her grumpy lover, got down on the floor, stretched out flat and stuck her head under the bed.

Because Poldi had learnt the following lesson from her father, Detective Inspector (ret.) Oberreiter of the Augsburg Homicide Division: Always look under the bed! Clues are like cockroaches; they shun the light and scuttle off into the homely darkness. And sure enough, in the penumbra beneath the bed she discovered something that caught her attention. Namely, a fine layer of dust that had, in places, collected into little dust bunnies.

"Push me," she called.

"What?"

"*Madonna,* push me farther under the bed. I can't manage on my own!"

Montana hesitated, then crouched down and pushed Poldi by the legs until she stuck fast almost up to her hips.

"Farther!"

John lifted the bed a fraction, enabling Montana to push her a little farther under the bed.

"Now waggle me a bit. OK, now pull me out, but mind you don't drop the bed on my head!"

When Poldi regained her feet, the front of her leopard-skin catsuit was furred with dust, crumbs and stray hairs.

"Serves you right," Montana growled, wrinkling his nose.

Without deigning to comment, Poldi produced a lint roller from her handbag and gave herself a thorough going-over. The three strips she used, she carefully put into a self-sealing polythene bag — she never went anywhere without one, needless to say — and handed it to Montana.

"For the lab."

Montana waved it away. "For one thing, that dust has been there forever, and for another, this isn't a case yet." He had reverted to Italian so John wouldn't understand. "You're welcome to discuss this further with your husband, Poldi, but count me out. I'll drive you both back to Torre, but I don't want to hear from you for the next few days."

"But Vito . . ."

"No, I've had it. *Basta!* I don't feel like playing the cuckold. Until I know what is going on here, you can count me out."

So Poldi still had the three adhesive strips in her bag when Montana dropped her back at No. 29 Via Baronessa and sped off without a word.

"I like him," John said as he followed Poldi into the house.

"Oh, shut up!"

"Are you in love with him?"

"Not another word!" Poldi snarled, wagging her finger at him.

It was past lunchtime already — her neighbours in the Via Baronessa were having their siesta — so she felt a drop of

51

something wouldn't hurt her. She poured herself a beer, eyeing John morosely.

"You've got a nerve, coming here."

"I'd been meaning to call you for ages."

"So why didn't you?"

"It's not that easy, Poldi. You know how I'm placed."

Yes, she certainly did.

"How are Amina and the kids? Are you feeling at home in my house?"

"I'll explain everything in due course, Poldi, but first I have to find Thomas."

"It doesn't look as if Thomas wants to be found."

"I'm a good cop. I won't leave without him."

"But what if he . . . I mean, you heard what Vito said."

John cleared his throat before coming out with it. "Kigumbe threatened to kill Amina and the girls unless I bring back what Thomas stole. You know what he's capable of, so I've no choice. I must find him come what may, alive or . . . well, preferably alive."

Poldi drained her beer in a series of little gulps. "Bullshit," she said. "I don't believe a word you say. This whole Thomas business stinks to high heaven." She put her glass down and rose. "No, don't say anything. I'm going out for a bit. I want you gone by the time I get back. Is that clear?"

"But I need your help, Poldi!"

"Bollocks. The whole thing stinks — I want nothing to do with it or you. Get out of my life, John. Go to hell and don't come back."

Before he had a chance to argue, she swept out of the *salotto,* snatched up her handbag and left the house.

Her objective was sad Signora Cocuzza's café bar. It wasn't *passeggiata* time yet, and the little town looked deserted as Poldi strode along the esplanade and past the little church of Santa Maria del Rosario, heading for the piazza. The morning had been sunny and agreeably mild, but now the sky was overcast. Very appropriate, thought Poldi, shivering. An emotional tempest was raging inside her, and an onshore wind was driving salty spindrift into her face. I'll give my Auntie Poldi one thing: it takes a lot to knock her sideways, and I'm not talking about booze, but that Sunday morning had really done the trick. Which was why she was looking forward to a warming *corretto* — an espresso laced with a double shot of brandy — and an air-clearing conversation with her friend.

Predictably, the bar was almost empty. The sad signora, who was doing a crossword puzzle behind the cash register, heaved a sigh just as Poldi came in. Seated over a game of cards in the far corner were three elderly *signori* who looked like extras in a fifth-rate Mafia movie, and presiding over his umpteenth espresso in the middle of the room, like a grumpy, chain-smoking king of the zombies, was the padre. He gave Poldi an ungracious stare.

"I missed you at Mass this morning," he boomed. "I suppose you preferred to remain tucked up in a warm bed with your commissario."

Poldi ordered a *corretto* and flopped down on a chair beside the padre.

"Hell's bells," she said, "if I told you what really happened to me this morning, you'd turn Protestant."

With a speed and agility that she mightn't have been thought capable of, Signora Cocuzza left her stool behind the register and joined them at the table.

"What's happened?" she asked in a hoarse whisper. "Another murder?"

"That remains to be seen," my Auntie Poldi said portentously, and proceeded to unload.

She concluded her account by depositing the self-seal bag containing the hairy adhesive strips on the table.

"You're a woman of mystery," growled the padre. "You're quite something!" Signora Cocuzza whispered delightedly, earning herself a reproving glance from the padre.

"Thank you, my friends, but believe me, I could have done without what happened this morning. The signor commissario was just getting up steam, if you know what I mean, when —"

"That's enough!" snapped the padre. He crossed himself and shook another gasper out of the packet.

Signora Cocuzza picked up the zip bag and examined the adhesive strips. "What's that?" she asked, pointing to a small red dot nestling amid the dust, hairs and flakes of skin.

Poldi, who hadn't noticed it before, took out the adhesive strip and inspected it more closely. "Looks like a sequin or something."

"From an evening gown," whispered the sad signora, "worn by a murderous femme fatale."

Poldi found this theory a trifle premature, but since a volcano of passion and romantic fantasies so obviously seethed beneath her friend's mouse-grey exterior, she let it stand. The little red sequin reminded her of someone or something, but she couldn't think who or what.

"Just to be clear," growled the padre, "we now want to hear all about your Tanzania episode. You aren't getting off so easily, not this time."

"Another time," Poldi said dismissively. "Right now I need your help. We must find out who Handsome Antonio is."

"Read Brancati!" cried the padre.

"And that," my Auntie Poldi informed me, "brings us to Sicily's most abiding myth: the Sicilian male. Or rather, Sicilian masculinity. A lot has been written about it, of course, but no writer ever poured more entertaining scorn on the Sicilian machismo and virility craze than Vitaliano Brancati in his novel *The Handsome Antonio*. There's also a film starring Marcello Mastroianni and Claudia Cardinale, in case the book's too difficult for you. But get this: second only to Tomasi di Lampedusa's *The Leopard, The Handsome Antonio* is one of the most important romans à clef about Sicily ever written. It's set in Catania, too."

My Auntie Poldi took a swallow of grappa. As ever when talking about her favourite subject — i.e., men — she had the bit between her teeth.

"Brancati must have had a melancholy streak as well as a great sense of humour —

I'd have fancied him myself. He was an idler, an elegant, sensitive idler, a small man with a moustache — and a moustache would suit you too, by the way. I can picture him in the 1940s, sitting in the Via Etnea with his wife Anna — she was a famous actress — sipping an *aperitivo* and laughing at the idiotic courtship displays in the Piazza Duomo. Not much has changed since then. This novel, the one about Handsome Antonio, is a symphony — a melancholy, erotic, political, baroque portrayal of the Sicilians and their mores. Of their sensuality, their piety, their love of country and their aversion to anything new and strange. It's also a textbook on patriarchy and the incarceration of women and girls in their own homes."

"But what's it *about*?"

A reproving glance. "You're always so impatient. If you ever finished that novel of yours, you'd be glad if it couldn't be boiled down to a short list of contents, wouldn't you?"

"*Forza* Poldi," I sighed.

"Brancati's novel," she went on deliberately, "tells the story of young Antonio Magnano, whom everyone in Catania idolises because of his preternaturally good looks, get the picture? In reality, however,

57

Handsome Antonio is just a schmuck, a dull-witted and — get this — totally impotent dimwit. His success with women, his legendary sexual exploits in Rome, et cetera — they're all just a series of lies and excuses. Why? Because he's dead downstairs. When this eventually leaks, Catanian society is hit by a shock wave. Antonio's marriage to the lovely Barbara is annulled in short order, his father commits suicide in a brothel, and Antonio comes to a bad end. Onto the scene come fascists and communists, priests and aunts, drum-playing grandads, mothers, lovers, murderous rivals, snobs, failures, illegitimate children and party officials. The story has everything — it's very cinematic, so make a note of that for your novel. But always in the foreground, mind you, is the sexuality of the Sicilian male. Now you may think, Good Lord, what does it matter if you can't get it up for once? What happened to Antonio was just a minor lapse. And you'd be right, it happens to every man once in a while. Except for Vito, but he's not only Sicilian, he's a detective chief inspector, and so, being a supreme specimen of human evolution, he's also —"

"A sexual force of nature," I sighed.

"Full marks. But in Sicily Antonio's particular little failing can amount to a tragedy. Why? Because — and you're no exception, being half Sicilian, so don't squirm like that — the Sicilian male has only one thing on his mind: *it.*"

And my Auntie Poldi knew a thing or two about men in general and Sicilians in particular.

Sometimes, when I can't get to sleep on very warm nights, I wonder if Poldi is right about this. If she may have had a similar experience with Vito Montana. If the descriptions of her frenzied nocturnal excesses were all invented for appearance's sake. If, to avoid offending Montana, she idolises him more when less goes on behind closed doors. But this is all groundless speculation. Not only does it get me nowhere, but it's none of my business. At all events, Montana has undoubtedly fathered two children, and he's no moppet, far from it.

Not being a moppet, he didn't like being cuckolded and made a fool of, so Poldi was glad he had gone. Because, needless to say, John was still there when she got back from the bar that Sunday morning. What was more, he had no intention of leaving.

"It's like this, Poldi," he told her calmly. "You seem to know something that could lead me to Thomas, and besides, you've got a guest room upstairs."

"Fine," said my aunt. "Then sign those divorce papers and buy me out of my house."

To her surprise, John extracted a crumpled envelope from the pocket of his puffa jacket and held it out. "Go on, open it."

Poldi hesitated before taking the envelope. It contained several official documents, now signed by them both, and a cheque drawn on the First National Bank of Tanzania.

"Are you being serious?" she said when she saw how much the cheque was made out for. "The house is worth twice that, and you know it."

"That's all I've got, Poldi. Regard it as a token of my goodwill."

Poldi was on the point of tearing up the cheque, slinging John out on his ear and hitting the bottle with a vengeance. But because she knew from painful experience that a bird in the hand is worth two in the bush, wanted to put paid to the Tanzania business once and for all, and could in fact use a small infusion of cash, she condescended to replace the cheque in the envelope.

"I hope it's good."

"It is. And as soon as I've got Thomas safely back home, you'll never hear from me again, I promise."

Well, yes, that's the sort of promise no one really wants to hear, and no one believes, either.

Despite her misgivings, Poldi didn't send John packing. After all, she wasn't made of stone. She possessed feelings and a tender, vulnerable soul. Moreover, it went without saying that her displeasure at John's sudden reappearance was mingled with another emotion, a familiar emotion not unlike nausea. Plus, of course, the thrill of the chase. Although Montana disputed this, my Auntie Poldi could smell a crime ten miles upwind.

"Seriously, I can smell them," she announced proudly when telling me all this later on. "Petty crimes smell faintly of sweat or stale food. More serious crimes, like fraud, abduction or bank robbery, smell like leather or hot iron. But capital crimes smell pungent and acrid — they sting my nose like ammonia or sulphur."

"I see," I said incredulously. "And what did you smell this time?"

Poldi sat back and closed her eyes. "Burnt rubber."

3

Tells of insomnia, old vices, the queen of Sicilian cuisine and — who would have guessed it? — of men. Poldi receives a visit and an indiscreet tip from an old acquaintance, convenes a meeting and has a fit of the giggles. Montana has something of interest to impart. Poldi proves to be remarkably agile and takes a nocturnal walk to the esplanade.

No one will be surprised to learn that my Auntie Poldi couldn't get to sleep after such an eventful day. Taking a nightcap with her, she went to her ground-floor bedroom at an early hour, closed the shutters, lay down on the bed in her favourite floral pyjamas and waited in the twilight for her double whisky to take effect. In vain. For a while she heard John showering, gargling and telephoning in the guest room upstairs. Then, as night came down over Torre, the house fell silent.

Now that all Poldi could hear was the muted sound of waves sluggishly breaking on the shore, Signora Anzalone's television burbling across the street and an occasional moped, she couldn't prevent herself from summoning up memories of certain hot African nights. That is to say, she pictured John, still her husband, stretched out on the bed upstairs in all the splendour of his nakedness. Maybe . . . No! Stop! No, she forbade herself to entertain such an idea. No, she was determined, *just for once,* not to think of *it.* She didn't want to think at all, she simply wanted to sleep and *basta.*

But it was no use, Johnnie Walker let her down. Thoughts went trooping through her head like a band of vociferous youngsters on a school outing. Together with a mishmash of random observations, the little red sequin had become lodged in the lumber room of her recollections. Poldi felt sure it hadn't come from a dress; on the other hand, where but on dresses did one see sequins?

To distract herself, she conjured up an image of Vito Montana. This time, however, he refused to appear in the form of a mature Adonis with virile body hair, a compact little tummy, big, demanding hands and a large dose of pulsating, insatiable *sicilianità,* but instead as a jealous, scowling, bad-tempered commissario in a creased and crumpled suit. This promptly aroused feelings of guilt and annoyance — emotions which, as we all know, are hardly conducive to sleep.

Poldi tossed and turned from left to right, south-east to north-west, but nothing helped. To take her mind off John and Montana, she got out one of the albums containing her photographic collection of dapper traffic cops from all over the world and wallowed for a while in sensual, sentimental memories of many a uniformed, mustachioed guardian of the law. She was even on the point of activating the cuddly electrical gadget in the drawer of her bedside table when she was brought up short by quite another problem — something that awaited her on the morrow and filled her with about as much joyful anticipation as a session with the dentist: she was going to have to speak to the aunts and give her sisters-in-law some explanation of John's presence.

This finally put paid to her pleasurable memories and sleep. There was only one thing for it. Sitting up in bed with a sigh, Poldi opened the drawer of the bedside table and got out her little tin of weed.

64

■ ■ ■ ■

"What?" I yelped incredulously when she told me this. "Are you being serious?"

It was late by now, but we were still sitting on the sofa in Femminamorta, as if the world around us didn't exist and time was taking a short breather.

"Jesus wept," she exclaimed, "if only you could hear yourself! You sound like a fuddy-duddy of the first order. Of course I smoke a spliff now and then, so what? We always used to in Munich, and on the beach at Pattaya, and in the ashram. Have I ever told you about the time in Las Vegas when your aunt and Jack Nicholson —"

"No, I'm not that interested, to be honest. Where do you get the stuff?"

"It isn't 'stuff,' it's grass. Marco got it for me. Finest quality, organically farmed grass. Grown where? Here in *bella Sicilia,* of course. *Denominazione di origine controllata,* so to speak. Like to try some?"

"No thanks. Forget it."

"You mean you've never smoked a spliff?"

"It's not compulsory, Poldi."

"So how can you pass judgement? What an anally uptight control freak you are! I mean, now you've started smoking cigarettes and wearing coloured shirts, you could at least try one once, no? You should be amassing experiences, being a writer. Maybe it would help your novel along. And besides," she added in a hoarse whisper, "it can be a real sexual supercharger, know what I mean? Mind you, it's no use without a girlfriend."

To be clear, I've had some experience of cannabis, albeit inadvertently. It happened at a party in the digs I shared, when I mistook a bag of pot cookies for a contribution to the buffet and was so hungry I scoffed the lot. I spent the rest of the party first on the loo and later in the hospital. I was never invited to parties there again, nor have I ever touched the stuff since.

It's not that I've got anything against pot smoking. Nearly all my cousins and friends in Sicily smoke, and they've got jobs and families and get along fine. Cannabis plants thrive in the Sicilian climate, and since the average Sicilian doesn't drink a lot, a joint in the evening is almost as normal as a stein in a Bavarian beer garden. One summer holiday many years ago, my Aunt Teresa proudly showed me a gigantic cannabis plant on the balcony outside Marco's room. "Look at that lovely plant," she said. "It's a cannabis plant, but it's only ornamental.

You can't smoke it." Marco, who was standing behind her, merely rolled his eyes.

Poldi was just surfing the first gentle billows of a high when she heard someone clear their throat right beside her.

"Hellsbellsandbucketsofblood!" she squawked in alarm. Death was sitting on the bed next to her with his knees drawn up.

"Sorry," he drawled. "Afraid it's part of the job. I call it the hoopla effect. Not the Doppler effect, but —"

"Yes, yes, dammit, I get it!"

Poldi's friend Death visited her from time to time, giving her some perspective on the life she sometimes tried to drink away, and the lives of those who went before her. This time, Death was wearing a kind of tattered monastic habit with a coarse woollen cowl. His clipboard with the list of names was casually laid aside on the bed, which Poldi construed as a promising sign. She also thought he'd put on a bit of colour recently. He made a fresher and more rested impression than usual, but that might have been an illusion. Judging by his cheesy BO, nothing had really changed.

"Good evening. I hope I'm not intruding."

"Course not," Poldi lied. "After all, we're . . . well, we're old friends by now. We are, aren't we?"

"What a nice thing to say, Poldi," said Death, scratching his armpit. "One doesn't often hear it in my job. On the other hand, I can also detect a certain quite understandable but nonetheless emotionally hurtful uneasiness in your voice. Somehow, that always forms a barrier between us."

Poldi pointed to his list of names. "Are you surprised?"

"What if I also possess feelings and a sensitive soul?"

Poldi sighed. "What are you suggesting? That we fall into each other's arms?"

"No, no," Death said hastily, "that would be against compliance regulations."

She gave him a searching stare. "You realise we're still right at the start of our relationship, don't you? We still have to build up a lot of mutual trust, and I think we should, er, take our time. Lots of time."

"Very nicely put, Poldi. Thanks."

She shook her head in puzzlement. "So what brings you here?"

Death indicated her whisky glass and joint. "Things aren't going too well with you again, are they?"

"That's one way of putting it." She held

out the joint. "Like some, or are you on duty?"

Death hesitated, took two polite drags and promptly had a violent coughing fit. Poldi refrained from thumping him on the back because she would probably have sent him tumbling off the bed.

"So it occurred to me," he gasped, "that I might somehow" — another paroxysm — "be of help to you."

"Help? You? Good God! Thanks for the offer, but I'd sooner no one had to die just because I'm in the middle of another fine mess."

"Now, now, Poldi, you know I don't have any influence on *that!* But" — Death peered round as though someone might be watching and lowered his voice to a whisper — "maybe someone has *already* died." He tapped his clipboard meaningfully and winked at her. "It's possible I may recently have escorted someone to the other side, someone who was compelled to depart this world by a blunt instrument."

"Oh? Who might we be talking about?"

Death threw up his hands with the histrionic brio of an Italian full-back who has just fouled an opposition striker. "No names. Red line. Sorry."

Poldi thought for a moment. "So it's a

murder case now?"

"It might be."

"One connected with John's surprise appearance?"

"Possibly."

"Come on, sonny, that's no good to me."

Death hesitated. Then, quite suddenly, the strip of adhesive tape with the little red sequin materialised in his hand. "Well, let's put it this way. Why don't you ask your friend Russo?"

As so often happens in a life beset by nosedives and heartbreaks, Poldi awoke the next morning with a plan. My aunt may be accused of many things — boozing, sexploits, volatility and hippieness — but she has always, throughout her life, had some kind of plan. Although most of her plans don't work, they enable her to navigate as if there were a distant beacon in the darkness.

So the first thing she did was to send a text to the chat group she maintained with her sisters-in-law, my Aunts Teresa, Caterina and Luisa, plus my Uncle Martino.

Meeting 5 pm today at Femminamorta
Something to tell you

She sent a similarly cryptic text message

70

to Valérie. Needless to say, the chat group went at once to code red. The aunts naturally wanted to know what was up, but Poldi merely intimated that she intended to give them a kind of sitrep. This, of course, sent them into a state of high excitement. Although they still spoke excellent German with a slight Bavarian accent, they'd heard terms like "sitrep" only on the news and in crime series on TV, so they were perturbed. I imagine that shortly after they received Poldi's text, their mobile phones went red hot as they jointly strove to make sense of it.

Then Poldi poured herself a preliminary Scotch. She needed another immediately afterwards, when John came into the kitchen. He had already showered and was wearing nothing but a small towel around his waist.

"Morning, baby," he said, picking up the *caffettiera* as if it were the most natural thing in the world.

Poldi couldn't believe her eyes and ears. He displayed no sign of embarrassment and acted like the house belonged to him already. My aunt was badly thrown by this casual act of appropriation, plus the sight of his glossy chest and the six-pack beneath it, which might have been sculpted in ebony.

Rage and lust — a thoroughly undesirable mixture, and one that in her case tended to trigger a booze reflex. However, Poldi had herself more or less under control.

"Baby be damned!" she snarled. "You can cut that out! And don't show yourself down here unless you're fully dressed, is that clear?"

Espresso cup in hand, John came over to her, and she had to admit that he could have modelled for some luxury Italian label. But he wasn't a model, he was a detective inspector, and we all know what that means. Poldi knew it too, and the bulge in the small towel did not escape her notice.

"Don't you care for me any more?" John purred.

Poldi's preferred response would have been to tear the hand towel from around his loins and . . .

But, as already said, she had a measure of self-control. She forced herself to look up and bravely lock eyes with the man who was still her husband.

"No, John, I don't care for you any more. I don't like this performance of yours, or the way you've been prowling around the house as though you own it, or the way you drink your coffee. I don't like you being here at all."

John said nothing at first, and he'd have done better to leave it at that. Zip the lip, drink up his coffee, get dressed and vamoose. Instead, he made a very silly mistake. "We're still married, Poldi," he purred in the soulful voice he'd always used when trying to talk my aunt around. "No worries, baby, just go with the flow." He not only came still closer but had the chutzpah to launch into a Tanzanian-accented rendering of Marvin Gaye's "Sexual Healing" and waggle his hips at her.

That did it. Poldi stared at him — and burst out laughing. She choked, caught her breath and went on laughing. And when my Auntie Poldi laughed, the earth shook. Cyclopes flinched and Sirens squealed, for she laughed with the whole of her body. Every last part of her shook and wobbled in time to her peals of merriment. It didn't worry her that her laughter was overly loud and brazen, that she pulled faces, that tears came to her eyes and she broke out in a sweat, that her wig slid askew and her bosom heaved like a North Atlantic swell. When my Auntie Poldi laughed there was no restraining or escaping it. Her laugh penetrated walls and bodies with ease. It rolled like cosmic thunder, warped space, soared to the stars and plunged back to earth like a comet of bliss and joie de vivre that simply — *whoosh!* — swept away all grouchiness, cussedness, boneheadedness and deviousness. One could sometimes see the laughter building up inside her, accumulating in the depths of her body like glowing plasma — see it throbbing and swelling, that throaty, ultra-Bavarian laugh which always erupted from her without restraint, for when she laughed she seemed to burst like an overripe fruit. Her laugh billowed along the Via Baronessa, setting shutters and hearts atremble. Laughter came purling out of my Auntie Poldi like iridescent bubbles, and one could bathe in its unalloyed gaiety. My Auntie Poldi's laugh was a gift from ancient gods: extravagant, prodigious and altogether excessive. And, as is the way with divine gifts, anyone who spurns or ignores them is not to be trusted and beyond help.

John froze. The bulge in the hand towel disappeared and he retreated a step, grinning sheepishly.

"You haven't changed," he said when her laughter gradually subsided, like her desire for him. He tightened the hand towel and turned. "I'll go upstairs and get dressed."

"You do that, John," Poldi said. "And then we'll go for a little walk."

In order to put something of a bridle on local gossip, which was inevitable, Poldi took him on a brief tour of Torre Archirafi's hot spots: Signora Cocuzza's café bar, Signor Bussacca's *tabacchi,* the esplanade and the old mineral water bottling plant. Poldi cheerfully introduced John to everyone they met as an American film director scouting locations for an art-house action musical.

"Who's going to believe that?" John protested. "I don't have an American accent and I know as much about films as a marabou stork."

"Don't worry," Poldi assured him. "Anyone who speaks fluent English is automatically assumed to be an American, and the locals know I used to be in the film business, so it makes sense. Besides, the funkier a backstory is, the readier people are to credit it. That's because they don't believe anyone could have made it up. I know how people's minds work. This way, no one will think twice if you make a few inquiries here and there."

She was right, as usual. John's cover allayed people's curiosity and spared her a lot of unwelcome snooping. Thereafter John fitted smoothly into the townscape. He strolled along the esplanade, partook of an occasional coffee and almond milk in the bar, went to church daily and said a friendly hello to everyone. After two days he received his first invitation to a meal, and by the third day several mothers had asked him to screen-test their daughters.

After taking a brief siesta, Poldi mounted her brightly painted Vespa and sped off to Femminamorta to make a confession. She had chosen a suitable outfit: a high-necked white woollen dress with diagonal blue stripes and lilies daintily appliquéd in gold. Intended to convey humility and lack of affectation, it made as understated an impression as the comet that wiped out the dinosaurs. But as my Auntie Poldi always says, "Moderation is a sign of weakness. If you've got something to say, raise your voice!"

When Poldi got to her friend's enchanted pink house, she saw my other three aunts and Uncle Martino already chatting to Valérie in her neglected paradise of a garden. Someone else was also sitting there: Vito Montana, who was just laughing at some wisecrack of Martino's. Poldi peered through the dense oleander bushes with a lump in her throat, for she realised that the six people sitting there on weather-worn plastic chairs, nibbling *cannoli* amid the jasmine, hibiscus, bougainvillea and young lemon trees, were her family. They were the people who steadfastly loved her in spite of her boozing, melancholia and falls from grace. Who cared for her, scolded her, admired her, escorted her to the fish market, took her mushroom picking, invited her to meals, laughed and quarrelled with her. Who had summoned her uptight nephew to keep an eye on her, who kicked up jealous scenes and looked after her. And for whom, in return, she made life difficult with her escapades, her plans for suicide and her secrets. Poldi suddenly felt mean and childish. She would have liked nothing better than to turn away, ride home and get thoroughly sozzled, but at that moment she was spotted by Oscar, Valérie's friendly little mongrel with the underbite. Barking hoarsely, he scampered towards her, jumped up and cavorted around her like a clockwork toy.

With a sigh of resignation, Poldi emerged from behind the oleander bushes.

Instantly, the cheerful chitchat died away, replaced by a hint of tension.

"Mon dieu!" Valérie exclaimed when she saw Poldi's dress. Montana's smile faded.

Poldi bravely bestowed *mwah-mwahs* all

round. In Italy, kissing is performed from left to right — not, as in Germany, from right to left. Where German-Italian relations are concerned, this can easily lead to central clashes of a painful nature.

When kissing Montana on both cheeks, Poldi felt his hand rest briefly on her hip, which restored her courage a little.

"Teresa called me this morning," the commissario said in explanation of his presence, "to pump me about this meeting, or" — he cleared his throat — "to ask if the two of us had an announcement to make."

Madonna! sighed Poldi when she realised what theories the aunts must have entertained in the past few hours.

"But then," Montana went on, "it occurred to me that you would want to enlighten your family about John and your time in Tanzania. That would interest me too."

Then came the moment of truth. Poldi let Valérie pour her an espresso, consumed a *cannolo* filled with ricotta, orange peel and pistachio nuts, and surveyed each of her assembled dear ones in turn.

"I had a farm in Africa," she began eventually, and dusk was descending on Sicily by the time she had finished.

"And that's it?" I said, rather perplexed. "What about your story?"

"I'd sooner keep it to myself," said Poldi.

"Pardon me, but you told it to *them.*"

"Yes, but they're my inner circle."

"And I don't belong to it?"

"No."

"OK, though I'm a bit surprised to hear that. Don't take this the wrong way, Poldi, but —"

"You don't understand, sonny. I told them because at that moment I had no choice. Besides, I made them all swear never to breathe a word about it."

"But why not? Tell me, Poldi."

"Because it's my own business, for God's sake! Is that so hard to understand? You're a thorough social media junkie, always posting everything, always unloading private stuff as if it was garbage. But it isn't, understand? 'Sharing is caring, postprivacy'? What fatuous nonsense! Some things are so private that every time you broadcast them you lose a bit of yourself. Everyone has a right and a duty to keep secrets, and the same applies to the characters in your novel. If you spill all you know or have found out about them right away, you might as well make them jump over a cliff after ten pages. Without secrets we're zombies, whether as persons or characters in novels. Make a note of that."

She told me in the end, of course; she simply couldn't help it. The only thing she withheld was her precise reason for moving to Tanzania. All I gathered was that it had something to do with a secret mission relating to Kigumbe, and that she'd had to quit Germany and disappear at short notice on account of some private matter. When speaking about Tanzania, though, I saw her eyes light up.

"It's such a wonderful country," she said fervently, "you've no idea. All that space and light — it's like the first day of Creation. Africa is the cradle of the human race, after all, you sense that at once. It sucks you in and seems to whisper 'Welcome home.' The thing is, Tanzania is a country without fences. You never see a fence — it goes on and on forever." She stared pensively into the blue as if surveying the wide-open spaces of Tanzania. "Well," she went on softly, "and then I met John. It was like I'd been struck by lightning, and not just because of the sex and so on, as you're probably thinking, but because he's a really wonderful, warm-hearted man — strange as that may sound right now. John is one of the smartest, kindest people I've ever met. One of the best detectives, too. He isn't in the same league as Vito, admittedly, but I hadn't met Vito at that stage."

"Well," I ventured, "considering he kept quiet about his family and cheated you out of your house, John doesn't sound too wonderful to me."

"There are two sides to him, that's all." She sighed. "And I know a thing or two about split personalities. Besides, maybe I didn't *want* to be too clear about a couple of things."

I nodded. I now knew plenty about blinding oneself to unwelcome reality when one's in love. I'd practically invented the technique.

Poldi's comprehensive revelations about her brief episode in Tanzania — her marriage to John, her purchase of a house, the murder case, the business with Kigumbe and her painful discovery that John secretly had another relationship and two kids on the side all the time, plus had fraudulently acquired her property — aroused three emotions in her listeners at Femminamorta: dismay, sympathy and an appetite for supper.

For my aunts had not, of course, come empty-handed — no fear of that! As soon as Poldi had concluded her account, they swiftly improvised a few tidbits, especially as they had assumed there would be something to celebrate. As the last of the sunlight faded behind the dark-angel silhouette of Etna, they brought out cooler bags, baskets and plastic bowls, and Sicily's delicacies emerged like a fragrant magma composed of tomato sauce, fresh pasta, Parmesan, bottled olives, deep-fried oyster mushrooms, *sarde a beccafico, involtini di pesce spada, polpette in foglie di limone,* dried apricots and my Aunt Caterina's home-made *limoncello.* Accompanying these was a well-chilled Chianta from Trecastagni, and no such picnic would have been complete without a very special jewel of Sicilian cuisine: *caponata.*

It sounds unspectacular. A lukewarm vegetarian dish of fried aubergine, paprika, celery, raisins and pine kernels, it tends to appear on restaurant menus in the small print appropriate to a side dish, but *caponata siciliana* is a complex taste bomb combining all sorts of flavours: salty, sour, sweet and bitter, all in a single mouthful. The trick is to deep-fry the various vegetables separately. The oil is then poured away, and it's not until the end that the ingredients are combined and dressed with fresh olive oil, balsamic vinegar, a squeeze of lemon juice and some parsley. No one wanting to get to know Sicily can avoid eating *caponata*.

Despite Poldi's comprehensive confession, the aunts were still eager for more. Aunt Luisa, who is a great fan of thrillers, asked for further details of the Kigumbe affair. Not even Vito Montana could disguise a touch of admiration. The aunts and Valérie naturally insisted on being introduced to John, but Poldi rejected the idea.

"All in good time, my dears. Right now, Vito and I have to find out what's happened to Thomas."

It didn't escape Poldi that Montana had grown steadily more taciturn and irritable. He drank nothing and smoked one cigarette after another, a clear sign that something was bugging him and that he was on the verge of exploding. Poldi didn't want it to come to that.

"Will you drive me home, Vito?"

"You came on your Vespa."

"Yes, but I've had a bit to drink."

"That doesn't worry you usually."

"Vito, please."

It isn't far from Femminamorta to Torre

Archirafi, less than ten minutes by car, but neither Poldi nor Montana uttered a word until Poldi pointed to an unlit stretch of ground just off the road.

"Please park over there. Yes, there."

"What for?"

"*Dai!* Don't ask, just do it. That's right. Now switch off." Before Montana could say anything, Poldi raised the locking bar under his seat, pushed the seat firmly back to its fullest extent and proceeded to undo his belt.

"What the devil!"

"Zip the lip, *tesoro.*"

For, exactly as she had expected, Montana's pride and joy emerged from his open fly in all its baroque form and dimensions, like a mythical hero released from the chains with which dark powers had secured him to the walls of Hades.

"*Madonna!*" he gasped, clearly surprised by the violent reaction of his throbbing *sicilianità.*

"Alleluia!" cried Poldi, stripping off her dress with a practised hand. Squeezing somewhat awkwardly past the steering wheel, she straddled her commissario's mid-point.

Resistance was useless. Montana was only a man, after all, and a Sicilian detective chief inspector to boot. Nor was he afflicted by Handsome Antonio's failing as described by Brancati. Breathlessly, Montana reached with both hands for the fruits of paradise so unexpectedly offered him, buried his face in her ample bosom, inhaled the scent of warm flesh and eau de cologne, and greedily sampled the nectar of lust.

"I want you!" Panting in his ear as she buried her fingers in his luxuriant greying hair, Poldi felt his breath fan her breasts and his Odysseus thrust its unerring way into Polyphemus's Cyclopean cave.

I always find it difficult to imagine Poldi and Montana having sex anywhere, let alone in the driver's seat of an Alfa. One is bound to be a bit inhibited when one's aunt is involved, I admit, but lust and passion were as much a part of Poldi as depression and booze, murder cases and her wig. A monstrous black beehive that loomed above her head like a thundercloud, the wig went with her like a hot dog with sauerkraut. According to family legend, no one had ever seen what lay beneath it.

The Alfa wobbled, creaked and groaned in every nut and bolt as the windows steamed up inside. Laboured breathing mingled with terms of endearment and cries of rapture pulsated their way out into the surrounding darkness like the heartbeat of some nocturnal creature in quest of redemption. This symphony of lust startled a few stray dogs and may have seeped into the dreams of a slumbering neighbour until every movement and all the little sounds culminated in one big, convulsive crescendo — in a throaty primal cry from my Auntie Poldi, which rose into the night sky like an animal *namaste* thanking the universe for the fact that multiple orgasms were still available to a sexagenarian.

"Because you know," Poldi added later on, when giving me an embarrassingly detailed account of her quickie in the car, "the female body is a mythical universe. No offence to you men — it wouldn't be half as nice without you, and you also get something out of it — but female sexuality is far more complex."

"Good for you."

"Heavens, don't be so uptight! Do you want to learn something or don't you?"

"Look, Poldi, give it a rest. That's enough for now, OK? I mean, I'm happy for you and everything, but there's such a thing as too much information."

"So female sexuality scares you, does it?"

"Certainly not!"

"You're undersupplied, then. All right, it happens, but that's just why you should listen carefully, so you're prepared when the time finally comes. A woman can have up to a hundred orgasms in quick succession, but on three conditions: she must be relaxed or slightly smashed, do a bit of yoga and have a partner she's fond of."

"Since when have you been doing yoga?"

"Oh, I don't need that, I'm talented by nature. A bit of tantra and kundalini doesn't hurt, but neither does a couple of drinks."

And my Auntie Poldi knew a thing or two about sex and booze.

When their overheated, perspiring, no longer youthful bodies had finally disentangled themselves and Poldi had with some difficulty resumed her place on the passenger seat, contented silence reigned in the Alfa. Montana smoked, Poldi adjusted her wig. Pleasurably, she felt desire flowing out of her like a great ebb tide. She felt simultaneously drained and satiated, a wonderful sensation that always, for a few brief moments, reconciled her with fate. She was conscious of Montana beside her, conscious of his warmth, his physical presence. Wondering what name to give this sensation, she came to only one conclusion: love. Without looking at Montana, she took his hand and asked him to give her a cigarette.

"I've made a few inquiries," he said.

Poldi said nothing.

He took another drag before continuing. "The mobile phone the number belonged to was logged in three days ago. In Sant'Alfio."

"That's up on Etna."

"Exactly. I then asked all the car rental firms at Catania Airport whether a car of theirs was missing. A Panda belonging to EtnaCar had been overdue. Guess where they found it."

"Sant'Alfio."

"It was rented by a Thomas Migiro."

Montana went on smoking in self-satisfied silence.

"Yes, and?" Poldi asked impatiently. "Was anything found in the car?"

He shook his head. "No, it was empty. I'm having it checked over right now, but so far there's no indication of an involvement with crime."

"You don't believe that, Vito. Have you asked around in the town?"

"I haven't been there myself, Poldi. It isn't a murder case."

"Let's hope you're right." Poldi sighed. "The car was bound to have a satnav. Have you checked the trip recorder?"

"No, I haven't. Anyway, how do you know such a thing exists?"

Poldi didn't pursue the subject. "What about the mobile provider's call stack?"

"That's enough, Poldi. I'm on it, OK?"

Montana tossed his cigarette end out the window and pulled up his trousers, then drove Poldi the last few hundred metres.

"Want to come in?" she asked when she was standing outside the house.

He shook his head. "Just don't do anything stupid, Poldi, OK?"

"I promise, *tesoro.*"

Poldi kissed him and waved until the Alfa disappeared around the next corner. She lingered outside her door, shivering a little in the cool night air and listening to the waves breaking on the beach beyond the next row of houses. There was no other sound. Torre Archirafi was fast asleep.

"Right, let's do it," she muttered to herself, and set off for the sea front.

On the esplanade, someone was already waiting for her in front of the church of Santa Maria del Rosario.

4

Tells of a nocturnal conversation, of alpha males, English fashion classics and mistrust. Poldi makes an alarming discovery and is compelled to hurry. She acquires a new fellow resident and undertakes investigations in a place famous for its cherries. But, as it turns out, it also has a miracle to offer.

Poldi made out the swanky Mercedes SUV from afar. Clearly visible, it was parked beneath a street light outside the church, but the man who owned it was seated on a boulder below the sea wall, watching his dogs, which were half-heartedly looking for rats or crabs among the rocks. His cream-coloured polo shirt was the only bright spot on the beach. When the two German shepherds spotted my Auntie Poldi laboriously picking her way over the rocks in his direction, they made for her like bullets from a gun.

"Scat!" snarled Poldi, at pains not to wake anyone because she wanted to conduct the forthcoming conversation in camera. "Piss off, you goddam brutes! Scat, you flea-ridden mutts! Scat!"

Hans and Franz seemed somehow to be committed to preserving the clandestine nature of this meeting, because for once they didn't bark, nor did they jump up at my aunt as usual, but merely panted hoarsely. An ugly sound, thought Poldi, and eloquent of cunning and cowardice, except that this time the German shepherds didn't seem so hostile. On the contrary, they circled my aunt, wagging their tails subserviently like obsequious waiters in a tourist trap.

"You're late, Donna Poldina," said Italo Russo as she sat down on the boulder beside him, breathing heavily.

"I had another engagement."

"Then I hope *our* engagement proves to be the highlight of the day."

Russo looked far from annoyed at the delay. He handed my aunt a small paper bag of pistachio nuts. "From Bronte," he said. "I never thought we'd have a romantic assignation on the beach as soon as this."

91

"You can drop the 'romantic' right away. This is merely one of our informal consultations."

I should mention that, although Poldi believed Russo to be a capo Mafioso, or boss of bosses, she had agreed to meet with him occasionally after his assistance in the Avola case, in which they brought down a wine grower with a penchant for murder. A risky business, one might say, for my aunt hoped to learn more about Russo's wheelings and dealings so as to be able to prove his Mafia connections. For his part, of course, Russo wanted something else. *It,* naturally. To get into her knickers, what else?

I mean, although my Auntie Poldi is sixty years old and cross-hatched by life, depression and booze, she still, for some reason, exerts a positively miraculous effect on men of all ages. She gets ogled even by the pomaded young peacocks from Catania who spread their feathers in Torre on summer weekends — honestly, I've seen it for myself.

My sole explanation for this phenomenon is, like many things in Sicily, mythological. Behind a bulletproof window in Vienna's Museum of Natural History one can see the limestone figurine of a corpulent female known as the Venus of Willendorf. Barely eleven centimetres tall, with thin arms, huge breasts and plump thighs, she was sculpted by a Neolithic artist around thirty thousand years ago, during the last Ice Age, when central Europe was so short of food that the whole population migrated south en masse and may have reached Sicily. I can imagine that those people, who knew only hunger and privation, revered corpulence as a divine ideal of beauty. After all, until the advent of the Phoenicians and Moors, Sicily was for thousands of years a barren land in which only olives and almonds grew. Memories of widespread hunger may have etched themselves into Sicilians' DNA, with the result that, notwithstanding all passing fashions and slimming crazes, body-shaming campaigns and low-carb diets, the sight of sensual corpulence still arouses lust in the male beholder. It certainly seemed to in Russo's case.

Tanned, shaven-headed and in his midfifties, Russo owned a veritable empire of palm trees, olive trees, strelitzias and oleanders. Covering hundreds of hectares between Acireale and Riposto, the large-scale nursery known as Piante Russo grew all the flora required by hotels, firms and municipalities in order to beautify their parks and gardens. Situated in the midst of this monocultural hell was Femminamorta, which

Russo had long been wanting to annex, either because he aspired to live there himself, as befitted his social status, or merely as an entrepreneur's final triumph over the decadent Bourbon nobility. Russo's business was obviously going great guns, because his need for land was almost insatiable. He also seemed to have his fingers in a number of quite dissimilar pies, or so Poldi surmised. She had likewise surmised that Russo was after Valérie, but it seemed he had altogether different prey in mind. He was a Sicilian in his bones.

At all events, my Auntie Poldi's businesslike call to order left him cold. He serenely went on chewing pistachio nuts. That was something she found impressive about him, his imperturbability. Wherever he went, he created the impression that everything belonged to him. He even seemed to own the darkened beach plus the whole of slumbering Torre Archirafi into the bargain.

"Do you have something for me, Donna Poldina?"

"What would you like?"

Russo smiled. "It's late, Donna Poldina. Perhaps you'd better just get to the point."

"I'm looking for someone, and I thought you might be able to help me."

"What would be in it for me?"

Poldi had been expecting this question.

"Because," she once told me, "you can offer guys like Russo a blow job and they'll still ask, "What's in it for me?""

"How does ten million dollars sound?" she said, and she saw him stiffen like a pointer taking scent.

"I'm all ears, Donna Poldina."

So Poldi held forth and Russo listened attentively with an impassive expression. He patiently heard her out, seeming to triage all the information in his head as she spoke. He also glanced at the mobile phone photo of Thomas and the photo Poldi had made of the phone number on the postcard.

"Have I got this straight?" he asked when she had finished. "Your Tanzanian husband turns up out of the blue, looking for his brother here in Sicily, of all places. The latter has disappeared without trace after stealing something from a big-time gangster in Arusha. Nobody knows what it is, but according to the gangster it's worth ten million bucks. And that's what this Thomas now plans to sell to someone called Handsome Antonio."

"Bravo, Signor Russo. And I want to know who Handsome Antonio is."

Russo shook his head. "I'm sorry, Donna Poldina, but it sounds like a cock and bull story to me. What's more, I don't see how I can help you."

"I thought you might have certain connections who would pretty soon get wind of the fact that someone wanted to sell something that valuable."

Russo drew a deep breath. "Even if I did, the whole story would have to be true."

"It's true all right, believe me."

"You mean you know what was stolen?"

Poldi bridled. "No. Not exactly, I mean, but I know Kigumbe. He's a really unpleasant type, an unscrupulous criminal, but there's one thing he isn't: a liar."

Russo shook his head again. "I remain unconvinced, Donna Poldina. These hypothetical connections of mine — I couldn't sell them such a vague story."

"There's that phone number!"

Russo shook his head again.

"But the police have recovered Thomas's rented car up in Sant'Alfio," Poldi said. "Surely that could be a useful starting point."

Another shake of the head. "I'm sorry, but I honestly don't think I can be of help to you." Russo got to his feet. "It's late. Come."

He took her hand and escorted her back over the rocks to the esplanade. Hans and Franz, looking somehow relieved they were going home at last, gambolled happily at their heels.

"But I've got to find Handsome Antonio," Poldi said wearily when they reached Russo's car.

"I think you're becoming obsessed, Donna Poldina," Russo replied.

That was precisely the sentence Poldi had been hearing all her life. From her parents, her teachers, her colleagues and bosses. From men. Men seemed to love talking her out of all kinds of things, from her choice of profession to the ways in which a woman, too, can get her due in bed. And, as ever when a man told her, "You're becoming obsessed, Poldi. Just drop it," my aunt dug in her heels.

"You know," said Russo, "I'd love to cook supper for you sometime."

That, in Poldi's experience, was another coded sentence much employed by men. It clearly meant, "I'd love to hear you praise me to the skies for my delicious pasta before jumping into bed with me. You don't even have to stay the night." Well, Poldi was normally the last person to turn down a nice dinner with lots of wine and subsequent nookie, but at the moment, especially after her quickie in the car with Montana, she felt disinclined to flirt. She had genuinely hoped that Russo could help her, and now her hopes had been dashed.

"Signor Russo . . ."

"Call me, Donna Poldina." Suddenly pressed for time, or so it seemed, he whistled up his dogs.

Before Hans and Franz made themselves comfortable in the back of the Mercedes, they both jumped up at my Auntie Poldi, bidding her a contemptuous farewell by soiling her dress with their paws and licking her face. In an attempt to fend them off, she grabbed the dogs by their collars and held them away from her. And then, in the glow of the street light, she saw something sparkle.

Rather at odds with the exalted image Russo usually cultivated, both dogs were wearing collars adorned with sequins. Red sequins, as Poldi saw as soon as she bent down for a better look. She could also see that some of the sequins had already become detached.

"Nice collars," she said when the initial shock had subsided.

"Oh, they were a present to the brutes from my daughter. They won't last long, though — my house is already littered with those shiny little things."

"You don't say." Poldi straightened up.

"Good night, Signor Russo. Think of it: ten million. I wouldn't want you to be miffed because I was quicker off the mark without you."

"Sleep well, Donna Poldina."

Russo got into the Mercedes, and Poldi watched the mega-nurseryman drive off with the uneasy feeling that she'd given away far too much to a capo Mafioso, thereby putting Thomas in even greater danger.

"Dammit!"

She realised that she must be quick and, as so often in her life, take matters in hand herself, so she hurried home.

Where someone else awaited her.

Poldi stole into No. 29 Via Baronessa as quietly as a cat burglar, hoping to catch John nosing around in her things. The whole house was hushed and in darkness apart from a dim, flickering light in the little inner courtyard. All that broke the silence was a murmur of voices. Tiptoeing nearer, she saw John and Montana sitting there by the light of a citronella candle. The two men had helped themselves to bottles of beer and appeared to be chatting. Conversation ceased as soon as Poldi entered the courtyard.

"Poldi!" John exclaimed like the master of the house greeting a belated guest.

"Am I intruding?" Poldi demanded rather irritably. "Enjoying yourselves? Anyone want another beer?"

"Where have you been?" Montana retorted, stubbing out his cigarette.

"What are you doing here, Vito?"

"I asked you a question."

Another sentence in the tone of voice my Auntie Poldi couldn't stand. It smacked of jealousy, claims of ownership and bullying.

"I've been for a little walk," she snapped.

"I'll leave you to yourselves," said John, pushing back his chair.

"No, don't get up, I'm sure you've got a lot to discuss. Like how to keep an eye on me, for example. Like how to prevent me causing trouble and interfering. You're bound to think of something."

"Good night, the two of you," said John, and went to his room upstairs.

"Calm down, Poldi," Montana said in Italian. "I was merely bringing John up to date with things."

"Couldn't it have waited till tomorrow?"

"And I'm moving in with you for a while."

Poldi stared at him. "Strange, I don't remember us discussing it."

"It's only while he's here," Montana went

on calmly.

"What are you, Vito, my chaperone? What happens when John goes — will you pick up your vanity case and say, *Ciao bella*?"

"I thought" — Montana cleared his throat — "I thought you might be pleased."

She really was. Of course she looked forward to the prospect of going to sleep in Montana's arms every night and waking in their embrace every morning. She looked forward to the scent of his eau de cologne in the bathroom, to neatly folded towels, bottles of shampoo arranged in order of size and a tidy kitchen. Because, in contrast to my aunt, Montana suffered from mild OCD. He even possessed a designer salad spinner, in Poldi's view the epitome of middle-class mentality and control freakery. She looked forward to the prospect of a little routine and normality in Montana's company. All the same, she would have preferred to have been asked beforehand.

"Why can't I rid myself of the feeling that you're spying on me, Vito?" she said with a sigh, and fetched herself a beer.

"Where there's a will, there's always a way," Poldi used to say, but everything became more complicated with two alpha males in the house. She wanted to keep no secrets from Montana, avoid doing anything stupid and be a good girl. The only trouble was, my Auntie Poldi simply wasn't made that way. There were few stupidities she hadn't committed in her life. She'd always had her secrets, and she'd never, as one can imagine, wanted to be a good girl.

Nevertheless, she enjoyed going to sleep beside Montana, or rather, watching him go out like a light and lying awake beside him for ages.

"It's like this, you see," she told me once. "Men always sleep better beside women, but women sleep worse. It's an evolutionary thing. From a woman's point of view, a guy in bed is a kind of overgrown child that might need attention at any minute."

The next morning she got up early and made the two men breakfast. She was irritated to find that, after wishing her the barest of good-mornings, they hardly exchanged a word. What bugged her most of all was not the jealousy that flickered between them like an electrical discharge, but their unspeaking alpha-male demeanour. In other words, their claim to ownership. And then she sensed another vibe between John and Montana. More like a faint scent, it was a musky whiff of camaraderie. And Poldi didn't like that at all.

So she chivvied Montana off to work as soon as possible, gave John a long shopping list and completed her toilette. True to her motto "Never underdress," she embarked on her investigations suitably attired. In view of the chilly weather and low clouds that boded an unpleasant drizzle up in Sant'Alfio, Poldi this time favoured a British look: a respectable ensemble comprising a yellow and black tweed suit, a scarf adorned with hunting scenes and a broad-brimmed felt hat from Styria, which was indissolubly anchored to her wig with countless hairpins, since she refused on principle to ride her Vespa wearing a helmet. A helmet would only have flattened her wig and it might have got stuck. Besides, if a woman intends to drink herself to death sooner or later, petit bourgeois health and safety measures cease to matter much. Poldi has never been stopped by the police for failing to wear a helmet, to the best of my knowledge, presumably because the wig resembles a helmet anyway. She wore pumps with this outfit, needless to say, and for protection from the rain she chose her mac. The mackintosh has been the traditional rainwear of English traffic cops since the nineteenth century, and Poldi knew a thing or two about traffic cops and fashion statements. A garment of this kind, which is made of patented rubberised and vulcanised cotton fabric, is entirely waterproof and guaranteed nonbreathable. It doesn't keep out the cold, but as soon as the outside temperature exceeds ten degrees centigrade the wearer sweats like a pig. The macs worn by English traffic cops are a sober blue in colour. Poldi's mac, by contrast, was pink — neon pink, to be exact. A unicorn from a Japanese manga with a glittering tail of stardust could not have been more conspicuous, and Poldi looked like an inflated flamingo. But, to quote her again: moderation is a sign of weakness.

Freshly fortified by an espresso laced with cognac — almost sober, in other words — she mounted her Vespa and zoomed up to Sant'Alfio.

Devoid of any special features, Sant'Alfio is a small, sleepy town on the eastern slopes of Etna. Apart from a bit of baroque in the local church, it has little to offer but fog, boredom, suspicion and fatalism. As in many small Sicilian towns, the shutters are kept defiantly shut all year round, and at noon the place resembles a ghost town. The closed shutters are due to the Sicilians' idea of privacy. Privacy is sacred and one's own home a refuge from economic crises and summer heat, neighbours and tribulations. The shutters function like translucent membranes through which one can peer out at the world without being spotted.

Sant'Alfio is noted for only two things: its cherries and the Hundred-Horse Chestnut tree.

Sant'Alfio's cherries are — you've guessed it — the best in the world. I didn't believe that myself, but some years ago Uncle Martino brought home a whole punnet. In my critical German way, which is much appreciated in the family, I was quick to doubt the cherries' superlative quality. That is, until I tried one and groaned with delight. No fruit could have tasted more voluptuously cherryish, and that's a fact.

The Hundred-Horse Chestnut is one of the oldest living things on earth. Dendrologists put the age of the gnarled and overgrown monster at somewhere between two and three thousand years. The trunk is twenty-two metres in circumference and has developed a kind of central clearing in which the aristocratic landowners used to hold banquets until the nineteenth century. Almost destroyed by fire a hundred years ago, the tree is now protected by a conservation order and enclosed by a fence. Seen from the fence, it looks more like a small copse comprising several partly stunted trees, but it is nonetheless a single, ancient plant that has stubbornly defied storms, volcanic eruptions, feasts, fires and climatic vicissitudes.

The road to Sant'Alfio is winding and circuitous, and Poldi took nearly an hour to get there. So it was hardly surprising that her back was aching, and the first thing she did on reaching the place was to pull up in front of the bar next to the church. Like a Wild West gunslinger who tethers his horse outside and stomps into the saloon, Poldi was met by the stares of the men who were sitting over their *caffè* in the interior. She might have been a creature from Mars — or from a Japanese manga.

"Morning all," she said affably, and ordered a double *corretto.*

No reaction. The men just stared at her in silence. That's to say, they didn't *stare,* of course. Sicilians never stare, they have panoramic vision. Through the centuries of occupation by various foreign powers, they have developed indirect rubbernecking into an art form. Sunglasses are helpful, naturally, but even without them Sicilians can keep an eye on everything within 180 degrees while looking as aloof and uninvolved as cats on a windowsill. They are

106

capable of carrying on a conversation while entirely focused on their objective — in other words, the potential threat, whether it be a Mafioso, debt collector, plainclothesman, neighbour or simply someone who might cause trouble. The only people exempt from this cultural technique are showbiz celebs, who may be gawped at, slapped on the back, invited home and forced to participate in selfies.

The young barmaid behind the counter, who was chewing gum incessantly with her mouth open, had less self-control. She couldn't stop staring at the exotic-looking stranger.

Poldi showed her the mobile phone photo of Thomas. "Have you by any chance seen this man here in town recently?"

No answer. The girl just chewed and stared, chewed and stared.

"Perhaps you could take a good look at this photo, signorina. He must have been around a few days ago. Maybe he had a *caffè* here."

The young barmaid shook her head, still open-mouthed. Poldi tried the men at the counter and the two tables, but just as unsuccessfully. The most she elicited was a dismissive shake of the head. It dawned on her that this form of questioning wouldn't get her far elsewhere in the town either. She would have to adapt her tactics to local conditions, so she ordered another café cognac.

"The person I'm really looking for is Handsome Antonio," she said casually, but in a louder voice. Having paid for her two *corretti,* she said a friendly goodbye and left the bar.

She adopted the same procedure in three other bars, the fishmonger's and the fruiterer's, in two *alimentari* smelling of mortadella and chlorinated cleaning fluid, and with the elderly gentlemen in the piazza.

Having gone for a protracted stroll around town in this way and accosted just about every inhabitant, Poldi seated herself on a bench in the piazza, consumed a panino and a can of lemonade, and waited. Micromovements in the general scene told her that her tactic was working. One of the elderly men called a little boy over and whispered something to him, looking in Poldi's direction, whereupon the boy ran off as if his pants were on fire. The stolen glances to which she was subjected, hitherto merely suspicious, had become alarmed. Poldi registered all these developments with satisfaction. She had tossed a pebble into a pond. It had caused ripples, startled a few somnolent fish and finally come to rest on the bottom, stirring up mud that might have been better left undisturbed.

Nothing much happened for the next half-hour, but Poldi could definitely sense she was being watched from all sides through closed shutters. It was almost noon by now, the clouds had dispersed, and it was getting hot. Poldi was sweating in her tweed suit, so she took off her mac, grunting with the effort. There wasn't a soul in sight apart from the old men on their bench.

Poldi considered abandoning the whole venture when a patrol car drove into the piazza and pulled up. The patrol car disgorged a young carabiniere in his early thirties, or so she estimated. He looked around as if checking on the weather and donned his sunglasses, but eagle-eyed Poldi had of course noted that *she* was the first thing he looked at. This electrified her, especially as he was quite good-looking, not to say sexy, not to say an absolute humdinger. He had classical, bronzed features, a nice Adam's apple, a not overly slim, overly gym-toned figure and even — Poldi noticed this at once — a teensy-weensy tum-tum of the kind for which she had a well-known predilection. His hands looked strong and gentle at the same time. All in all, he was a sight for sore eyes and a definite candidate for inclusion in Poldi's photo album devoted to policemen. She stealthily got out her mobile phone and activated the continuous shooting function.

The smart carabiniere set off and strolled across the piazza in a studiously unobtrusive manner, nodded to the old men on the bench, meandered around rather obviously and then came towards Poldi. Poldi was ready. She covertly aimed her phone at the policeman and waited until he was near enough, then pressed the button and took a series of photos of him. The carabiniere noticed nothing. He strolled past Poldi, glanced briefly at her and walked on. Poldi saw him get into his patrol car, but he didn't drive off.

Satisfied with the impression she had clearly made on him, Poldi was about to examine the photos when she saw the errand boy return in high excitement and whisper something to the old man on the bench. Soon afterwards a woman came up to her. Middle-aged, not very well dressed, tired-looking. Could be a hospital nurse coming off a long shift, thought Poldi. The woman sat down on the bench beside her and blew her nose.

"Are you from television?"

That question was the last thing Poldi had expected.

"Do I look like it?"

"So who sent you?" the woman asked wearily without looking at her.

It occurred to Poldi that this was Sicily, and that she might be in for trouble, so she pulled herself together.

"No one," she replied as coolly as she could manage. "I'm just a desperate woman hunting for someone who stole something from me, something I'd like returned."

"Nobody here has stolen anything from you, signora."

"I'd sooner question Handsome Antonio in person," Poldi retorted stoutly.

Another shot in the dark, but it obviously found its mark.

"Antonio won't speak to you."

"Then I'll wait here until he changes his mind. Or would it be better if I called him, do you think? I've got his number, after all." Poldi held out a slip of paper bearing the phone number she had copied off the postcard found in the hotel. "That is his number, isn't it?"

The tired-looking woman didn't even look at it. She seemed to be thinking.

Then, turning towards Poldi, she scrutinised her closely. "Nice suit."

"Thanks."

"You're wearing a wig."

It didn't sound like a question, more a confirmation of something already known. Poldi was at a loss how to reply.

"Er . . . yes."

The woman shook her head with an incredulous air and got to her feet. "Come with me."

Without looking back at Poldi once, the putative hospital nurse strode out of the piazza. She led Poldi along several small side streets that zigzagged across town until she came to an unremarkable gateway and went through it into the courtyard beyond. Poldi plucked up her courage and followed. She just had time to see the woman enter a one-storey, windowless building on the far side, possibly a car repair shop, judging by the oil stains and the tyres lying about. When the woman opened the big iron door a few inches and slipped inside, the sound of choral singing drifted out through the crack.

In B movies this is always the time you long to shout, "Don't do it! Call for backup!" Poldi knew it was pretty silly to go in there without calling Montana first. On the other hand, the singing made the presence of Mafia killers rather unlikely.

So she bravely entered the workshop,

which was lit by neon tubes overhead. The interior smelt of rubber and petrol and — ever so slightly — incense as well. It looked as if it had recently and hurriedly been converted into a place of worship. The workbenches, mobile hydraulic hoist, body panels, tyres, waste oil containers and scrap metal had been pushed up against the side walls to make room for a group of around thirty people seated on folding chairs. All quite normal in appearance, they were softly singing a chorale in Italian, holding their rosaries or aiming their mobile phones at a child sitting in front of them, who was perched on a massive wooden chair — almost a throne, one might have said. Attired in a white dress and veiled like a bride, the child was holding a sketch pad and drawing something with a felt pen, seemingly lost in thought.

The singing ceased when Poldi came in, and everyone turned to stare at her. The tired-looking signora, who was standing beside the child, beckoned her over.

With a slight but understandable feeling of reluctance, Poldi went closer. The woman lifted the veil to reveal the chubby-cheeked, petulant face of a boy no older than eight or nine — Poldi was no expert on children.

The boy stopped drawing and pouted.

"Why have they stopped? Make them go on singing! Go on, make them!"

"They will in a minute, Antonino," said the tired-looking woman. "The signora here would just like to ask you something."

"Is this Handsome Antonio?" Poldi asked in disbelief.

"It's what he likes being called," whispered the woman, who was evidently his mother, "ever since the Madonna appeared to him and told him to wear dresses. That's why we call him that. If we don't, he gets bad-tempered, and when he's bad-tempered he draws disasters." She crossed herself.

It occurred to Poldi that she had heard of this strange child. The local papers had printed sporadic accounts of "Handsome Antonio of Sant'Alfio," who had also been the subject of a report by a local radio station. The Mother of God had allegedly appeared to him one morning and commanded him to do two things: wear nothing but white clothes and draw pictures of the imminent Apocalypse. Previously quite untalented, the boy had from then on produced some masterly drawings, all of which depicted dire future happenings. As though in demonstration of his prophetic gifts, he had identified a stolen car and its thief, prevented an accident on a construction site, cured a blind man and located the hidden savings of a recently deceased person. However, the blind man and the savings had quickly proved to be hoaxes, which was spitefully publicised by the press. This had considerably reduced the media's interest in the subject and left behind a certain dislike of its representatives, and this, in turn, accounted for the local mistrust of Poldi.

Child prodigies to whom the Madonna manifests herself are forever turning up somewhere in Italy. They occasion a brief outbreak of local hysteria and then sink without trace. Poldi regarded the whole thing as pure eyewash, a scam perpetrated by unscrupulous parents who exploited their children on trashy TV shows and hoped to make a killing out of them. She wasn't too keen on Catholicism and its belief in miracles to begin with, and this pouting brat in a bridal gown confirmed her prejudice in spades.

The child glanced at Poldi, then turned back to his mother. "Tell her to go away," he whined. "She's bad and she tells lies."

Poldi heaved a rueful sigh. Great, she thought, dead end. She wasn't a big fan of children, and she felt like giving this specimen a hiding. But she was on an official mission here, so she showed the brat and his mother the mobile phone photo of Thomas.

"Was this man here recently?"

"I won't say!" snapped the boy. "Only if she takes her wig off, I want to see what's underneath. Tell her to take it off, Mamma!"

"Nothing doing, you little shit," Poldi hissed in German, glancing angrily at the mother.

"He was quite different before," the woman insisted. She looked genuinely exhausted. "I know the Madonna chose him, but there are times when I'd like to have my old Antonino back."

"If you really want to do him some good, take him to see a doctor," Poldi told her. She turned to go.

Antonino's mother caught her by the arm and held her back. "Wait!" She pulled a small portfolio from under the chair, leafed through some drawings and then handed one to Poldi. "Antonino did this one last week."

"You must call me Handsome Antonio! Tell her to take off her wig or I'll draw something nasty."

Poldi had had enough. All she wanted was to leave before she slapped the boy. Reluctantly, she glanced at the drawing.

And uttered a startled squeak. "He drew this?"

The woman nodded. Poldi broke out in a sweat. The drawing might have been executed by a Renaissance master, not a child. Done with a felt pen, it was extremely detailed, delicately cross-hatched in a way that perfectly captured the light and shade, and the coloration was beautiful. It was a portrait of Poldi on her Vespa.

That would not have been enough to give her such a shock on its own: her photo had appeared in sundry local papers in the past few months, so it was quite possible that little Antonino had chanced to see it. No, what really put the fear of God into her was that the week-old drawing showed her in today's outfit: a yellow and black tweed suit, a scarf, a felt hat and a pink mac.

5

Tells of adaptation to the inexplicable, of hidden talents, enchanted places and — yet again — of men. Poldi's nephew becomes inspired and she takes her wig off. Then she disturbs the elves and loses something. Soon afterwards, she finds something.

The human brain is the real miracle. Especially that of my Auntie Poldi, which in spite of booze and advancing age, protected from extreme climatic vicissitudes by her wig, works with the precision of a high-performance machine. My Auntie Poldi's brain can, within seconds, pounce from a standing start like a panther on the prowl, operate flat out, detect patterns, draw conclusions and then just tick over again. My aunt's brain is a triumph of adaptation and induction. If she concentrates on something, her expression undergoes a change, becoming abstracted and not of this world. This is deceptive, however, because not only are all her senses on the ball; she is wired, her body is a highly sensitive antenna, no detail escapes her, and beneath her wig, in nanoseconds, all items of information are filtered, ordered and deciphered. When confronted by the inexplicable, below-average normal guys like me would naturally flip out at once — say if, on a comfortable train ride through the Black Forest, they suddenly saw Godzilla appear from behind a hill and come trampling along the tracks. Or if the zombie apocalypse broke out, as I sometimes imagine it will. Someone like me would simply freak out: lips flecked with foam, convulsions, collapse. Not so my Auntie Poldi, because her brain has already attained the next stage of evolution and possesses an innate, very Bavarian attribute: serenity. Germans from farther north construe the Bavarian mantra "Well now, let's see" as ignorant complacency. In fact, it's a brilliant buffer off which every enormity bounces and can be calmly examined with due pragmatism. My Auntie Poldi isn't easily thrown off balance by anything but the sight of a strapping traffic cop on point duty — certainly not by some impudent brat's Old Masterish drawing, which shouldn't by rights have existed.

The fact remained, though, that it *did* exist. She was holding it in her hand.

"Interesting," she said when she'd recovered her composure and was examining the drawing more calmly. When one's brain has come to terms with the inexplicable, it provides a basis for further considerations. For instance:

"Are there any more like this?"

Antonino's mother nodded.

"Tell her to take her wig off!" squawked Antonino. "Wig off first! Wig off first!"

Poldi's palm itched, but she restrained herself and showed his mother Thomas's photo again.

"Did Antonino draw him too?"

"It's possible."

Poldi pointed to the portfolio. "May I look through that?"

The woman handed it to her with a shrug.

"No!" Antonino whined shrilly. "Only if you take off your wig!"

"What if I don't?" Poldi hissed at him. "What if I simply look at your drawings and be damned?"

"Then I'll draw something very, very nasty — and it'll happen!"

Poldi didn't believe that, but the people on the folding chairs did. She saw the horror in their eyes and their determination to prevent the Apocalypse from happening at all costs. She didn't want it to come to that.

"You disgusting little twerp," she hissed in German.

And took off her wig.

"Wow!" I said when she told me this on the sofa at Femminamorta. "Did you really?"

"Why, I had no choice."

She took a drink.

I have no idea how long we'd been sitting on the sofa. I only remember it was very late at night by then. I didn't feel in the least bit tired, just slightly bemused by my aunt's story. I needed to straighten out my thoughts.

"Poldi?"

"Yes, my boy?"

"You once told me I was to be your chronicler, so to speak. You did, didn't you? I was to put everything down on paper sometime. For posterity, I mean. And to gain us an international reputation. Well, you more than me, of course."

Poldi eyed me suspiciously. "What are you getting at?"

"Well, if I'm to write everything down, I must know everything to begin with, that's only logical. I mean, you've already given me detailed descriptions of your quickies and things, but if I'm to present a really authentic picture of you, you'll have, for better or worse, to —"

"Forget it."

"— bare all, Poldi. Simone de Beauvoir said that too. So off with that wig of yours!"

I grinned at her. And promptly earned myself — smack! — a cuff on the ear.

"You cheeky young devil! I'm still your aunt, and that means I deserve some respect, got that?"

We stared at each other.

And simultaneously burst out laughing.

"You almost had me fooled!" Poldi spluttered. There was mischief in her expression and, to my surprise, a touch of benevolence.

I'm sometimes questioned on the subject by the aunts. Uncle Martino harbours a particularly lively interest in it.

"You see her all the time," they'd say. "Surely you must have seen her, well, *without* it?"

But no, I haven't. Well, not *directly,* but I don't have to say as much to the family.

Tired of talking by now and slightly tipsy, Poldi went off to bed.

I, on the other hand, was wide awake, my mind in turmoil and awash with inspiration. My equivalent of *The Forsyte Saga,* which had lapsed into a coma for so many weeks, was summoning me back to the keyboard at the top of its voice. Adjectives were seething inside me and demanding to surface. An adjectival volcano, I had hoped for this sudden impetus and was far from unprepared when it smote me. On the flight to Catania I had made some notes on my novel's structure and incredibly complex plot, for the whole work was to be a brilliant epic spanning a century and three generations. Nothing less than a marvel of overlapping story lines and narrative skill, of ingenious twists and turns and subtle social criticism, replete with conflict, drama, humour, action and eroticism, it was to be a monstrous, purring, Kafkaesque machine whose perfectly oiled components meshed with a satisfying click — in short, a page-turner destined to be translated into thirty languages. Something of that kind naturally needs careful planning. I felt like an engineer who has just been employed to build a steelworks in China and now, without more ado, sets to work with confidence, determination and a light hand. With utter professionalism, in fact. So I hurried off to my stuffy chapel room, jury-rigged the wobbly desk and opened my laptop in readiness to unleash a typhoon of intriguing metaphors.

To recap: My virile young hero and orphaned great-grandfather, Barnaba, emigrates from Sicily to Munich in 1919. With the assistance of the alchemist Pasqualina and the preternaturally beautiful Cyclops Ilaria, he builds up a wholesale fruit-importing empire based in Munich's central market. In so doing he avails himself of certain unscrupulous business methods and shady insider dealings. This, in turn, introduces the cantankerous Munich police inspector Vitus Tanner, who implacably hunts Barnaba from now on.

Barnaba has not only fathered a child with the buxom barmaid Rosi but passes up no opportunity to acquaint the belles of Munich with the delights of *sicilianità* and the eruptions of his mighty Etna. (I had yet to write these passages, but I'd inserted marks to show where I would flesh them out in a sumptuously sensual but tasteful manner. All very cinematic.)

Barnaba loves Munich. He loves German reliability. He visits Catania only once a year, travelling with a suitcase full of cash, the better to reinforce certain business connections. He also re-impregnates Eleonora, his first love, who never sets foot outside the house and spends his entire visit tearfully begging him never to leave. I shall later elaborate on these moving, heart-rending scenes in potent language. For the present I mark the place with a weeping emoji.

Puny little Federico, his son with Eleonora, weeps the whole time too, and is scared of the strange man he has to call Papa. But he also has to call other strange men Papa — for instance, John Kigumbe, a Tanzanian diplomat, word of whose regular visits to the house on Corso Italia must on no account reach the ears of the papa named Barnaba.

Barnaba wears tailor-made suits, gloves, fur coats and snakeskin shoes, and lends unbureaucratic assistance to impoverished Sicilian families who lack the money for a doctor or coal when their children fall sick. Still under thirty, Don Barnaba is revered and feared like a Cyclops. If some obstreperous hothead dares to compete with him, it isn't long before the Munich fire brigade has to put out a blazing market stall or fish some unfortunate person out of the Isar.

Munich in the 1920s is, in fact, a place where no omelettes are made without breaking some eggs. A gold-rush, life-in-the-fast-lane atmosphere prevails. The city vibrates and fizzes with promise and joie de vivre. In smart bars foxtrots are danced and morphine is injected, and in beer halls a little man with a toothbrush moustache delivers hysterical, rabble-rousing speeches. He always wears a long raincoat and a broad-brimmed hat and packs a clearly visible revolver. He also likes to brandish a riding crop. Barnaba knows him by sight from the Osteria Bavaria, the restaurant owned by his partner Deutelmoser, in Schelling-strasse, but steers clear of him on Pasquali-na's advice. He isn't much interested in politics anyway, and his Cyclopean instinct whispers to him that the little man is very, very dangerous — and not just because of the revolver. So for safety's sake Barnaba considers getting some of his most reliable associates, two ruthless brothers from Ra-gusa, to take an interest in the little man. The Munich streets were ill lit in those days, and someone could easily have an accident, get their neck caught in a garrotte and fall into the Isar. However, Barnaba abandons this plan when Vitus Tanner's investigations into the brothel incident become more and more of a problem to him. At that point I underlined the word "investigations," typed three interrogation marks in the margin, staggered off to bed and instantly fell into a feverish sleep.

"Take it off! Take your wig off!"

126

Poldi suddenly felt sorry for Handsome Antonino. Behind his theatrical attire and tearful expression she detected a very lonely child. She might not know much about children, but she knew plenty about loneliness. She knew what it meant to grow up in the provinces, and the Sicilian provinces, with their narcissistic *sicilianità* myth, were the bitter end. Poldi saw a little boy whose parents had done their best to spoil him, mainly with sweets and plastic toys, but whose latent talent they had never recognised, still less encouraged, until the Madonna appeared to him, for the Madonna was Italy's universal fixer — or so it seemed to Poldi. She felt sorry for Handsome Antonino because this wouldn't make it any easier for him to escape someday from the confines of his one-horse home town. His breathtaking talent was a sufficient complication without the addition of a gift for prophecy. Poldi had known enough people with that gift to know that it only made them lonelier. Nobody really wants to know what the future looks like, because it could look even lousier than the present state of affairs.

"Take it off!"

"All right," Poldi said with a sigh, turning round.

The group of people on the folding chairs gawped at Poldi and held up their phones like fans at a pop concert.

"Put 'em down!" she called sharply. "On the floor, under your chairs."

Reluctant compliance. When all the phones were sufficiently hard to reach beneath their chairs, Poldi removed the hairpins that anchored her hat to her wig, bent down a little so Antonino could see and bared her head.

"Whee!" Antonino gasped in awe, and a collective murmur made itself heard in the background. The boy put his hand out, but Poldi retreated and clapped the wig on again.

"That's enough. Now for the other drawings."

Antonino stared at Poldi open-mouthed, as if she were the Madonna in person, and nodded.

Poldi opened the portfolio and looked through it. The drawings' quality of execution still astounded her. Antonino might be an impudent brat, but there was no doubting his talent. Many of the drawings were of everyday scenes in Sant'Alfio. They captured the individual attitudes and gestures of the human figures with great skill, and the whole impression they created was one of life and movement. They were genuinely beautiful.

Looking up, Poldi saw that Antonino was watching her closely, as if awaiting some form of redemption. And that was when she had a prophetic moment of her own: she could clearly see Antonino as an adult. His talent would rot away like leaves under snow. He would do as he was told and bury his secret aspirations so as not to stand out any more. He would resign himself to his fate.

Perhaps he would lose his chubby cheeks and even, for a while, become a handsome fellow. Having scraped through his school-days, he would later design advertising leaflets for a third-rate agency or, at best, become a carabiniere or a municipal police-man. He would get married young to a proxy for his mother and have children. He might occasionally draw unicorns for his kids, but that would be it. He would develop a tummy and wear Reptile sports shades like his peers. He would never view Renaissance art in the Uffizi or travel abroad, because he would never leave Sant'Alfio. Perhaps he would never cease to dream secretly of drawing, and that would make him suspicious, envious and timorous — in other words, turn him into the sort of Sicilian male Brancati so scathingly portrayed in his novels. And that Poldi found almost heartbreaking.

"Promise me something," she whispered to him. "Make sure you get away from this place as soon as possible, OK? You're good at this, so go away and make something of it. OK?"

Sometimes it takes only a word or two — at least, Poldi hoped so. Antonino grinned and nodded. Poldi gave the boy a conspiratorial wink and went on leafing through his drawings.

He had sometimes drawn monsters, or monsters fighting monsters. Or monsters devouring people and crushing cars. Children do that, it's quite normal — except when such drawings are executed with a precision worthy of Dürer; then it turns your stomach. Poldi did not find much that was prophetic, however. That might explain the waning media interest, she reflected. Perhaps the tracing of the stolen car, the prevention of an accident on the building site, the curing of the blind man and the discovery of the nest egg were all simply faked, she thought. Perhaps that drawing of herself was just . . . She stopped short, staring at the drawing in her hand. It too depicted my Auntie Poldi. Still in the same suit, but skirtless, she was standing in a little wood or copse and holding a spade in her hand. And she wasn't alone. Someone was standing beside her — someone she knew only too well.

"When did you draw this?"

"Last week." Little Antonino suddenly made a far more lucid impression.

An appalling thought occurred to Poldi; it was as if the effects of some drug were wearing off.

"Why aren't I wearing a skirt in your picture?"

Antonino shrugged. "I only draw what I see."

She tapped the copse. "Where's that?"

"That's the Hundred-Horse Chestnut tree," the mother said. "Do you know the man standing beside you?"

"I certainly do," Poldi said. Taking out her mobile, she dialled a number and waited. "Pick up, for God's sake!"

But Montana didn't pick up, not even after the tenth ring. Poldi turned to Antonino's mother again.

"Tell me where this chestnut tree is. Oh yes, and I'll probably need a spade."

She mounted her Vespa and ten minutes later reached a small area on the outskirts of the town that had been converted into a sort of botanical amusement park, complete with nature trail, noticeboards, car park, information desk and refreshment kiosk. Not far away stood another very ancient chestnut tree, the Ship Chestnut. The municipality had wanted to make a bit of tourist capital out of Italy's two oldest trees, but now, on a Tuesday afternoon late in October, the car park was empty and the kiosk shut.

Poldi soon located the Hundred-Horse Chestnut.

"Well, tickle my ass with a feather!" she exclaimed when she was standing in front of it, because the sight of the possibly three-thousand-year-old chestnut seemed to send the millennia coursing through her veins. She gazed at the huge tree, whose crown was autumnally aglow and rustling softly in the breeze, with a humble, awestruck sense of how small she was.

Actually, the Hundred-Horse Chestnut looked more like a small, circular copse, a ring of gnarled tree trunks surrounding a shady central clearing. Poldi could not get any closer because it was entirely enclosed by iron railings topped with spikes. She rattled the gate for form's sake and circled the tree once. Having viewed its wonderful tracery from all sides, she almost felt it was speaking to her, singing her its ancient song of solitude, the seasons and eternity. As one of the noticeboards explained, such living trees can replace dead parts with new shoots, so they're fundamentally immortal, provided the climate remains stable and no one sets fire to them.

Poldi tried to detect some unusual or suspicious feature, but all she spotted was a squirrel. It was no use, she had to get closer, if only because Antonino's drawing had shown her standing plumb in the middle of the clearing with Montana.

She called Montana again, but he still didn't pick up. She turned round. There was no one to be seen; she was alone. She took hold of one of the rails and gave it a half-hearted shake, looking up at the danger-ously sharp spikes.

"Bugger it, what a daft idea this is!" Resolutely, she hurled the spade over the fence and tried to wedge a foot between two rails and pull herself up a little. "There's always a way," she growled defiantly.

The fence was not all that high. Two metres, perhaps, so not exactly the north face of the Eiger. However, Poldi was no Messner or Kammerlander, and rock climb-ing had never been her thing.

Without really meaning to, I can never resist picturing my aunt as she grimly scaled that fence in her high heels and tweed suit. I see her slip, swear, start again, slip, adjust her wig and, panting and cursing, inch her way gradually higher. The more she fulminates, the stronger she gets, because my Auntie Poldi can become a pit bull when she has to. Tenacious to the end, once she has sunk her teeth in something, she never lets go.

So she struggled, clawed and hauled herself upwards, bit by bit, until she got to the spikes. What now? Poldi had had an idea. Before embarking on her climb she had draped her pink mac over the spikes, because the rubberised cotton fabric was pretty tear-resistant and provided reasonable protection against being impaled when folded twice. Grunting, Poldi rolled over the mackintosh padding and slithered to the ground on the far side. But alas, her skirt caught on a spike, and when she exhaustedly surrendered to gravity, it ripped the material from waistline to hem.

"Hellsbellsandbucketsofblood!"

She examined the skirt to see if there was anything to be done, but no joy. However, my Auntie Poldi possesses the Bavarian gift of doggedly, steadfastly pursuing an objective, come what may — skirtless if necessary.

Scrambling to her feet, she looked around to see if anyone was watching and tweaked her tweed jacket straight. Now clad only in that and her semi-translucent pantyhose, she looked vaguely like an ageing revue dancer trying to resuscitate her career in a 1950s movie. But Poldi couldn't have cared less about that, not now. Picking up the spade, she marched towards the chestnut tree.

The nearer she got to it, the louder it seemed to whisper to her. A warning, perhaps, or just a friendly greeting. Its multiple crowns were still rustling softly in the breeze, and when Poldi entered the clearing she felt as if she had left the whole world behind, together with her skirt. She would have liked to strip down and be entirely naked and free in this magical place, which was devoid of melancholy and passion and pervaded only by the murmur of the passing years. It was peaceful here, a cool and silent place where one would have liked to build a hut and remain forever. For a moment Poldi just stood there, turning on the spot and gazing up into the dense foliage overhead. A squirrel scampered excitedly hither and thither; flies, beetles and flower petals shimmered in the air; and yellow chestnut leaves fluttered slowly down on her.

It was an enchanted place where elves and trolls danced by night and wanted their peace and quiet during the day, thought Poldi, and she felt like an uninvited guest trampling through paradise. On the other hand, she herself resembled a sort of elf in her short jacket and pantyhose, so she almost went with the ensemble. Determined to avoid unduly disturbing the clearing's invisible, pointy-eared residents, she resolved to get on with the job.

Tricky, when you don't know what the job is.

She looked around. With a spade in her hand and butterflies in her tummy, a female ace detective can usually see what's what. Sighing, Poldi focused her gaze on the ground and paced its soft, mossy, leaf-strewn surface, which was threaded with roots like sinews. The clearing looked as if no one had set foot there for ages, but that, alas, was only an initial impression, because Poldi discovered the spot on her second circuit.

It was just in front of one of the tree's main trunks, on the edge of the clearing, and she noticed it only because the squirrel

136

was staring at her from there in a hostile, defiant way. Poldi saw that the fallen leaves looked as if they had been strewn there by design — an almost imperceptible breach of the natural order of things. She scraped the leaves aside with her spade and, sure enough, the soil had been dug up at that point, then filled in and tamped back into place.

"Not again . . ."

With another sigh, Poldi prepared to dig.

"Stop! Don't move!" called a strident male voice from behind her.

She froze.

"I want to see your hands! Show me your hands!"

Poldi groaned with annoyance. Someone had obviously been watching too many American cop shows.

"*Madonna!* You can see my bloody hands!"

The owner of the voice seemed briefly at a loss.

"Get rid of that . . . whatsit — that spade. Then put your hands up — slowly!"

Poldi complied.

"Now turn round. Very slowly."

Turning, Poldi found herself facing the carabiniere from the piazza. He had levelled his service pistol at her and was trying to look ferocious.

137

More timid and less criminally experienced persons like me might now have been shitting a brick. Not so a professional like my aunt.

She saw at once that the good-looking young carabiniere kept his finger off the trigger for safety's sake. Besides, she was an expert on policemen, especially carabinieri.

They aren't regarded in Italy as the brightest bulbs on the Christmas tree. This is a cruel preconception, of course, but poking fun at masculine authority is permissible in any democratic society and does no one any harm. The following are classic examples of the jokes Italians tell about their guardians of law and order:

Carabiniere Mezzapelle is attacked and robbed by a couple of crims while on duty. Money, wristwatch, patrol car — all gone. "But what about your gun? Didn't you have it with you?" asks his superior officer. "Of course, sir," Mezzapelle replies eagerly, "but fortunately I managed to hide it in my trousers."

Or this exchange between two carabinieri: "Hey, Gianni, why are you pulling such a long face?" — "Because I've got a blood test tomorrow." — "So?" — "Well, I never learnt it at school."

The carabiniere keeping Poldi covered was

apparently cut from different cloth.

"What are you up to?"

"What does it look like?"

The guardian of the law looked more puzzled still. "What do you think *you* look like?"

Poldi essayed a coquettish pin-up pose. "Fancy me?"

"Don't move, I said! What are you doing with that spade?"

Poldi sighed. "Just taking a soil sample. I'm a biologist, and I'm doing research into the oldest living things on earth."

This seemed to give the carabiniere food for thought. He knitted his brow and screwed up his eyes. Poldi, who found him more and more handsome, was pervaded by a familiar tingling sensation. Smitten by the sight of his Adam's apple bobbing up and down with agitation and the luxuriant dark hair peeping from under his cap, she wondered what it would be like to . . .

"You climbed over the railings," he said. "I also noticed you in town earlier on. You were acting suspiciously." Then, sharp as a knife, "You're no biologist."

"Cento punti!" said Poldi. Then, more benevolently, "What's your name?"

This appeared to floor the carabiniere even more than her flimsy lie. "Er . . . Brigadiere Magnano."

Poldi's eyes widened. "Not . . . *Antonio* Magnano by any chance?"

"Yes. How did you know?"

She smiled. Sicily seemed to be teeming with handsome Antonios.

"Why are you grinning like that?"

"Because you're so good-looking," Poldi blurted out. "Well, Brigadiere Magnano, seeing as you've been looking at me all this time, you could have opened the gate for me. Then I wouldn't be compelled to stand here in front of you without a skirt on."

The brigadiere screwed up his eyes again. "Name?"

"Isolde Oberreiter, but you may call me Poldi."

"You're German?"

"*Madonna,* is that a crime these days?"

"I'm glad *I'm* not German, anyway."

"Why?"

"Because I can't speak the language."

Poldi stared at him, then burst out laughing. She simply couldn't help it. It was all too much — she couldn't wait to tell Montana about this episode.

Brigadiere Magnano found her laughter less to his taste. "I'm arresting you for breach of the peace, trespass and, um . . . preparing to commit a criminal act."

"Oh come now, brigadiere," Poldi gasped, mopping her eyes, "you surely can't be serious. Do I look like a jihadi?"

"No arguments. Come with me, but nice and slow." Brigadiere Magnano retreated a step, never taking his eyes off her.

Poldi pulled herself together. Perhaps it would be better to straighten things out at the station, she told herself. Sighing and still rather out of breath after her paroxysm of mirth, she followed the carabiniere. High heels and uneven ground made it hard to preserve her dignity.

Her attempt to do so failed utterly, because one of her heels caught in a root. She tripped, uttered a squawk of alarm, threw up her hands and fell flat.

This initiated a peculiar series of mishaps and misunderstandings. The impact had dislodged Poldi's wig, which came to rest on the ground beside her. At the same instant she heard a shot. Already startled by her crash landing, Brigadiere Magnano had clearly pulled the trigger by mistake, thereby startling himself still more. He then tripped, flailed his arms and fell over backwards. His gun flew through the air and he ripped his trousers on a projecting branch. In a hurry to retrieve the weapon, he crawled on all fours towards Poldi, who was also on her hands and knees by now and had hastily donned her wig again. The policeman's gun had landed right in front of her, she saw, so she picked it up with the intention of handing it to him. He, for his part, completely misunderstood this gesture. Promptly putting his hands up, he pleaded for his life.

"Please don't shoot! That shot just now was a mistake!"

"You stupid clot! I could be dead by now — dead as mutton!"

And then Vito Montana's thunderous voice put an end to this undignified performance. "What the hell's going on here?"

Poldi could scarcely believe her eyes when she saw him marching towards them like a wrathful Greek god of vengeance.

"Vito!" She scrambled hurriedly to her feet. "I tried to get you on the phone."

"Yes, I saw." Montana turned to the brigadiere. "What's going on here? Why did you fire at this woman?" he demanded angrily. "Why are the two of you in a state of undress?"

"It's not what you think, Vito," said Poldi.

Magnano was looking more bewildered than ever. "And who might you be?"

"I'm your worst nightmare, Brigadiere. When I inform your boss that you opened fire on an unofficial associate of mine, he'll kick your butt till it's so blue, a baboon would fall in love with you."

He flashed his ID under Magnano's nose, and the hapless brigadiere was reduced to silence.

Poldi's heart leapt, she found Montana's anger so awesome.

"Did you just call me your unofficial associate, *tesoro*?"

Montana stiffened and looked her up and down. There was something on the tip of his tongue, but he merely shook his head. "Oh, the hell with it," he growled, like someone who has come to terms with chaos. "I made a few inquiries in town. I discovered you'd already been there and also where you'd gone. Now, will you explain what's going on here?"

Poldi pointed to the spade in the clearing. "I'm afraid we've got some digging to do, Vito."

"Why?"

"Because I think there's something under there, and I'm afraid we won't like it."

As ever where dire premonitions are concerned, my Auntie Poldi was right.

Montana removed his jacket, rolled up his sleeves and picked up the spade. With my aunt and Magnano looking on, he started digging in the spot Poldi had indicated. It wasn't difficult, because the soil was loose and he didn't have to go down far. A human body came to light after only a few spadefuls had been removed. A dark-skinned body. A man's body. It was recognisable as such despite the removal of some important components. The hands and the head, for instance. It appeared that the chest had been opened and some organs removed too.

Poldi couldn't tear her eyes away. As though from afar, she heard Montana groan and handsome Brigadiere Magnano throw up behind her.

6

Tells of corpses, hypotheses, phone numbers and Bantu tribe medicine. And, of course, of men. John, though more or less under house arrest, does some investigating on his own account and creates a rather unsettling atmosphere in Poldi's home. Montana goes ballistic, Poldi wards off an accumulation of negative energy, and her nephew — for once — asks a not entirely stupid question.

It was three days before the results of the DNA analysis confirmed what Poldi, Montana and John had long taken for granted: the dead man was Thomas. John had already identified his half-brother in pathology by a small tribal tattoo on his right upper arm.

The cause of death could only be guessed at, because, discounting the amputations and the deep cut in the chest to remove the organs, the body displayed no injuries, though the autopsy revealed that the heart was among the organs removed. The only remaining possibility was a head wound, but the head was missing, unfortunately, so it was impossible to tell whether Thomas had been beaten to death or shot. Not that it mattered in the long run.

John, who looked shocked but retained his professional composure, asked Montana if he could assist with the investigation, but Poldi's beloved commissario declined his help.

"I'll get back to you in due course, Mr. Owenya. You can't do anything for the time being. Your best plan is to stay in the house so I can reach you any time."

Poldi construed this as a form of house arrest, as did John.

"Does this mean you suspect me?"

"Should I?"

"He was my half-brother, Commissario Montana. You really think I could have done . . . all that to him?"

Montana gave John a searching look. "All the same, I'd like you to remain available."

"*Hamna shida.* No problem. Your case, Commissario."

John was very quiet after his visit to the morgue. He drank half a beer but wouldn't eat anything.

"I'm so terribly sorry, John," Poldi murmured. "He didn't deserve that."

"It was Kigumbe's people," he replied dully. "I've seen something of the kind before."

"Muti?" asked Poldi, and he nodded.

"Muti? What's *muti?"* I said, rather at a loss, when Poldi was describing further developments to me on the morning after my arrival.

Somewhat impatiently, she had woken me at the crack of dawn — even before sunrise. She seemed in a hurry to get on with her story. Nothing was stirring outside, not a bird could be heard. We were on our own in Femminamorta like a couple of ghosts, or so it seemed to me after a busy night and less than three hours' sleep. Poldi handed me such a strong black coffee, it squeezed my heart like a lemon. She appeared to have just got up too, because she was wearing a snug pink terrycloth onesie, complete with a hood and rabbit's ears. In other words, the sort of garment one would really prefer to see on a baby, not on one's sexagenarian aunt.

"It's an ancient superstition prevalent among certain Bantu tribes," she went on imperturbably. "A kind of magic medicine.

They make it out of all manner of plants and herbs. Some you have to chew, others you must smoke, and many of them the traditional healer mashes up into a sort of porridge or brews into a nice cup of tea. Western medics regard it as totally ineffective, but many people believe in it, including doctors. It's rooted in the African soul, this belief in magic and spirits. I didn't believe in it to begin with. But then there was the murder in Kilombero Market. Witchcraft was definitely involved, I tell you."

"Just a minute. What's this murder you're talking about?"

"The murder I solved in Tanzania. Anyway, *muti* is mostly made of plants, but many healers also use goat fat, bones and certain kinds of offal. These are ground up or made into a paste and then smeared on the skin. In Africa there are whole *muti* markets where you can buy all these things. Imagine a load of lions' pizzles and monkeys' hearts offered for sale in the sweltering sun and stinking to high heaven. It was said that certain shady healers also use human body parts occasionally. The hands or eyes, mostly, or the heart and the . . . well, you know."

Shuddering, I asked, "A kind of organ

donation, you mean?"

"Don't be so naïve! Those body parts have to be procured freshly, of course. People are killed for them. They're called *muti* murders."

"Oh no!" I pulled a face.

"I never believed these took place; I thought it was just a rumour. But the way Thomas's corpse had been mutilated left John and me in no doubt, because that's what Kigumbe was believed to do to his enemies. It was said he not only killed them, but would cut off their most valuable parts and flog them. That kind of thing can be intimidating, believe you me."

John's suspicion stood to reason, and Poldi shared it. If Thomas really had stolen something so incredibly valuable, Kigumbe would undoubtedly have launched a manhunt for him. Being afraid that he himself had put Kigumbe's people on Thomas's track in Sicily, John was filled with remorse.

Poldi tried to set his mind at rest. "It's equally possible that Thomas got in touch with Kigumbe in the hope of making a deal with him."

John just gave her a wry smile and went to his attic room. A little while later she heard him sobbing.

Poldi saw and heard nothing of Montana in the days that followed. He moved back into his flat in Catania or slept at headquarters, as she was told in confidence by Assistente Zannotta.

Zannotta became Poldi's keyhole into Montana's office, so to speak. He sent her secretly taken mobile phone pictures of Montana at his desk or in the field, so she knew that her grumpy *tesoro* had sunk his teeth in the case and would turn up at her house in due course.

All she could do was be patient, which was not in her nature. She also had John in the house, and inactivity was driving him, too, to distraction.

"Investigations will soon be complete," she told him. "Then you can take Thomas home for burial."

To her surprise, John dismissed this. "Not until I've solved the case."

"Here in Sicily? You can't do a thing. Go home and arrest that bastard Kigumbe."

"I must prove he was responsible, and the evidence is here in Sicily."

Poldi thought for a moment. "Vito won't let you work in harness with him, you know that. Besides, Kigumbe's people will have left here long ago."

"Perhaps, but I've got to do something,

150

Poldi. I'm a policeman, I can't just sit around doing nothing."

"There's nothing you *can* do, John."

"Yes, there is, but I'll need your help."

She stared at him. "Why do I get the feeling I'm not going to like your suggestion one bit?"

"Thomas must have had some contact here if he planned to sell an object of such value," John went on. "That contact either killed him or at least knows something about his death."

"You can bet Vito had the same idea and is onto it already," Poldi replied, but John shook his head vigorously.

"I don't think he'll get anywhere near the man. It's another world."

"What do you mean?"

"I mean that Thomas's contact must be a Tanzanian. Thomas had never been abroad. He didn't know anyone here. But if his contact is a Tanzanian, the man will be living in an African community in Catania or some other seaport. Montana won't get his foot round the door, he can forget the idea. But me, I could."

Even Poldi could see that.

"Where do I come into it? I'm an outsider too."

"I'll need a bit of cash when I start making inquiries."

Poldi emitted an audible sigh. "You can't be serious."

"I am, Poldi. I'm asking for a loan, not a gift."

"Use your own damned money!"

"Poldi! My credit card won't stretch far enough here in Italy. I wouldn't ask if there was any other way."

Poldi had to sit down. "I'll be damned if I will lend you a single cent of my meagre savings, let alone my pension."

"You don't have to. You've still got the cheque I gave you."

"You want it back?"

He sat down beside her and gazed into her eyes. "You'll get it back, I swear."

Poldi inserted another brief interlude in her narrative and, as if sluicing away a bad taste, took a big swig of coffee laced with grappa.

"How did he react when you refused to produce the cheque?" I asked, eager to get her back on track.

She gave me a meaningful look.

"Oh, no," I cried. "You didn't!"

"Yes," she said quietly, "of course I did."

"But that was bloody stupid of you. The man had already cheated you out of your house. You'll never get that cheque back."

She nodded. "I realised that."

"So why . . . ?"

"God Almighty, because the money meant nothing to me," she snapped. "I couldn't care less about money. I never have. That's because I decided early on in life that it's nothing but negative energy. Utterly, utterly negative. And what do you do when you get a build-up of negative energy?"

"You get rid of it," I said, because I realised she was completely right. "I never looked at it that way."

"But you get my point now, don't you, I can see. *Benissimo,* we're making progress. At least the cheque was covered, so that was one less lie."

She grinned at me and I grinned back. "Feeling like a *cornetto* now?" she asked.

I nodded, and as she heaved herself out of her chair with a grunt and toddled off to the kitchen in her terry-towel onesie, I realised something else. Even though my Auntie Poldi was always bullying me, criticising me, showing me up and scolding me to her heart's content, I knew more than ever that I loved her. I loved her and was proud she was my aunt, and I knew I'd never be able to refuse her anything. What I didn't know, however, was how much trouble this would land me in.

■ ■ ■ ■

John went off to Catania the next morning and did not return until late that evening, looking tired and tense. Poldi tried to pump him — where had he been, whom had he met, what had he found out — but he merely shook his head.

"It's better you don't know," he said, and went up to his room.

That was yet another thing Poldi detested about men. The way they met up with other men to settle important man things. The way they never wanted to reveal their hand, least of all to a woman. It was as if these matters were too important and complicated to divulge to a woman, let alone allow her to participate in them. In Poldi's experience, what eventually transpired was seldom anything good. Not from the female perspective, anyway.

The same thing happened the next day, and the day after that. John went off to Catania and returned, tight-lipped, in the evening. Noticing a slight bulge in his puffa jacket, Poldi deduced that he had somehow acquired a gun. Not a really welcome development, she thought, and she couldn't wait for Montana to move back in.

Montana reappeared on the third evening with the final report on the DNA test and details of what he had discovered so far. They didn't amount to much. He looked as grumpy as ever, but Poldi detected something else in his expression: a kind of suppressed rage.

"Your brother's body has been released," he growled at John when the three of them were sitting together in Poldi's living room. "You'll be able to take him back to Arusha in the next few days."

"Thanks," John replied. "I've already made the necessary arrangements, but I'm staying on for a while. You received the communication from my ministry?"

"I certainly did," Montana snarled, and Poldi saw him flush with anger. "But there were no grounds for it."

Yet again, two men were discussing man things in Poldi's presence, as if she were thin air.

"Hey, guys," she broke in angrily, "mind telling me what communication you're talking about?"

"The Tanzanian Ministry of Home Affairs oversees John's police force," Montana explained. "It has sent the Italian Ministry of the Interior a request that he be taken on as an observer. Rome passed it on to me as an order, not a request."

Poldi could imagine how much that idea had appealed to Montana. Like not at all.

"Go home," he told John in English. "We aren't fools. There's nothing you can do here."

John leant forward. "Listen to me, Commissario Montana. You're stuck with me whether you like it or not, and you'll have to live with that. The sooner we wrap up this case, the sooner you'll be rid of me."

That was when Montana lost it. The man was a Sicilian with a low flammability limit, after all, and things had clearly been building up inside him in the past few days. These now had to be vented.

"There is no 'we'!" he bellowed — in Italian, because his English wasn't up to a thoroughgoing hissy fit. "I'm sick of you! I only have to take one look at your self-satisfied mug! You waltz in here with your pack of lies, try to ingratiate yourself, screw up Poldi's life, and mine into the bargain, and someone promptly gets killed. Bugger the order from Rome! Bugger your co-operation! I don't want you here! Get lost! Piss off!"

At first John just glared at Montana, but then he yelled back — in Swahili, because when delivering a tirade he reverted to his

156

native tongue, a Bantu language of which Poldi had mastered a little. Although she didn't understand the whole of John's outburst, it was obviously a cascade of the vilest oaths, curses and insults involving excreta, animal comparisons and considerable doubts as to Montana's virility. Swahili was a beautiful language, Poldi thought. Even a paroxysm of rage sounded as melodious and rhythmical as a herd of galloping gnus.

While John was still bellowing, Montana bellowed back. The two men jumped to their feet, jugulars swelling, fists clenched and jaws jutting, but neither seemed inclined to come to blows — rather a shame, Poldi thought. She savoured this form of Italo-Tanzanian cultural exchange for a moment or two, then she'd had enough. Since her voice would have been drowned out by this hullabaloo, she resorted to another expedient. Going over to the sofa, she picked up the firmest of the cushions and hit her two policemen over the head with it. To be more precise, she flailed away at them until her arm grew tired.

"Put a sock in it, for God's sake! Pipe down!" she yelled at them in her mother tongue. "I've had enough of your bickering! This isn't a bloody kindergarten! Siddown, both of you!"

As ever, Bavarian-accented German had its tried and tested effect. The two fighting cocks instantly fell silent. Staring at Poldi transfixed, they subsided, seething, onto their chairs.

"That's better," she growled. "Now shake hands," she went on in English. "Go on, or I'll kick you out — both of you."

Montana and John hesitated. Then, registering Poldi's ferocious expression, they obeyed like schoolboys, though it seemed they did their best to crush each other's fingers.

"Good. Now repeat after me: *Namaste.*"

Their jaw muscles twitched.

"Namaste."

"Namaste."

"There," said Poldi, and order was restored.

While the two men were kneading their aching fingers, she fetched three beers from the fridge.

"We haven't found a murder weapon," Montana reported, "and there was very little blood. We found no clothing either, so that chestnut tree wasn't the scene of the crime. Thomas Migiro was probably murdered a week ago."

He took a swig of beer and waited for

158

Poldi to quiz him, as usual, but she merely nodded.

"His rental car's tracking function shows that he had driven all over the place since his arrival in Sicily. I followed his route and questioned one or two people. Some of them could remember seeing a striking black man, but that's as much as we've learned to date."

"Where did he go?" asked Poldi, her curiosity aroused.

"He was on the road for four days. We know his route, but we don't know where he stopped or for how long. He first went south to Siracusa, then on to Noto, then west to Gela. From there he drove to Agrigento, and from there back east to Enna. Then he drove to Catania, and then" — Montana drew a deep breath — "then he did something very odd."

He was looking straight at Poldi, who sensed that this boded ill.

"Well?" she asked in a low voice.

"He drove here, Poldi."

"What?"

Montana took another swig of beer. "He was here in Torre Archirafi."

"You mean . . ."

"Yes, I think he meant to pay you a visit. Was he here, Poldi?"

"No!" she cried. "I'd have told you if he had been!"

Montana seemed to believe this. He nodded.

"But because he didn't get to see you, he drove on." Montana turned to John, who had been listening intently. "The thing is, how did he know Poldi's address? How did he even know she was living in Sicily?"

"Why ask me?" John retorted.

Montana held his gaze. He was now looking very calm. It was the special kind of serenity so familiar to Poldi, who knew when all of a detective inspector's senses were in receiving mode.

"After that," Montana continued without taking his eyes off John, "your brother drove up to Sant'Alfio. In the ensuing days the car went on short trips, one of them down to the sea, but it didn't leave the town after that until your brother's death."

"Doesn't anyone there remember seeing Thomas?" John asked. "I mean, he must have stood out like a sore thumb."

Montana shook his head. "It seems not."

"But that doesn't make sense!"

"You can say that again."

"What if it was all quite different?" Poldi suggested quietly, because she knew from personal experience how disastrous it can

160

be to cling too tightly to a hypothesis at the start of a murder inquiry, no matter how plausible it is.

"What do you mean?" asked Montana.

"Well, what if it wasn't Kigumbe's people? Purely in theory, what if it was simply meant to look like a *muti* murder? What if something went badly wrong and the murderer suddenly had to improvise?"

"Poldi!" Montana exclaimed, and she could have screwed him on the spot for the look he gave her. It was a look filled with amazement, admiration and, yes, affection.

"Because," my Auntie Poldi told me once, "nothing makes a *commissario di polizia* randier than a mixture of baroque eroticism and intellectual brilliance."

I think she meant herself.

"The way I see it," John said, "Thomas tried to sell this ten-million-dollar object somehow, probably without success. He was tracked down by Kigumbe's people and eventually murdered. Why so complicated? If there are several explanations for one and the same state of affairs, it's always better to go for the simplest."

"Thanks for the lesson," Montana said caustically.

John leant forward. "Look, Signor Montana, let me help you. We're on the same side."

Montana shrugged his shoulders. "You're an official observer now. It bugs me, but there's nothing I can do. Oh yes, there is one thing: I can confiscate your passport. So hand it over, Mr. Owenya."

"Did Montana seriously suspect him?" I asked.

Dawn was breaking over Femminamorta, and Poldi had disappeared into the bathroom to get ready for the day.

"Get on with you!" she called through the closed door. "It was pure harassment on Vito's part, of course, but John didn't turn a hair. That's because he'd have done exactly the same, understand?"

I thought for a moment. "Did you tell Montana about the inquiries he'd made among the African community in Catania, and about the red sequin and your suspicions of Russo?"

Poldi sighed. "The thing is . . . no. Why should I have? When you come down to it, John only did what a detective does: investigate. And because that was likely to cause some aggro, he carried a gun. It was quite normal."

"Hm," I said, because I didn't think it was

as normal as all that.

But then, I'm not an ultra-virile, sharp-witted, tough nut of a cop. I'm just her nerdy nephew in a navy-blue polo shirt, with a sticking plaster on my nose.

"Besides," Poldi went on from the bathroom, "I thought he might really pick up some items of information Vito would never get at. John's big enough to look after himself."

I detected a trace of admiration in her voice.

"You still find him attractive, don't you?"

This question seemed to bother her. I could hear her clattering around in the bathroom, but that was all.

"You may be right," she said at last in a rather odd voice. She started to add something else but thought better of it. "Yes, it's possible."

"But surely you should have told Montana about Russo and the sequin?"

"Should I bollocks!" she snapped from inside the bathroom. "Don't you understand? I knew Vito would dismiss it as another piece of crackpot, typically German Mafia mania, not to mention the jealousy factor. No, I realised I would have to go into action myself."

I waited in suspense for her to get dressed.

She was now wearing black stretch pants and a black roll-neck sweater. She stared at me in silence for a moment.

"Er, what is it? Is my nose bleeding again?"

"No, it's all right. It's just that if you can ask such smart questions — like why I did or didn't do this or that — I'm sure you can tell me what *you* would have done next."

"Is this supposed to be a test, or do you want my opinion?"

"Both, of course."

That idea appealed to me as little as someone prodding me in the chest or pinching my cheek. I don't like exams, which is why I think being a best-selling author would be a suitable profession for me. I'm certainly no detective, but my Auntie Poldi's expression left me in no doubt that she wouldn't let me off without an answer.

"Well, in your place I think I would try to find out how Thomas got hold of my address."

"Cento punti!" Poldi exclaimed. "And who might know that?"

"I'd try to sound out Russo," I said, off the cuff and without giving it much thought. "He was in Thomas's hotel room, presumably, and right now that's your best line of

164

inquiry."

"Spot on!" She nodded approvingly, and was about to continue when something else occurred to me.

"What about that phone number on the postcard? Did Montana run a check on it?"

For the second time, my aunt's expression implied that I was a really bright lad.

"Congratulations," she said quietly. "Of course Vito had the number checked, but the strange thing is, it was unallocated because it had never existed. And the strangest thing of all is that John checked Thomas's Tanzanian mobile phone number and found that he'd made one call to the nonexistent number. A call lasting a quarter of an hour."

7

Tells of Poldi's idea of discretion, of basic
dance moves, Montana's silence, Russo's
lips, CCTVs and post-traumatic stress
disorder. And of male hormones. Poldi
proves she has a big heart, is compelled
to wait and coincidentally prevents a
tragedy. Then she comes to a decision
and loses her mobile phone.

The next morning Poldi rode her Vespa over
to Russo's place to talk turkey. She puttered
through the big gateway that led into the
Piante Russo nursery and along the avenue
of olive and palm trees, heading for the
squat administration building. She performed an elegant swerve to avoid a big
digger laden with a palm tree which suddenly crossed her path. *Beep! Beep!* Two
toots, and she puttered resolutely onwards.
In passing, she treated Turi, an elderly
member of Russo's workforce whom she

knew from the Valentino case, to a nonchalant wave. He and his fellow workers stared after her with a slight frisson. It was as if they were watching a cross between a fairy and a Fury descend upon the world in her cosmic chariot, intent on restoring order. Nobody barred her path, not even the security guards or the young receptionist, though she quickly reached for the phone. Poldi saluted smartly, like a general taking in a parade, and marched straight into Russo's office — or rather, invaded it like a supertanker with rudder damage crashing into a jetty.

"Donna Poldina!" cried Russo, faintly annoyed, when the door flew open and my aunt burst in. He was still holding the phone from which his receptionist's agitated voice was issuing. "You might have announced yourself, or even knocked."

He was seated at the old desk in his little office, whose unadorned simplicity had surprised Poldi on her first visit. Seemingly unchanged in appearance, it still smelt of musty files, coffee and white camellias in a big floor vase. But Poldi's investigative senses did, after all, register a minute change, a minor structural shift and focal displacement, but she was so furious, it took her a moment to detect what it was.

"Why are you messing me about?" she snarled while still in the doorway. Reaching into her handbag, she removed the zip bag containing the red sequin and slammed it down on the desk.

"I've no idea what you mean, Donna Poldina. What's that?"

"It came off your dogs' collars. I found it in a hotel room in Taormina. You were there, don't deny it! I could tell you knew — it was written all over your face. So . . . who killed Thomas Migiro, and did you give him my address?"

Russo screwed up his eyes. "Are you referring to that ritual murder up in Sant'Alfio? Awful business, but what am I supposed to —"

"Stop playing me for a sucker! That sequin proves you're mixed up in it!"

Russo looked at her. "How about a coffee, Donna Poldina?" Without waiting for an answer he picked up the phone and gave the order. Then he rose and went over to the old leather sofa facing the desk. "Sit down and catch your breath."

Poldi complied. She sat down — beside him, but at an appropriate distance — and mopped her brow.

"That sequin proves nothing at all, you realise that, don't you?"

168

"You were there," Poldi insisted. "You were in contact with Thomas, and I want to know why."

Russo gave her another long look. And then he did something that took her completely by surprise. It was like being hit on the back of the head in a game of dodgeball. The ball simply knocks you down and takes your breath away, and at first you've no idea what's what. Russo moved closer, leant over — and kissed her.

Poldi was so taken aback she didn't react at first. She was, to all intents and purposes, paralysed. Russo's lips felt surprisingly soft, yet firm. It wasn't just a fleeting kiss. He applied a certain amount of pressure and didn't release her immediately. Poldi could smell his aftershave, which was mingled with a trace of sweat, and she could sense the nearness of his potent masculinity. And, once the initial shock had worn off, she reacted as she usually did at such moments: she parted her own lips.

To be clear, this was a purely instinctive response, not a sign of acquiescence, far less an invitation. It was merely a reflex which Poldi, being the emotional, sensual, susceptible person she was, had never been able to control.

Just as her lips parted, Russo removed his

own and sat back, at a decorous distance once more. "That's all I wanted to know," he said. "Now we can talk turkey."

Half indignant, half thrilled, Poldi couldn't get a word out. Nor did she have to, because just then the coffee arrived.

"You rotten swine," she hissed as she stirred some sugar into her cappuccino.

Averting her gaze, she noticed that there had been a change in the decor. Hanging by the usual picture of the Madonna was a framed art print of Amy Winehouse onstage.

"She was an absolute dear, Amy was." Another digression on Poldi's part. "Multi-talented, though very few people know that. So amusing, too, but lonely as well — so lonely, poor girl. Did you know that Amy also had a phoenix tattoo on her left breast? She copied that from me. Like the beehive wig, incidentally."

Here we went again. I'd been afraid of this. Poldi and her cockamamie showbiz reminiscences. I didn't believe a word of them, of course, but I was well aware that the only thing to do when she shunted herself onto one of these sidings was to keep cool and let her have her head. Resistance was futile.

"Oh yeah?"

"You don't believe me, but I knew Amy before she was really well known. We were soulmates, almost. I tried to talk her into rehab, because it was obvious her boozing would be the end of her, but all she kept saying was "No, no, no!" So I sat down with her and helped her at least to write a song about it."

"You're not seriously saying you wrote 'Rehab.' "

"I didn't actually write it," Poldi conceded, "but I inspired Amy to do so. And then I showed her some dance steps, because Amy was no great dancer."

I pretended this piece of effrontery was water off a duck's back to me.

"Cool," I said. "Let's see you, then."

"See me what?"

"Sing 'Rehab' and show me those dance steps."

"Get away with you!" she parried, wagging her finger at me. "It's so long ago, I couldn't any more. With my knee? What an idea!"

"You're going to sing 'Rehab,' Poldi. And dance. Now, this minute. I want to see it. If you don't, I'll go home tomorrow, I swear."

"This is blackmail."

I threw up my hands as if the future course of events was beyond my control.

" 'Rehab' or I'm out of here. 'Rehab,' 'Rehab,' 'Rehab'!"

"You little shitbag!" Poldi glared at me and, with a grunt, heaved herself off the sofa.

"Forget it, Poldi," I said, laughing. "It was only a joke. Sit down and go on with your story."

"Shut your trap!" she snapped, and disappeared into the bedroom for a minute or two. When she returned she was wearing a skin-tight green stretch dress that only just hid her backside. Not particularly flattering, given my aunt's proportions. She shoved the coffee table aside, rolled the carpet back, took off her shoes and rammed a CD into the CD player. Moments later a karaoke version of 'Rehab' filled the air.

I mean, seriously. My Auntie Poldi! Sixty years old and on the plump side, wearing a wig and not entirely sober, she waggled her hips, spread her arms, swayed a bit, performed a few twist steps and sang Amy Winehouse's famous, sad, defiant song from beginning to end.

She sang it like it was her own life story, in a slight Bavarian accent. Although she didn't hit all the notes, it sounded deep, dark and true. I hadn't known my Auntie Poldi possessed such a nice voice, and I must confess it gave me goose-bumps. I couldn't tear my eyes away and ended by applauding loudly.

"Man! Wow, Poldi! You really nailed it!"

"Now you."

"Er, what?"

"We'll now sing 'Valerie' together. As a duet."

'Valerie,' of all songs! I was panic-stricken.

"No way. I can't sing."

"God Almighty, how I hate that! 'I can't, I can't'! You'll never get anywhere with that novel of yours if you're frightened of your own shadow. Everyone can sing, it's quite easy. Come on." She dragged me up off the sofa. "Shoes off!"

She made me learn the lyrics, showed me a few basic steps and how to look cool without fidgeting around too much. And then we sang "Valerie" together, and I pictured a certain mysterious French beauty as we did so.

I can still manage the song and the basic steps. In fact, I sometimes sing it all alone in my apartment, just like that. I was about as graceful as a giraffe on roller skates, and Poldi needed all the patience she could muster, but we eventually sang the song as if to the manner born, and I don't think I've ever felt so light on my feet.

Satisfied, my aunt flopped down on the sofa again.

"Accuse me of lying one more time, sonny," she growled, "and I'll have your guts for garters."

"So you're an Amy Winehouse fan?" Poldi asked Russo in a conversational, tea-party tone of voice.

"Amy was the greatest," he replied.

"She still had so much more to give us."

Russo looked at her. "I can't tell you everything, Poldi. Maybe I really was at that hotel in Taormina, maybe not. Maybe I know what this Thomas Migiro was doing here, maybe not. What is quite certain is that it's better *you* don't know, believe me, and that I myself don't know who killed him. I didn't give him your address, either. Word of honour."

"The word of honour of a liar and manipulator."

Russo raised his hands in the traditional Italian gesture signifying innocence.

"OK, I wasn't entirely honest with you. Perhaps I did hear something about an extremely valuable object making the rounds here in Sicily with various people after it. More than that I really don't know. In return, you must swear to me that no information I give you ever reaches the ears of Commissario Montana."

"That's too wishy-washy," Poldi said dismissively. "I want something I can work on."

"You'd be dealing with some very dangerous people, Poldi."

Instead of replying, Poldi did something that took Russo, in his turn, completely by surprise. With amazing agility, she sat astride his lap, cupped his head in her hands and kissed him back. It was a regular kiss, complete with tongue and all the trimmings — my Auntie Poldi knows her stuff in that respect. When she felt his hand creep down her cleavage, however, she pulled the rip-cord. Releasing him, she acrobatically resumed her seat alongside.

"Do I look as if I couldn't cope with some very dangerous people?"

Russo shook his head and laughed. "Just swear Montana won't get to hear."

Poldi solemnly raised her hand. "I swear by the innocence of Our Lady and Amy Winehouse."

"No blasphemy, please." Russo sounded as if he meant it. "But all right, I know from a reliable source that what Thomas Migiro was trying to sell is still in the country. Here. In Sicily."

Seated facing Montana in his stuffy office at the end of the passage in Acireale's police headquarters two hours later, Poldi told him what she had learned. This naturally reflects badly on her reliability as regards words of honour and oaths of secrecy, but she felt they needn't be taken too seriously when given to liars and Mafiosi. Besides, she had sworn by something that didn't exist in her cosmos, not believing in the Immaculate Conception. And where Amy Winehouse's innocence was concerned, she simply knew better.

"Who told you this?" Montana demanded.

"I can't say, *tesoro.* I have to protect my sources."

"I insist on knowing who told you."

"I'm sorry. Just trust me, it came from a reliable source."

"Is the source a man?"

"Why do you want to know?"

"Is it Russo?"

"*Madonna,* why rake him up again?"

"Are you having an affair with him?"

"Vito, no! Cool it! I've just given you some important information on a silver platter — you must follow it up at once. It probably means Thomas's killers are still in the country and we've a chance of catching them."

But Montana wouldn't hear a word of it. Absolutely not.

"*Madonna,* why does everyone always talk of 'we' when they mean 'I'? Just when I think everything's sorted, you muddy the waters again. You promised not to do anything stupid, and now this. I have a murder to solve and I've got your John breathing down my neck. I don't have time to deal with your cockamamie theories as well."

"I've solved two murders, Vito."

"And I've solved dozens! You were lucky, Poldi, that's all. In fact, you were lucky not to buy it the last time."

That did take some of the wind out of her sails.

Assistente Zannotta poked his head round the door. "Everything OK?"

"Get out!" yelled Montana, and Zannotta fled.

"Vito, I . . ." Poldi began, but he raised his hand.

"It's like this, Poldi. I need a bit of peace and quiet. We won't be seeing each other for a while. Not so long as John is staying with you, at any rate, and not while you're playing the detective yourself and seeing

Russo or whoever. Above all, not until this case is put to bed. After that, we'll see. I need a bit of time."

"Time . . ." Poldi whispered like a mournful echo, and she felt her heart give a lurch. "Peace and quiet . . ."

"I just need some time to think things over," he said. "Don't worry."

But that only made her heart lurch still more. Whenever men had told her they needed time to think and not to worry, nothing good had come of it.

"Because that's another man thing," she told me serenely. "Whenever the situation gets too stressful or tiring or complicated, but most of all when the smallest thing pisses you off, you men make decisions without consulting anyone, least of all a woman. As a woman, the most one gets is a bit of mansplaining. Still, that's just the way you are, irrational and incorrigible. I know what I'm talking about, too. I'm an expert on men."

"Men are irrational? Come off it, Poldi."

"Hello? It's like yin and yang. Women are rational creatures. You, by contrast, pure chaos and irrational activism. That's how the male brain works, though. You have to chew away at a problem on your own until you know you're right and come out with some daft decision. If you didn't, you'd simply despair of us and the world in general, but you do it all the same. It's a hormonal problem."

"That's an utterly ridiculous theory, Poldi."

"No, it's the fruit of purely empirical experience. It's understandable, too, because man hasn't reached the same evolutionary stage as woman. And that's that."

Poldi knew there was nothing to be done. She had often enough in her life been slapped down and rejected like a donated liver, but it rent her heart every time. She was a person who always had to be creative and ready to set off fireworks of love, to give of herself and take the sexual initiative. This had always attracted men, but it also scared them when their image of her no longer conformed to reality — when, as they sometimes sheepishly put it, the rose-tinted spectacles came off and they saw nothing but shades of grey instead of wonderful, iridescent colours. There was no point in asking for explanations, Poldi knew, because irrational behaviour is inexplicable. She could only let go, painful though it might be.

At the same time, Poldi did understand Montana, because she had experienced the same sensation many times herself. For instance, when a man's proximity became too much for her, when she feared for her freedom, when gifts became too flashy and protestations of love too frantic. Her first husband, Peppe, had grasped this, albeit very belatedly, and had contrived to open up spaces for them both in which gravity no longer applied. She had loved him for that — and, of course, for his *sicilianità*. She sensed that Montana still had some way to go. Maybe he would come to understand, maybe not. Meanwhile she could only wait. That was the hardest thing.

At least she could drink, and that night she did so. She shut herself up in her bedroom with Mr. Johnnie Walker, abandoned herself to tears and got thoroughly smashed.

The next morning, when she tottered into the kitchen with a diabolical headache, a dead rat in her mouth and a rent in her heart, "I Will Survive" was blaring from the little Bluetooth speaker and the floor was littered with an unappetising mixture of undigested food, broken crockery, torn photos and red wine. Unable to remember how this still life had come into being, she turned the music off.

The silence was broken only by the distant sound of two bickering female neighbours.

"John?" she croaked. And, a little louder, "John?"

He wasn't there, and his bed had not been slept in. He had obviously spent the night elsewhere, but that was nothing new; John came and went as he pleased. No explanation was to be expected.

She made herself some coffee, took two aspirin and went and sat outside in the courtyard, waiting for the fresh air to dispel her nausea and subdue the evil dwarf rampaging inside her skull. Then she went to the bathroom. Peering at her from the mirror was a zombie, a sad old zombie. Not a pretty sight, but the tattooed phoenix on her left breast spread its wings with every breath, as if trying to tell her something.

That reminded Poldi what she was: a phoenix. Her whole life oscillated between two extremes, freedom and excess. She had always taken whatever she wanted and plunged blithely into each new escapade, not only neglecting many of life's little wayside flowers, but sometimes trampling on them. Family, friends, unopened letters and bills, job, reading, music, healthy eating, tap-dancing. Until life had had enough and she went bust and couldn't bear the sight of herself in the mirror any longer. I reckon Poldi was like one of those children who, when they're too well off, go up to a precipice and can't resist peering over the edge. They look down and shiver, but don't jump. And because she knew all about the phoenix and freedom and excess and the abyss, and because there was always a way, she didn't jump this time either, but took a last look down, shuddered and turned away.

She had a bath, put her wig on, perfumed herself, slipped into her red good-mood dress with the white polka dots, dumped the spirits bottles and came to a decision of her own: to be good to herself again from now on. To drink less. To be disciplined. To solve the case. That was the only thing one could do in such situations: be good to oneself and concentrate on important matters. And believe it or not, my Auntie Poldi knew a thing or two about the art of liking oneself and concentrating on essentials.

A quiet time began, interrupted only by some strange events. Lemons were now ripening in the orchards around Femminamorta, as were mandarins and blood oranges beyond Catania. The consumption of gelati in sad Signora Cocuzza's café bar declined, but her two sons increased their production of colourful pastries and marzipan fruit of deceptively realistic appearance. At Poldi's jocular suggestion, they enthusiastically modelled some little pink marzipan penises, inscribed *Bell'Antonio* or *Viva l'Italia*. They proved to be a real winner. The so-called "Torre Archirafi dicks" became something of a craze with day-trippers from Catania.

A stormy wind blew moist, salty air through Torre more often now. It rained a lot, and the nights soon became so cold that Poldi had to put on her central heating for the first time since moving to Sicily. It turned out that, as so often in Italy, the architect had made the radiators far too small. The house never became really warm, and the single-glazed windows let in terrible draughts. Sicilians subscribe to the belief that they inhabit an oasis in the middle of a sun-scorched desert. Their homes are consequently paved with cooling tiles or flagstones, and they turn up their noses at sissy Teutonic radiators, completely dismissing the months between December and March. These can be devilishly cold and rainy, and even if the twenty-degree barrier is occasionally broken in December or January, the nights remain cool and dank. So Sicily isn't the ideal place to spend the winter.

Poldi did what most Sicilians do in this case: she acquired three *stufe,* or mobile gas heaters, and kept them going full blast. The butane supplier became her best friend.

Assailed from time to time by depression as chill as the east wind that plucked at the shutters, she asked herself questions one should never ask: Is he missing me? What's he doing now? Has he met someone? Less and less often, though. She sometimes still caught herself playing the what-if game, which never leads to anything. What if he said this and she replied that in a truly wise, gentle, perspicacious way? But this kind of mental movie is anything but perspicacious. She was told so by Aunts Teresa, Luisa and Caterina, by Valérie, by Signora Cocuzza, even by the padre, though Poldi wondered how he knew about such things. For all that, she was very touched by the affection of the family and her new friends, and, if only out of respect for them, she limited her consumption of booze. She waged a brave fight against excess, kept her home spick and span, dutifully opened all her mail at once, played gin rummy with the sad signora, visited Valérie, joined the *passeggiata* every afternoon and attended Sunday Mass again.

At some point text messages started arriving from Montana. *"Ciao cara!" "Come stai?"* And, once, "I miss you." But Poldi never replied to either his texts or his phone calls. Not out of umbrage or defiance or because she wanted to resume the old game of male courtship and female bridling, but because she simply wasn't ready. Because for once in her life she wanted to see things as they really were, free from expectation, for as long as she had left.

And then, one night, she had a dream. She was standing in front of a tall steel tower in the middle of a wide plain. Marie Antoinette, a bewigged figure with powdered cheeks and an elaborate gown, was climbing the tower. Poldi tried to call her back, but in vain. She was compelled to watch as Marie Antoinette, having reached the summit, threw herself off the battlements. She knew she now had to scale the tower herself. Higher and higher she climbed until she reached the top, where she was overcome with terror. She was so alone, so terrified of having to jump, that she called Montana on her mobile phone. But he didn't reply — all she could hear was white noise and indistinct, whispering voices. *Oh, well,* she thought, *he must be asleep and he's turned his phone off.* And so, despite her fear, she hunkered down on the battlements and eventually fell asleep. Awakened by a noise, she saw Montana climbing up to fetch her, having picked up her message in the morning.

Quite a nice dream, actually, but dreams are only dreams, and the consoling effects of this one soon evaporated. Montana never appeared.

Throughout this time she lived under the same roof with John as a kind of lodger. She made him breakfast and sometimes supper. He was civil and behaved correctly, but they found little to say to each other. John often spent the night elsewhere. Poldi, who guessed that he had met someone, was surprised at how little she cared.

Some new neighbours moved into the Via Baronessa, the world was out of kilter and would probably soon succumb to rising sea levels, an American millionaire came up with another answer to everything, and the days grew shorter.

Poldi, who heard nothing more from Russo either, made no progress with her inquiries. She couldn't, not without any firm leads, but she had put two and two together. The late Thomas Migiro had rung her bell to ask for help, that was clear, and if the mysterious ten-million-dollar item was still in circulation, she thought that Handsome Antonio might sooner or later do the same. That being so, she could only remain on the alert in that respect as well.

"But weren't you scared you might someday come home to find the murderer on your doorstep?" I asked.

"Of course I was, but get this: fear is where it's at. I've always lived that way. Besides" — she winked at me — "I'd twigged that Death still didn't have me on his list. And for safety's sake, as backup, so to speak, I got your cousin Marco to install the cameras."

"Eh? What cameras?"

"Why, surveillance cameras, the kind you can get on the internet. They're tiny — almost invisible. One in every room, complete with motion sensor."

She proudly showed me an app on her smartphone that enabled her to monitor the cameras individually. Once they were activated, the slightest movement would instantly trigger an alarm.

"So?" I said. "What if he'd come at night when John was away and you were alone in the house?"

"Well . . ." Poldi cleared her throat. "I wasn't alone in the house."

■ ■ ■ ■

The thing was, one evening about two weeks after Thomas's murder, Brigadiere Magnano from Sant'Alfio appeared at her door. Although he was wearing his carabinieri uniform and sunglasses and made as handsome and dapper an impression as Poldi remembered, he seemed to be in a bad way. He was looking pale, nervous, positively desperate.

"Well, this is a surprise," Poldi said.

"I don't mean to intrude, signora," he said haltingly, and removed his sunglasses.

The dark smudges under his eyes suggested that he hadn't slept in recent nights. Poldi saw at once that he had something on his mind.

"You'd better come in."

Magnano entered the house hesitantly, like someone picking his way through a swamp. Poldi shepherded him to the sofa and brought him a grappa.

"And you?" he asked, pointing at the glass.

"Not for the moment. And please call me Poldi."

"Thank you, Signora Poldi."

"Just Poldi."

The doleful young carabiniere looked

younger than Poldi remembered, almost childlike. He nodded obediently, took a sip of grappa and surveyed his surroundings.

"Nice place you have here."

Poldi sat down beside him. "All right, Antonio, out with it. What's eating you?"

That did it. The handsome youth uttered a sort of hiccup and then burst into tears.

"That corpse!" he sobbed. "That poor man's body! I just can't get the sight of it out of my head!"

Poldi could well understand that.

"The thing is," she told me, "your first corpse is particularly traumatic, especially when it's been mutilated. It doesn't get much better after that, but your first one can really knock you sideways. I know what I'm talking about."

It seemed that this was the first time in the course of his duties that handsome Brigadiere Magnano had come face-to-face with a dead body. He'd been traumatised by the sight of Thomas's torso, which pursued him into his dreams. Unable to sleep and on the verge of a nervous breakdown, he had thought it might be good to speak to someone who would sympathise. His paroxysms of sobbing were so violent, the whole sofa shook, so Poldi impulsively did what she did best: she dispensed warmth

189

and consolation. Taking the suffering young man in her arms, she clasped him to her bosom and felt his hot tears soak into her broderie anglaise blouse.

"Shh, Antonio, everything'll be fine."

Another sob. And then she felt his hands on her breasts. They clung to her like a drowning man to a lifebelt, and she let it happen.

"And then . . ." Poldi sighed when describing this episode to me at Femminamorta, but for once I cut her short.

"No details, please," I groaned. "I've heard it all before: policeman plus Sicilian equals sexual force of nature. The dam broke, and you were borne away on a torrent of passion, and his *pesciolino* became a magnificent swordfish. And so on and so forth, all night long. I know."

"My, my, what a shrinking violet you are," she grumped. "You know damn all — absolutely nothing, that's all you know, you muttonhead. You think I'm just a shameless, hormone-driven hussy, I know that perfectly well, but the truth is, I simply felt sorry for the poor young policeman. That's because I'm not made of stone. I'm a person with feelings and a big heart, understand? It was also because I happened to be a bit lonely and heartsick just then, and because I know from experience how best to help men cope with emotional pressure. May I go on now?"

"*Forza* Poldi!" I said, bracing myself for another sexual epic on my Auntie Poldi's part.

"Come," Poldi said softly. She got up off the sofa and tried to propel Magnano into her bedroom.

But the young man recoiled, positively panic-stricken. "Oh, no," he cried, "please don't, not that!"

The truth dawned on Poldi: handsome young Antonio Magnano, whose good looks were not matched by his intellect (he hadn't read Brancati, not that he read much of anything), was quite simply gay. She couldn't help laughing.

He looked puzzled. "What is it?"

She stroked his head and gave him a gentle smile. "Nothing, my dear, everything's fine. My mistake. Would you care for something to eat before you go? I could make you a plate of spaghetti."

He shook his head shyly. "Would it be possible . . . I mean, could I possibly, er" — he cleared his throat — "stay the night?"

And that was how it came about that, although not sexually attracted to women, handsome Antonio slept in Poldi's bed that night. When she stretched out at a decorous distance on her side of the mattress, the traumatised brigadiere snuggled up to her in his pants and vest and went to sleep in her arms like a baby. It wouldn't have surprised her if he'd sucked his thumb as well, but she had some understanding of mental upsets and realised that the young policeman simply needed some maternal affection. Experience had taught her that all men, whether gay or straight, were the same in that respect.

Handsome young Antonio visited her regularly from that day forward. Whenever John wasn't there for the night, he drove to Torre Archirafi from Sant'Alfio after work, enjoyed a good, dreamless sleep in Poldi's arms, drove back to work in the morning and thus became her temporary child and protector. It was a brief symbiosis, so to speak. Poldi mothered him, and he behaved with discretion. He came each time bearing vegetables from the market and fresh fish and other seafood from the fishmonger's owned by his family.

His mother had died some years earlier, he told Poldi. He had reluctantly helped out in the shop until gutting fish became too much for him and he joined the police. He hadn't acknowledged his sexual orientation until he fell in love with a fellow student at police college, and he had never yet had a really close friend.

"I don't know what to do."

"Where there's a will, there's always a way," Poldi told him. "Perhaps you should get out of Sant'Alfio."

Antonio thought this over. "I could apply for a transfer to Rome," he said.

And Poldi knew that the handsome brigadiere was on the right track.

November came and went, *salve, buongiorno, arrivederci.* Poldi averted a potential tragedy in the town after it transpired that Beyoncé Lombardo, who had only just come of age, was pregnant by an unemployed, muscle-bound dimwit named Toni Amato from Riposto. This had sparked off a vendetta between the parents and brothers of the pair — one that even the padre had failed to quell, like a bumblebee bouncing off a windowpane. The words "dishonour" and "disgrace" had been bandied about once too often, murderous threats were exchanged, and a Vespa went up in flames. It was all very dramatic. Then Poldi lost her cool. She brought the whole of her authority down on both families like Thor's hammer and pulled off a diplomatic miracle. First she got dimwit Toni a job as one of Piante Russo's security guards. Next she summoned the young couple's parents to partake of an apocalyptic joint of roast pork with beer sauce and dumplings, plus a Black Forest gâteau. She also invited a good friend of hers from Rome to join them. This was the politician and one-time porn actress Ilona Staller, better known in Italy by her pseudonym, Cicciolina. During the eighties she had often and gladly bared her breasts in public and had been elected to the Italian parliament as a polemical member of the Radical Party. Her status in Italy was legendary.

"Cicciolina," my aunt informed me, "campaigns for animal rights, environmental protection and free love. She's a very clever, kind-hearted person — genuinely wise, I'd call her. I introduced her in the nineties to Jeff Koons — that's how we know each other. And, of course, she's an absolute authority and expert on *amore*."

This time I forbore to comment.

Intimidated by Cicciolina and German cuisine, the guests were somewhat inhibited at first. That, however, was precisely Poldi's strategy, because once the roast pork and gâteau had been consumed, buttons and hearts popped open and the Via Baronessa rang to roars of laughter until late into the night. The Lombardos and Amatos, who raved for weeks about Poldi's cooking and the nice Signora "Cicciolina" Staller, promptly organised Beyoncé and Toni's wedding. If the baby turned out to be a girl, the question of a name had already been settled. No prizes for guessing it began with a C.

December. Nothing special happened, or nothing that Poldi cared to tell me about. She merely made some allusion to a musta-chioed policeman from Giarre who had shown her his collection of china knick-knacks. China knick-knacks, I ask you!

Poldi spent a quiet Christmas with the aunts and saw in the new year with Valérie at Femminamorta. She drank only in mod-eration and found to her surprise that Montana was becoming a stranger to her. She even had to concentrate hard to remem-ber what he looked like, and was obliged to consult the selfies she'd taken during their weeks together. Meanwhile, John had moved in almost permanently with a widow in Catania. Poldi resumed her habit of danc-ing around the house to the strains of "I Will Survive" — relatively sober, what is more.

In mid-January she sent the handsome brigadiere home, pronouncing him cured, and wished him the best of luck in Rome and his love life. She no longer believed any killers would pay her a visit, nor did she believe the case would be solved. But she forgot that Sicily is a volcanic island, that Etna can slumber quietly for months, emitting its melancholy plume of smoke, but that deep beneath the crust, pressure is forever building until, one day, *boom!* Inferno. Devastation. Chaos.

One mild, sunny Sunday in early February, when spring was in the almond-blossom-scented air, Poldi went mushroom picking with Teresa, Martino and their dog, Totti, in the Nebrodi Mountains. There were no mushrooms at this time of year, but details of that kind mattered little to Uncle Martino. The main thing was to be able to amble through the great outdoors armed with a basket, while the dog chased happily after wild boar or pine martens. "Mushroom picking" at this time of year was really just code for "We'll work up a bit of an appetite in the fresh air and then lunch on some nice lamb cutlets at a local inn."

The Nebrodi Mountains are a picturesque range and national park in north-east Sicily, with steep limestone cliffs and alpine pastures, waterfalls and dense woods of oak, cedar, maple, and myrtle bushes. A Sicilian Middle-earth, in other words. It is still home to the fallow deer and lynx, porcupine and eagle, and also to the chunky Sanfratellano horse. One can ramble or ride there for hours without coming across another living soul. It feels like being in a fantasy film. Uncle Martino firmly contends that at twilight one evening he encountered a party of trolls, who crossed his path without noticing him.

Outings with Aunt Teresa, Uncle Martino and Totti always follow precisely the same course. Uncle drives for hours (he enjoys driving) along winding, undulating roads until, in obedience to his instinct or the call of the wild, he spontaneously turns off and heads for the back of beyond. He drives on until he can't get any farther. Then the doors open like the hearts of two lovers, Totti lollops off, barking delightedly, and the trek can begin.

In contrast to Teresa and Martino, who always wear practical attire and stout shoes, Poldi has donned a white trouser suit and shiny silver sneakers, those being the most functional footwear she possesses.

It's a matter of principle with Totti that he

promptly rolls in the nearest puddle and jumps up at Poldi — not that this detracts from her benign mood, because she's feeling relaxed. She merely gives the dog a gentle slap, draws several deep, noisy breaths and strides resolutely on.

Ahead of her is a sea of lush green foliage and the first buds of spring, overhead a cloud-stippled sky so radiant that she has to suppress a little tear when they pause for an initial breather. It's like that sometimes on excursions into the wild; one feels so light and airy, so reconstituted and at one with oneself and the world in general. Poldi sensed that something, somewhere, was sloughing off her. Tingling all over, she seemed to hear a cheerful hum, a whispered assurance that all was well. That where there was a will, there was always a way. That she was alive. And free. She thought lovingly of her first husband, Peppe, from whom this sensation might be a sign, and she also thought, with warmth and benevolence, of Montana. She decided to text him at once — no, better, to call him. Then she noticed that she'd stupidly left her mobile phone in the car.

"Lost something, Poldi?" Teresa called when she saw her fumbling in her handbag.

"Oh no, it's nothing," Poldi called back,

loath to spoil the idyllic moment by dashing back to the car.

So the three of them adhered to their original schedule. They devoured a mountain of lamb cutlets at an inn, or rather, a glorified truckers' diner beside the road, and did not return to the car until mid-afternoon.

Poldi discovered her mobile under the passenger seat and saw at once that something was wrong. Wrong with a vengeance. The phone was buzzing and flashing. The app connected to the surveillance cameras in her house had reported a break-in.

8

Tells of chaos and power places, phone numbers and address books. And of nephews and uncles. Poldi keeps mum about something and makes a call. She realises that much has gone wrong, asks a favour and comes to a decision that defies all reason. Her nephew almost has apoplexy and she's suddenly in a hurry.

Standing dazedly amid the chaos in her living room, Poldi heard the distant voices of Teresa and Martino as they spoke with the police and made phone calls. The burglars had turned the whole house upside down. They had ransacked and vandalised it, emptying cupboards and drawers, slitting open cushions and mattresses, overturning cabinets and chests of drawers and even dismantling the fitted kitchen. They'd made a thorough job of it; the place was a battlefield . . .

At some point the figure of Montana swam into her field of vision.

"Poldi!"

She stared at him as if she didn't recognise him, but then her self-control of the past few hours collapsed. She flung her arms round his neck and sobbed without restraint. She trembled all over and felt her knees buckle, but Montana held her tight. He whispered to one of the policemen standing around to fetch a blanket. Then Poldi felt him gently shepherd her over to the sofa and cover her. A hand proffered her a cup of strong, sweet tea heavily laced with rum. She sipped and sobbed alternately.

"Vito, I —"

"Don't talk, Poldi. Just lie there and rest. I'll deal with everything."

And he did.

Two hours. That was all it had taken for the four burglars to make such a thorough mess of Poldi's home. The CCTV tapes showed how systematically they had gone about it, as if they'd had precise knowledge of the layout. The masks they wore made it impossible to tell their identities. Montana sent the videotapes to a special laboratory in Rome.

Poldi, lying beneath her blanket on the

eviscerated sofa, watched the house fill up. Policemen, forensics operatives with their fingerprint brushes, Dr. Finocchiaro, who took her blood pressure and gave her a tablet to swallow. The aunts roamed the house like ghosts, Uncle Martino bent the ear of one of the crime-scene techies, Totti gambolled around happily. Signora Cocuzza brought some cupcakes, the padre surprisingly said nothing at all for once, Signora Anzalone promptly burst into tears, and one or two inquisitive neighbours debated the probable modus operandi. They argued and gesticulated more and more vehemently until Montana yelled, "Shut up! Anyone with no business here, get out!"

Poldi spent the night at Aunt Caterina's in Catania, but Montana turned up to collect her the next morning.

He was thinner, she noticed. Thinner and a little greyer.

"How are you feeling, Poldi?"

"I don't know."

"Are you up to coming to Torre with me? We have to work out just what the burglars took."

"I don't know."

"Take your time."

Montana sat down with Caterina in the living room and waited patiently until Poldi reappeared, dressed to kill in black stretch trousers and a black sweater, ready to face facts.

During the drive Montana summarised his initial findings. "No fingerprints. We're still trying to identify the men. We haven't managed to identify what they took, perhaps because it was out of the cameras' range."

"But what could they have been looking for?" Poldi wondered aloud.

"Have you really no idea?"

She looked at him. "Are you being serious, Vito?"

"Forget it." He removed one hand from the wheel and lit a cigarette. "I'm putting you under police protection for a while. I'll billet a couple of my men on you."

"Only good-lookers, mind!"

"There now, you're obviously feeling better."

"Seriously, Vito, I don't want that. I'll move into Femminamorta for a bit. Valérie will be away visiting relations in France."

"What'll you do there? It's so isolated."

"It's a power place, a place charged with peaceful energy. Nothing will happen to me there."

"Then I'll drop the men off at Femminamorta."

"Just leave it, Vito, OK? I don't need

protecting, so *basta.*"

Montana opened his mouth again to argue, but she laid a hand on his arm and he got the message: resistance was futile.

Poldi did, for all that, feel choked by the sight of her devastated home, but she drank an espresso with a shot and was soon back in the zone. She inspected the house room by room, carefully subjecting the whole place to her eagle-eyed gaze, because she knew that every detail mattered. Montana remained in the background, but near enough for her to smell his aftershave. She roamed the chaos like a tracker, retrieving articles of clothing and bric-a-brac from the floor, replacing the occasional piece of crockery and wondering if her life would ever be plain sailing. She sensed she knew the answer.

She completed her survey in two hours. Montana had made coffee, tidied up the living room a bit and turned the gutted sofa cushions over.

"Well?" he asked impatiently. "What's missing?"

"Nothing," she replied with a shrug.

"Nothing at all?"

She shook her head. "I haven't spotted a thing."

That was a total lie.

She hadn't taken long to detect the disappearance of a certain thing she had kept in an unremarkable cardboard box in her bedroom cupboard. When she failed to find it anywhere, she realised that it could be vital and began to worry.

"OK," I said when she told me this, "I suppose you aren't going to tell me what it was."

"Why yes. It was just a little notebook."

"I see. What was in it?"

"The names and phone numbers of some good friends."

"So?"

"Well, they weren't just any old friends, but important figures, public figures, can you imagine? All the numbers were confidential, of course."

I whistled through my teeth. "I don't have to tell you what a shemozzle some spotty young hacker could cause if he got hold of them. Why didn't you tell Montana about it?"

"Who says I didn't?"

"I know you, Poldi."

She nodded. "It wasn't on. There are a few aspects of my life I can't discuss with Vito. That's because I've got a past of my own, understand?"

■ ■ ■ ■

In the afternoon Montana drove Poldi to Femminamorta, as agreed.

"I'll look in on you every day."

"There's no need, Vito. I'll manage."

"Don't you want to see me anymore, then?"

Poldi shook her head uncomprehendingly. "*You're* asking *me* that?"

"I'd like to straighten you out on a couple of things, Poldi."

Another sample from the poison cupboard of killer phrases that simply turn one's stomach.

"Perhaps that can wait, Vito," Poldi said with an effort. "I've had a lot of time to think in the past three months, but I'm not quite through yet."

That, of course, was a killer phrase from the same poison cupboard, but she had to send him on his way. The truth was, she didn't need more time to think at all. She only wanted to dissuade Montana from turning up at Femminamorta in the next few days. For certain reasons.

"Mon dieu!" cried Valérie when Poldi told her everything. *"Mon dieu, mon dieu! I*

certainly won't go to France. I'm not leaving you here on your own."

But Poldi wouldn't hear of it.

"Nothing's going to happen to me here, *chérie*. And I'll have lots of visitors all the time."

Another lie, but Poldi felt there was no alternative.

Late that night, when she was alone at last in her bedroom upstairs, she took her mobile phone from her handbag and opened the photo she'd taken in Taormina of the postcard with the phone number on it. The phone number that didn't exist.

HANDSOME ANTONIO
393403469364

It was only a conjecture. Nothing more than a weird premonition, but she knew she was usually right. Drawing a deep breath, she keyed in the number.

Once again, a recorded announcement regretted that the number did not exist or was unobtainable. Poldi hung up and waited. Half an hour later her mobile rang. The caller was withholding their number.

Poldi waited for the second ring. "Yes?"

A man's voice replied in English, "State

your code word." Which was just what she did.

I stared at her. "You what?"

"Why, I gave him the code word, of course."

"And how did you know what it was, pray?"

My aunt rolled her eyes like a schoolmarm when the class dunce at the blackboard says "Um . . ." yet again.

I was momentarily speechless when it dawned on me what she meant.

"You aren't serious, are you?"

"I am." She sipped her red wine with an innocent air.

"But how . . . I mean, who was on the other end of the line?"

"Let's call it a certain multinational information-gathering firm which occasionally employed me as a freelance outworker, but a long time ago. I'd almost forgotten the code word."

"An intelligence service, you mean? You're a secret agent?" My voice sounded a trifle shrill, I thought.

"You said that, I didn't. I can neither confirm nor deny."

"But which 'firm' are we talking about? CIA? MI6? FSB? Mossad?"

"Calm down, sonny. Deep breaths, OK? No need for you to get worked up. It's a sphere of activity you've no conception of. It can't be labelled just like that, even though you, with your narrow-minded, petit bourgeois mentality, have a thing about it. The truth is a bit more complex — make a note of that for your novel."

I still found it hard to believe. My aunt a secret agent! Sitting beside me on the sofa and sipping her wine, she looked like even butter wouldn't melt in her mouth. I tried to collect my thoughts.

"Who knew, or knows, about this?"

"Peppe knew, naturally." Poldi lowered her voice a little. "He always worried when another job cropped up. I sometimes wonder if it was that that made him ill."

"Couldn't you have stopped, or is it the kind of firm you can't resign from? Like in the movies, I mean."

"Life isn't a movie, my boy, bear that in mind. There were many reasons why not. The fact is, I was activated only once more after Peppe died."

"Is that the reason you moved to Tanzania?"

She nodded. "One of many. It was partly a necessary escape for me — more on that another day — but then I got activated and, well, what can I say? Then I fell in love. Anyway, I shouldn't say more about this."

We didn't speak for a while, and I tried to process all I'd heard. Not easy, because I'm not the type of person who's good at dealing with surprises. My head was spinning, and I had a sudden fear that all of Uncle Martino's half-baked conspiracy theories might be true. But then another thought flashed through my mind, galvanising me and putting me on the qui vive: this was great material for my novel! At that point I myself was in investigative mode.

"All right now?" Poldi inquired.

I looked at her. "OK, so what did the firm say?"

"Well, I was surprised too, because we'd been thinking along quite different lines. The thing is, Thomas hadn't stolen that attaché case —"

"Er, what attaché case?" I cut in quickly.

"The McGuffin! The object of desire. It was an attaché case, understand? A special attaché case, bombproof and almost impossible to break open. May I go on now?"

I gestured feebly.

"Well, Thomas hadn't robbed Kigumbe of that attaché case containing the McGuffin after all. That's because it had been stolen long before. Thomas wasn't a thief, he was one of the firm's freelance outworkers like me. I'd always suspected as much but never been sure. Because in this line of work there aren't any company outings or lunch breaks in the canteen . . . What's in the attaché case is probably incredibly valuable and capable of triggering an international crisis. That's why the firm activated Thomas — to recover the attaché case. Are you still with me?"

I nodded. "More or less."

"Bravo. And that's why Thomas was dispatched to Sicily."

"Why Sicily?"

Poldi sighed. "Lord, how slow on the uptake you are. Because it had been stolen by another multinational firm based in Sicily, of course!"

"What did Cosa Nostra want with the attaché case — the McGuffin, I mean?"

"To sell it to the highest bidder, what do you think? Cosa Nostra is a profit-oriented enterprise with a board of directors, human resources department and all the frills. All that interests them is the bottom line and shareholder value, get it? So my firm issued Thomas with another attaché case, but it contained something quite different."

"Like what?"

"Ten million dollars."

I whistled through my teeth, thought feverishly of my novel and cursed myself for not having a notebook handy.

"Can you fit that much cash into an attaché case?"

"In that kind of business deal there are better forms of payment than cash," Poldi said. "The only information my firm had was the name of the middleman who was to sell the attaché case — Handsome Antonio — and a phone number for fixing the rendezvous."

"Didn't John run a check on Thomas's mobile phone traffic?"

"Thomas used a cheap prepaid phone," Poldi explained, "that he could get rid of later, leaving no trace."

"Oh yes, of course, sorry."

"And so," she went on, "Thomas flies to Sicily with ten million dollars to make a deal with Handsome Antonio. So far, so good, but then everything goes pear-shaped. The firm loses touch with Thomas, the money disappears and the attaché case is still missing." Poldi took another swallow of wine, sat back and looked at me. "Any more questions?"

You bet. "The McGuffin is what, exactly?"

"That was the first thing I asked, naturally, but they wouldn't tell me. Top secret."

I found that unsatisfactory, but somehow reasonable under the circumstances.

"Why did Thomas call at your house?"

"The firm has no idea. One can only assume he was in trouble of some kind and needed my help."

"So why didn't he come back?"

She threw up her hands. "Because things went even more pear-shaped, maybe? His dead body doesn't really suggest that things went smoothly, does it?"

That was true too. I thought for a moment.

"Why should Handsome Antonio or the Cosa Nostra need your celebrity address book?"

"No idea, but I don't have a good feeling about it. I reckon things are heating up."

"Why did they wait so long before they broke in?" I thought aloud. "Your brigadiere wasn't there the whole time, after all."

"I don't know, but I suspect someone's patience snapped."

Plausible as that sounded, I still didn't understand.

"Any more questions?"

I shook my head.

Poldi rose. "In that case, let's get cracking."

"Er, get cracking how?"

"Why, I've got to find Handsome Antonio and recover that attaché case."

"*You,* relieve the Mafia of something worth ten million dollars single-handed?"

"No, *not* single-handed!" she snarled. "Why do you think I asked you here?"

I let that settle in, to grasp it in all its you-cannot-be-serious enormity. It was the sort of double take that afflicts you when you've accidentally flushed your mobile phone down the loo or dropped your only house key down a drain.

"You mean I'm . . . to help you . . . go hunting for a murderous Mafioso who's in possession of something worth ten million dollars?"

"There's no need to wet yourself."

I was panic-stricken. "You must be crazy, Poldi. This is a kamikaze idea! I thought I was your chronicler. Remember? You the cool lady sleuth who solves murders, screws policemen and likes to lift her elbow, me your nerdy ghost writer — you know, navy-blue polo shirt, middle-class values, sexually inhibited? And all nice and comfy on the sofa without any stress or Mafia or getting killed."

Poldi dismissed my objections with a sweeping gesture. "Nonsense, you're exaggerating. I'll handle the rough stuff, all you have to do is drive."

"My God, do your own driving!" I yelled hysterically. "Drive yourself and be damned!"

"I can't."

"What do you mean, you can't? Why can't you?"

"Because I don't have a valid driving licence, that's why."

"What? Since when?"

"Since two years ago. I went a little over the limit."

"But you *have* been driving — here in Sicily! We drove here from Munich last summer. We took turns."

"Of course we did, and I'm an excellent driver, but I can't risk running into a police check. On this mission we must be totally inconspicuous. Absolutely under the radar, understand?"

"There is no 'we'!" I screamed.

"Now you're sounding like Vito. You don't have the charisma for it, though, so better not. Take some deep breaths, my boy. Have a drink, it'll do you good."

I was trembling all over. At least, I think I was.

"No!" I groaned. "No way. Never. I'm not doing it. Count me out. I'm out of here. I'm going home tomorrow."

One thing was missing: an inconspicuous car. Poldi already had an idea, however. Her superbrain had been operating at maximum revs and paid as little regard to bourgeois scruples as it did to road regulations. She picked up her phone and dialled a number.

"Pronto?" said a sleepy young voice.

"Toni, Donna Poldina here. Listen, it's not that you owe me anything, but I have to ask you a favour."

Half an hour later, still outfitted in her black stretch pants and black sweater, she stole out of the house and into the darkness like a panther. She knew the way.

The old Bourbon landed estate of Femminamorta, with its few hectares, Valérie's neglected garden, small palm plantation, outhouses, vegetable beds and fruit trees, lies like an oasis in the middle of Piante Russo's grounds. A narrow path leads from the garden, past a sports ground, to the administration block. Poldi scarcely needed the torch function on her phone, and she got to Russo's office building within ten minutes. A small area in front of it was illuminated for the benefit of the surveillance cameras on the roof. Poldi, who could see no security men patrolling with dogs, waited in the shadowy lee of an olive tree for her mobile phone to buzz.

"Yes?"

"The garage is on the right, behind the main building, between gates three and four." The voice at the other end of the line belonged to the newlywed Toni Amato, who owed Poldi his job as a Piante Russo security guard. How or why she got him that job, I never found out. He sounded nervous. "You've got ten minutes until the cameras come back on. That's the most I can do for you."

"Thanks, Toni, and don't worry. I'll bring the car back in one piece in a day or two, and I'll take full responsibility for everything. Word of honour."

"You'll find the key rack in the office beside the gate. Ten minutes, Donna Poldina."

Poldi set her phone timer and took off in a hurry. As fast as her bad knee permitted, she scuttled into the illuminated area in front of the main building and found the garages behind it, where Piante Russo's tractors, agricultural machinery and small vans were parked. A van bearing the nursery's logo would have been far too conspicuous, of course, but Poldi knew that Russo

217

also kept his two private cars there: the beefy Mercedes and the silver-grey Fiat Tipo for business meetings where a more modest image was appropriate.

The garage gate opened as if by magic and the lights came on. Seven minutes left. Poldi lost no time in stealing inside like a ninja's shadow. She darted into the office, located the key rack, grabbed the Tipo's key and hurriedly looked for the car. The silver-grey Fiat was parked at the far end of the building. Five minutes to go before the CCTV came on again. Time enough.

But there were several quite different cars parked there too.

"Madonna mia!" she gasped.

For the crummiest, most inconspicuous car in the world was flanked by some regular speedsters. Two Ferraris, an Aston Martin and the orange Lamborghini Aventador Poldi had seen when the wedding pictures of Russo's daughter were shot at Femminamorta. There was also an old red Maserati Spyder. She hadn't known that Russo collected sports cars, but was unsurprised.

She stood there weighing the keys of the Fiat Tipo in her hand, but she couldn't take her eyes off the Maserati convertible. The sight of it brought back memories of outings with that Brazilian Formula One driver

— what was his name? She couldn't call it to mind. Three minutes left. She knew precisely what she needed for her mission: a reliable, inconspicuous car. She knew the idea that had just popped into her head was utterly crazy. Daft, irrational, risky, adolescent — and thoroughly cool. And my Auntie Poldi knew a thing or two about coolness.

There was also her inner voice whispering that although the idea was crazy, et cetera, it might pay off in the end. And, as we all know, Poldi's flashes of intuition are usually correct.

So she hurried back into the office, looked for the right key, failed to find it, swore, found it after all, then darted back as fast as she could. One minute to go. Grunting, she squeezed in behind the wheel, uttered a prayer to the god of starter motors and turned the ignition key. With unexpected reliability, the Maserati roared to life. All that remained was for Poldi to floor the accelerator.

I felt like a condemned man on his way to the gulag. Poldi told me to pack a few things and be quick about it.

"Just the bare essentials for two or three days," she decreed impatiently. "We won't be any longer than that, and the Maserati isn't a family sedan."

"But it'll be dark soon," I protested feebly.

I felt sick. Setting out on a suicide mission without much sleep was a nerve-racking prospect.

"Can't we leave tomorrow morning?"

She brushed my pathetic objection aside. "Every hour counts from now on. I've wasted enough time bringing you up to date, but there was no alternative. Please hurry."

Soon afterwards we shoehorned our small bags into the measly boot. The Maserati Spyder with its tiny rear seat affords only enough room for two adults and two hobbits, plus lunch bags, and the roof is so low that even a person of average height would repeatedly hit their head on it.

"I don't know why I'm doing this," I muttered. "I must be absolutely mad, getting myself involved in this caper."

"You're a regular Sancho Panza, did you know that?"

"Meaning what?"

"Meaning personalities have a binary structure, just like luck. You're either a Don Quixote or a Sancho Panza. One always wants to ride headlong into escapades, the other prefers to stay home. But every Sancho Panza needs a Don Quixote and vice

versa, believe me, so quit bellyaching and
drive."

"Drive to where, pray?"

"Catania. First we have to pick up the satnav."

"What satnav?"

"The special one covering Sicily, of
course. Stop asking stupid questions. Just
drive."

That meant nothing to me, but by now
I'd reached a stage where I just didn't care.
To soothe my nerves, I concentrated on my
novel. This would simply turn out to be a
grotesque research trip, I surmised, and I
pictured myself describing it later on chat
shows. If the truth be told, I didn't really
believe that Poldi was hell-bent on tangling
with a bunch of Mafiosi. She might calm
down during the drive, or so I hoped. In
any event, it would certainly be better if she
didn't embark on this hare-brained venture
solo.

Poldi directed me straight into Catania's
evening rush-hour traffic. I like that city's
blend of baroque and art nouveau and
volcanic basalt, especially on summer
nights, when sodium street lights cast a
magical glow over the city centre, the
cathedral, the black elephants, the Piazza
Università, the Via Etnea, the narrow side

streets, the palm-fringed avenues, the garbage dumps, the deserted fish market and the air of decay. One could believe one was somewhere in the tropics.

I recall long nights spent with my cousin Ciro and emerging into the Via Alessi in the small hours from the Trattoria Nievski, where all the well-tanned *jeunesse* of Catania hung out. Where they drank beer from plastic cups, smoked pot, canoodled and talked anticapitalism. Where the music was loud and the girls were pert and pretty — and where shy, inhibited me felt like the gooseberry of all gooseberries.

But before we puttered home on the Vespa, Ciro and I always stopped off at an old, art nouveau kiosk where an equally ancient woman stood amid a mountain of mandarins and lemons and juiced them. We bought ourselves mugs of *mandarine con limone* and fresh, warm *cornetti con crema* from the bakery across the street and sat down on the kerb. We didn't speak, but one doesn't have to with Ciro, who's good at saying nothing. And at those moments, with the taste bomb of mandarins, lemons, *cornetto* and vanilla cream in my mouth, I felt unburdened of all the youthful stress that comes from trying to impress and making sheep's eyes at girls — my utter failure to be cool, in fact — and I loved that shimmering black city and its nocturnal smell.

Poldi sent me zigzagging across Catania, seeming somehow to have lost her way. Catania's traffic always stresses me out, I admit. Everyone drives wherever they please, like a scattering of shot from a gun. You can forget your rear-view mirror and the lane markings. Onward, ever onward is the motto. You have to swim with the stream, spot gaps, honk your horn and dauntlessly force your way in. If you want to change lanes, the best thing is to hang your arm out and thump the neighbouring car, which will brake soon enough.

The Maserati had a rock-hard clutch and steering, and it didn't like travelling at low speeds. I was also worried I might scratch the paintwork of a Mafia boss's favourite, well-maintained old-timer. I was worried about a lot of things.

"Just tell me where we're going!" I said peevishly.

"To Teresa and Martino's, that's where."

"Eh? I thought we were picking up a sat-nav."

"Correct. The satnav is your Uncle Martino. No one knows Sicily better."

"You're planning to take Uncle Martino with us?" I squawked. "You realise what that means?"

Sheer horror overcame me. I'm fond of my uncle, honestly I am. He's the most affectionate, generous, clever, well-read, jovial, mischievous uncle imaginable. He knows all there is to know about Mediterranean fish, mushrooms, Sicilian history, the Mafia and the CIA. In terms of central European standards of good order and punctuality, however, one would have to call him mad. He spent the forty-plus years of his working life as a sales rep for a company that manufactured safes and other security equipment for banks, a job that had taken him all over Sicily. The fact is, nobody knows the island better than Martino. He does, however, have a downside, which is that he loves driving for hours on end, talking and smoking incessantly, without ever stopping for a drink or a pee.

I tried to reason with her: "But this car is far too small for three."

"Go on, we aren't sumo wrestlers."

I gave up. *What the heck,* I thought groggily, *you're going to chauffeur two lunatics across Sicily in search of a Mafia killer. Great. Anything else?*

Not that I knew it, but things would get far worse.

My Auntie Poldi and I must have visited

Teresa and Martino a hundred times, but the traffic in Catania follows tortuous, undulating routes interrupted every two minutes by roadwork of some kind, and I suffer from a lousy sense of direction — a family failing that Poldi appeared to share. We spent a full hour driving aimlessly around the city, and it wasn't until we happened, purely by chance, to pass the old Due Milla bar that I knew where we were.

Soon afterwards, feeling as relieved as a yachtsman safe in harbour after sailing through a hurricane, I parked the Maserati outside Teresa and Martino's house in Via Luigi Sturzo. I didn't pay much attention to the two men in the black Toyota that crawled past us at walking pace and parked a few metres farther on.

Neither did Agent Poldi.

9

Tells of tactics and apparitions, of tinfoil hats and parallel universes, of quests and discoveries and magical places. And, again, of men. Poldi hassles me and takes cover. Martino looks for his glasses and needs a coffee, and Totti finds something, but so does Handsome Antonio. Soon afterwards, Poldi makes a discovery of her own.

Aunt Teresa greeted me warmly with a kiss and a solicitous inquiry about my broken nose. Anyone would have thought that nothing was up — that we weren't on the verge of setting out on a suicide mission. Totti was beside himself with delight at seeing us again. I'm fond of the dog. There was a small hold-all in the hall. I could hear Uncle Martino moving around in the *salotto.*

"Don't tell me you approve of this insane idea," I entreated Aunt Teresa.

She looked at me with a mischievous twinkle in her knowing, boot-button eyes and chivvied me into the kitchen. Meanwhile, Poldi poured herself a grappa.

"Are you ready, Martino?" I heard her call. "We must be off!"

"Just a minute!" came a bellow from the *salotto.*

"Don't worry, my boy," Aunt Teresa whispered to me in the slightly Bavarian-accented German she and her sisters had preserved. "It's impossible to talk Poldi out of anything — I don't have to tell you that — so we thought we'd copy the Chinese when they're doing their tai chi, know what I mean?"

"Er?"

"Or their kung fu, it's all the same. What matters is to let your opponent waste their energy on thin air. If Martino comes with you, you won't get far."

And then the point of the aunts' tactic dawned on me. Although Uncle becomes more chipper every hour he spends driving and knows his way around Sicily better than anyone, he lives in a different space-time continuum than the rest of us. Time means almost nothing to him. He moves around in it in an entirely relaxed and unconstrained manner, sometimes backwards. On our excursions I have never known him to take the shortest route between two points. He despises motorways as instruments of suppression on the part of turbo-capitalism, delights in detours and side roads, farm tracks and the backwoods. He's a born explorer, doomed to eternal curiosity and missed appointments, a characteristic which those around him often construe as muddle-headedness.

Feeling highly relieved, I gave Teresa a hug.

"Brilliant," I sighed. "You're simply brilliant."

In the *salotto* Uncle was already providing a sample of what had inspired her tactic. With an unlit ciggy in the corner of his mouth, he was looking for his forty-third pair of reading glasses. He keeps losing them. You might think that even the biggest home would reach the saturation point where reading glasses are concerned, but not a bit of it. Uncle is a genius at misplacing them, and the same goes for lighters.

Poldi, who was pacing impatiently, looked as if she was about to explode.

Not so Uncle, who was calmness personified and completely focused on his quest.

"Teresa!" he called out from time to time, not because he wanted her to help him, but because he happened to be thinking of her at that moment. "Teresa!"

Teresa, who had naturally cooked us a meal, insisted that we eat something before we left, and when my Aunt Teresa cooks a meal, you don't say no. There was a fennel and orange salad with green beans and mint, followed by *pasta alla norma,* the Sicilian classic, and *lumache al sugo di pomodoro,* or little sea snails in tomato sauce, and a mountain of grilled red mullet, and ending with a heavenly fruit salad.

Another hour went by before we could leave.

We somehow squeezed Martino's bag into the Maserati's boot.

"Just a minute," he said, and disappeared into the house again.

Poldi was having difficulty controlling herself. Me, I was feeling fine — well fed and rather sleepy.

This changed abruptly when Uncle returned after another quarter of an hour. He was now wearing an olive-green photographer's gilet with pockets and zips all over it and leading Totti, whom he manoeuvred onto the back seat.

"Oh no!" Poldi protested. "That dog stays here."

"I'm not going without Totti," Uncle

declared stoutly, and Totti emitted a euphoric bark from behind. "Totti is the best tracker dog in the world. We're a team — we're almost joined at the hip. Without Totti I'm a useless old fart."

And he lit a cigarette.

You have to hand it to Uncle Martino. He's a cool customer.

Poldi was seething. "All right," she snarled, "but this car is a nonsmoker."

So we drove off at last, with Uncle Martino and Totti wedged together in the narrow back seat, Poldi in the passenger seat and me at the wheel. Poldi inserted a cassette, and we left Catania that night to the strains of San Remo pop — who'd have thought it? — from the eighties.

It got dark.

It started to rain.

Uncle started smoking.

Despite Poldi's vigorous protests, he puffed away throughout the trip.

Poldi kept front-seat driving, either stamping on an imaginary brake pedal or bullying me unmercifully into stepping on the gas and swigging from her hip flask between times.

I felt very lonely and pathetic.

Poldi's plan consisted of following the route Thomas had taken, according to his

230

phone tracker record. This led from Siracusa via Noto to Gela, Palma di Montechiaro, Agrigento, Enna and Catania. She proposed to employ Uncle as a kind of sleuth hound, because of the wide range of friends and contacts whom he could discreetly question about a "Handsome Antonio." It made some sort of sense.

Although condemned to thrombotic inactivity in the back seat, Uncle Martino seemed to be enjoying the trip. He jabbered incessantly. His latest conspiracy theory went:

"Sicily is the safest place in the world. Why? Because there's no terrorism here. *Ecco!* And for why?"

"Because of the CIA and the Knights Templar," I said wearily.

A triumphant laugh. "Ha! No, because of the Islamic State. ISIS has made a drugs and arms deal with the Mafia. But the Templars and the CIA are also involved."

"You don't say."

"I'm only citing facts," Uncle said coolly. "The links go back a long way. A very long way. When eastern Libya was still an Italian colony, Marshal Pietro Badoglio was the governor of the province of Cyrenaica. He later deposed Mussolini and paved the way for the Allied invasion of Sicily. This, as everyone knows, took place without much bloodshed, because Lucky Luciano got the Americans to air-drop yellow silk handkerchiefs with the letter L on them to tip off the local Mafia bosses. This definitely shows that Badoglio was also a boss and an agent of the CIA. Before that, though, he had put down the rebellious Senussi in eastern Libya after some very bloody fighting. The Senussi were a Sufi clan. They did as they pleased under Gaddafi and organised the first Islamist combat troops. All clear so far? *Beh!* Well, Badoglio was a Templar — everyone knows that. A Templar, a Mafia boss and a CIA agent, and what he was after in Libya was something quite other than the Senussi: the Templars' treasure, the Holy Grail. He wanted to bring it back to Sicily. That's why he made a pact with the Senussi, in order to —"

"Just a minute. I thought he massacred them."

"Yes, to begin with, but why do you think Italy suddenly withdrew from Libya? Exactly! Because Badoglio had done a deal with the Senussi, right? Badoglio, the Sufi, Templars, CIA, Mafia, ISIS. *Ecco!*" He sat back contentedly.

"Could you step on the gas a bit, sonny?"

Sighing, I tried to concentrate on the

232

road. We were taking the motorway to Siracusa, and I had just sighted the lights of the gigantic Augusta refinery when Poldi swore and started feverishly rummaging through her handbag.

"What's the matter?"

"Like a fool I left the goddam road map behind at Teresa's."

"Great. A fine secret agent you are. Lucky we've got Uncle Martino with us."

Behind us, Uncle Martino and Totti farted almost simultaneously.

Not that I'd noticed it before, Totti was a chronic farter. It wasn't long before the whole car stank of cigarette smoke and rotten eggs. My affection for the dog began to diminish a little. When I rolled down the driver's window, rain lashed me in the face and I couldn't see. To avoid fainting, I smoked as well. This made me feel sick.

Not far beyond Augusta, Uncle Martino announced that the motorway ahead was closed because of a bridge under repair, and made me turn off onto a secondary road, followed by an even narrower secondary road. At his instruction, I drove this way and that through the nocturnal backwoods.

"A shortcut," he insisted. "Trust me."

I guessed what that meant: Teresa's plan was now bearing fruit. This relieved and worried me at the same time. With every kilometre we drove, signs of habitation became rarer. After passing through a few villages, we soon saw no more houses at all. There was almost no traffic, no lights were visible anywhere, and the signposts were no help. If there were any, they were rusty, bent or riddled with shotgun pellets. We were driving on our own through the heart of darkness like Vikings rowing across the North Atlantic. The countryside was as dark, as pitch-black, as if it had swallowed all the light in existence. My heart sank. The rain grew steadily heavier, and the windscreen wipers became almost useless as I drove blindly through the February night. My eyelids kept drooping. I blinked and yawned and fought the urge to nod off. I needed every ounce of concentration not to send us all careering into the hereafter. An hour later Uncle abruptly stopped burbling and fell asleep, as did Totti and then Poldi. They all snored, but at least there was no more cigarette smoke or canine farting, just peace and quiet. I turned off the radio and was alone. Very alone.

After another hour I ran out of petrol. I was utterly lost. The car went steadily slower, the engine faltered, stuttered, and I just managed to pull over onto the verge. I had forgotten to keep an eye on the fuel gauge and cursed myself for not having borne in mind that a forty-year-old six-cylinder twin-turbo engine consumed around five times as much petrol as a Fiat Panda, though in any case I hadn't seen a petrol station for hours. Total darkness reigned around me. I could see only a small stretch of the narrow road ahead in the headlights' beam. Then rain and darkness swallowed that up too.

So I gave up. I simply couldn't cope any more. My personal supply of fuel had also run out. Apathetically, I watched the rain stream down the windscreen. It looked as though we were sinking.

I turned off the headlights, closed my eyes and recited one of my Auntie Poldi's favourite expressions: "The rest of the world can kiss my arse."

"Ah, Teresa!" Uncle Martino muttered in his sleep.

I didn't really sleep at all that night. Only my legs went to sleep. I shivered with cold, I was thirsty, and I needed to pee but shrank from getting out. But then I must have nodded off, because I had some chaotic dreams.

A brief flashback. Munich 1942. The little

man with the toothbrush moustache no longer patronises the Osteria Bavaria. He has plunged the world into total war and master-minded the greatest genocide in history. Barnaba is now a middle-aged, wealthy signore and Mafia don. He has even developed a little tummy, but he still looks very handsome. He has dependably fathered a child each summer with the ever-sadder Eleonora, and Rosi and many another fertile Munich belle rejoice in raising his splendid progeny, for whom Barnaba provides on a generous scale. Barnaba is at the zenith of his success, but he wants still more. He is searching for some meaning in his life.

He finds it one night when Aunt Pasqualina reveals her activities as a secret agent. Pasqualina, too, is older and has put on weight, but she has given up spirits, drinks only champagne, and maintains sexual contact with the Berlin film industry and leading lights of politics and industry. She also has conducted a passionate affair with Vitus Tanner. Tanner turned out to be an indefatigable lover of positively Sicilian calibre, which was not surprising in view of his status as a detective inspector. Pasqualina eventually broke his heart, which made him even more grimly determined to nail Barnaba.

As a top spy, Pasqualina has spent years working on the side for various governments. She has also prevented the discovery of Atlantis (Note to self: *Atlantis too much of a good thing?*), but all to no avail. The world is creaking in every joint and threatening to go to the dogs if the little man with the toothbrush moustache remains in power in Berlin for much longer. Barnaba bitterly regrets not having sent the brothers from Ragusa to pay the little man a visit. Something has to change.

For a start, Barnaba sends to Catania for puny Federico, now twenty-one, intending to hand over the business to him. Unfortunately, Federico proves to have no head for business. Anaemic and sickly, he's scared of his father and Munich in equal measure. So Barnaba sends for another son of the same age named Walter, an ultra-Bavarian, bull-necked bear of a man with gumption, and provisionally entrusts his empire to the two brothers. Although Federico and Walter could not be more dissimilar in appearance, they have one thing genetically in common: a blazing, uncontrollable temper that is unleashed when they are beset by the least disrespect or frustration, and can send them right round the bend. Business continues to be excellent.

Thereafter Barnaba, now a secret agent of the first order, goes travelling with Pasqualina under the protection of the magical amulet given him by the preternaturally beautiful Cyclops Ilaria. At the behest of Marshal Badoglio, the Knights Templar and the CIA, he finds the Holy Grail in eastern Libya, deciphers the Enigma code, ends fascism in Italy and paves the way for the Allied landing in Sicily. And that is only the start.

Dawn was just breaking when I awoke alone in the car. I saw that we had come to rest on a gently undulating plain. It was as if this wild expanse of countryside had shivered once at the beginning of time and then frozen. The whole plain was densely overgrown with spiky *macchia* bushes interspersed with bizarre limestone formations and isolated olive trees. In the distance I could make out some grassland and almond trees, and beyond that, casting long shadows, a small wood. The Maserati was standing beside the only road that meandered across the undulating terrain.

Not a soul to be seen. No Poldi, no Martino, no Totti. Groaning and shivering, I struggled out of the car, did a few knee bends, relieved myself and tried to get warm. Then I tried calling Poldi and Martino, only to find that my mobile phone had no reception. Surprise, surprise. That meant I couldn't find my location either. Great, I thought, and set off in search of the family.

Yesterday's rain was history. Although the road and its surroundings were still damp, there wasn't a cloud in the sky and the rising sun dispensed a little warmth. Swaths of mist were rising from the fields. The lighter it became, the more I discerned of this stretch of countryside, which seemed to have been asleep forever. The air was redolent of damp stone, resin and spring flowers. Feeling at once strangely light-hearted and far from home like a ship-wrecked sailor on a suicide mission, I paused for a moment to savour the sensation. Wherever we were stranded, I had never seen this part of Sicily before.

All I really know is the east coast around Catania, because that is where the family lives. My hours-long trips around Sicily with Uncle Martino on visits to his customers I remember only as nightmarish extremes of heat, cigarette smoke, headaches, sunburn and thirst. Sicily and I have always had a difficult relationship. Although I have often heard its call and felt more at home there than anywhere else, it has also mocked me often and treated me like a foreign body.

But now, standing in that beautiful wilderness, which might have been a forgotten leftover from the Garden of Eden, I felt a sort of kinship. It was as if I had just returned home and something was expecting me.

And then I saw him.

He was standing in the scrub some fifty metres away, facing the rising sun with his head back, possibly enjoying its warmth, possibly just daydreaming. He neither moved nor appeared to notice me. Or perhaps he was ignoring me — something I'm used to. In any event, I didn't make a sound, just stared at him the way one stares at an impossibility. In the dawn light he was not much more than a shadowy figure. I made out his thick-set, muscular chest, his long neck and long, matted hair, which fell to his shoulders. And I saw that his upper body terminated in the rump of a horse or donkey. I saw hide shimmering in the sunrise, saw four powerful legs and a short, restlessly twitching tail. The centaur pawed the ground with his left forefoot and scratched his chest like a Sicilian paterfamilias on the beach, but other than that he still didn't move. He might have been part of the *macchia*. It was as if he had sprouted from the scrub and would soon be reabsorbed by it. Steam rose from his equine back.

Then I heard shots in the distance. Startled, I turned in their direction. The scattered reports suggested that someone was firing at random. When I turned back to the centaur, the creature had disappeared.

At least the shots were real, and because the human brain is focused on reality, discounting occasional lapses due to lack of sleep or overexcitement, I hurried in their direction without another thought. That was where I would find Poldi, of that I felt certain.

Having followed the road over the brow of a low hill, I saw an old farmhouse nestled in the *macchia*.

An elderly man armed with a shotgun was standing outside the farmyard gate and yelling in Italian, "Piss off, you goddam trespassers!"

By that he evidently meant Poldi, Uncle Martino and Totti, who had taken refuge behind a boulder but were looking as relaxed as if they were on a picnic. Totti uttered a joyous bark when he saw me, and Uncle waved a little plastic bag at me like a tourist guide urging a dawdling culture vulture to catch up. He always carries this plastic bag in case he finds something of interest. A pair of glasses, for instance, or some wild asparagus, or oyster mushrooms, or the Holy Grail.

Poldi swigged from her hip flask and adjusted her wig. She looked rested and fresh, and her make-up was immaculate. I wondered how she managed it.

"Get lost!" The old man fired in the air again. "I can still see you, you miserable stooges of globalisation! I can detect your gamma rays, but they won't get inside *my* head!"

He was wearing a *coppola,* a Sicilian peaked cap, which he had wrapped in kitchen foil. I was beginning to get the picture, but by this time nothing surprised me.

Being the pragmatist I am, I debated whether to sprint over to Poldi and Martino at a crouch, like some cool SAS man in a movie, but decided on the less cool expedient of crawling.

"Hey, what are you doing?" Poldi called to me. "You'll tear your pants on the prickles! Stand up and come here."

I crawled on.

"I think I just saw an apparition," I said breathlessly when I finally reached the boulder.

Poldi, who knows a thing or two about apparitions, handed me her hip flask without a word, and I took a swallow.

"Will someone tell me what's going on here?" I asked.

"Why, you were sleeping like a baby. We didn't want to wake you."

"Thanks, very considerate of you."

Poldi and Uncle Martino are light sleepers, and spending the night in a Maserati hadn't helped. They had woken up shortly before me and surveyed their surroundings. Being explorers by nature and in need of exercise, Uncle and Totti disappeared into the *macchia.* Poldi fixed her make-up and marched off to find someone who could give us a tow. They discovered the farmhouse, but when they approached it the old man opened fire and they took cover. I had found them soon afterwards, and here we now were.

"Why is he blazing away like that?"

"He'll soon stop," Uncle said serenely. He gave Totti a dog biscuit from his pocket and fiddled with his plastic bag. "We'll wait for him to calm down a bit and then ask him politely if we can have some coffee. Hey, look what Totti found just now." He opened the bag and held it under my nose.

Inside it was a flat, pointed, longish flake

of shiny obsidian with sharp edges. A Stone Age spearhead.

"Wow!"

"I can still see you!" the old man yelled from his post outside the house. "You're transmitting my thoughts to the Illuminati, I'm well aware of that!"

"OK," I said, trying to focus on a solution to this impasse. "We're obviously unwelcome here. Let's make ourselves scarce."

"Not without coffee," said Uncle.

"And we can't just abandon the Maserati," Poldi put in. "If you hadn't got us lost and failed to keep an eye on the fuel gauge, we wouldn't be hunkered down here like a bunch of idiots."

"So what do you suggest?"

"A coffee would be good," said Uncle.

Poldi struggled to her feet with a groan. "Signore," she called, "we're simply tourists whose car has run out of petrol. It'd be kind of you to tow us to the nearest petrol station. Maybe you could also offer us a cup of —"

"Pah!" the old man said. "Think I'll fall for that story?"

"I'm coming over to you, then we can have a quiet chat," Poldi called, and she strode off across the *macchia*.

"Not another step, Satan!" the old man

bellowed. He fired another shot in the air.

"I need some coffee," growled Uncle, and he also stood up.

Before I could say another word, he set off for the house in Poldi's wake. This is just a bad dream, I thought, expecting the old man to gun them down the next minute, if only by mistake.

Then I heard Uncle call out, "Antonio, calm down!" I thought my ears had deceived me.

"It's me, Martino!" Uncle called. "Martino Cosentini from Catania! Put that gun away and make us some coffee. That old thing'll blow up in your face if you're not careful!"

"Martino Cosentini?" I heard the old man call back, flabbergasted. "Martino with the magic hands?"

"Yes!"

"I don't believe it!" the old man exclaimed delightedly. "Good heavens, what brings *you* here? It's been ages. Come here, man!"

I simply couldn't believe what I was hearing.

Half an hour later we were seated around a rough wooden farmhouse table. I'd ceased to be astonished at anything, certainly not the multiplicity of handsome Antonios in Sicily.

On the table in front of us were slices of fresh, home-baked bread and cups of coffee, which Poldi diluted with the contents of her hip flask.

"This is a good place," she announced. "It's charged with the purest positive energy. First-rate karma."

Poldi knew about such things.

The old farmhouse consisted of little more than the room in which Antonio slept, cooked, lived and pursued his "project." The few pieces of furniture were worn and plain, the walls plastered with cut-out illustrations of mythical creatures, old maps, and sheets and scraps of paper covered with spidery handwriting. There were piles of books everywhere. I had expected the house to reek of age and neglect, but instead the whole place radiated peace and strength and smelt of fresh laundry, crusty loaves and the *salsiccia* Antonio was just frying for us. He had hung the tinfoil cap and the shotgun on a hook on the door and now looked quite lucid and businesslike. Close at hand he made a far less loopy impression, and the laughter lines around his eyes spoke volumes. *He looks a bit overgrown, with that beard and moustache and all that tousled hair,* I thought, *but in his youth he may actually have been a good-looking man.*

Antonio explained where we were: not as far from our intended route as I had imagined. Only a hundred and fifty kilometres astray, we were somewhere south of Enna, in the middle of Sicily.

"What brings you here?" he wanted to know.

"We're looking for —" Uncle Martino began, but Poldi cut him short.

"We're doing a bit of a tour with our nephew here, who's writing a novel about Sicily. Really hot stuff — the next international bestseller. A family saga covering three generations, it's filled with myths, drama, culture and history — and brim-full of sensual *sicilianità,* if you know what I mean. We're helping him with his research into the island and its people."

That finally convinced me I'd wound up in a parallel universe.

"Bravo!" cried Antonio. "Mind you, youngster, I can't say you look like a novelist. What happened to your nose? Run into a door, did you? Look at your uncle — that's what a real novelist looks like."

That, of course, was music to Uncle's ears.

It turned out that in another life, many years ago, Antonio had been the branch manager of the Banco di Sicilia in Milazzo, and that Uncle Martino had sold him a new safe every few years.

"And whenever the bloody thing jammed and we couldn't meet any withdrawals, Martino Cosentini would come racing to the rescue with his magic hands," Antonio recalled. "He had only to touch the safe — click! — and it opened again. Simply magical. How long ago was it, Martino?"

"Thirty years?"

"Thirty years, *Madonna*! And you recognised me even so!"

Poldi unceremoniously interrupted their sentimental chitchat. "Why the charade with the tinfoil cap and the gamma rays?" she demanded.

"Oh, because these smart young realtors and tourism promoters keep turning up here, wanting to *develop* everything — I can't stand the word — and that upsets an old codger like me. I bought this property for peanuts twenty years ago, when I started to devote myself to my project. They can't do a thing without my signature. I've been offered the earth, but I'm not leaving. Not for ten billion lire!"

He had evidently failed to register the introduction of the euro.

"The loopier I act, the more seriously they take me," he said gleefully. "Anyway, I'm still here, and I'm defending my paradise against all comers, whether investors, luxury hotels or Mafiosi."

"But aren't you afraid the Mafia may . . ." Poldi began.

A dismissive gesture. "Bugger them. Just let them try it. I know I'm nearing the end of my shelf life, but till then, signora, I'm up for anything."

"What exactly is this project of yours, Don Antonio?"

"I can't talk about it."

"Please, Don Antonio. Your whole house testifies to it."

"Tell her, Antonio," growled Uncle Martino, knocking back his third espresso.

"Very well. I'm pursuing an evolutionary niche theory which anthropologists consider absurd," said Antonio. "I'm looking for evidence of the existence of a certain lateral branch of *Homo sapiens* that lived only here in Sicily."

"Aha," said Poldi. "And what sort of lateral branch is it?"

"The Cyclopes," Uncle said drily, and lit a cigarette.

Antonio nodded vigorously. "I'm convinced they existed. I just *know* it, but they've left nothing behind, so people think they're purely mythical."

A parallel universe, I thought.

But Poldi nodded earnestly. She knew a thing or two about niches and not being taken seriously.

"According to my research, they must have evolved in Sicily some two hundred thousand years ago," Antonio went on. "Nobody knows what happened then, possibly an epidemic wiped out the entire population. At any rate, my research indicates that one group lived on Etna and another in the middle of this island. Right here, in other words. That's why I refuse to be ousted."

Uncle had an idea. "Totti found something earlier. Perhaps it could be of some help."

He fumbled in one of his innumerable pockets, fished out the plastic bag and put the flake of obsidian on the table.

Antonio stared at the spearhead. "*Madonna,* where did you find that?"

The spot was not very far from the road and roughly where I'd seen that apparition of a centaur. The ground sloped gently down to a half-hidden stream that wound through the *macchia.* The rain of recent days had softened the soil sufficiently to cause a minor landslide and expose some muddy gravel. It was from this gravel that Totti had unearthed the spearhead.

Antonio started digging feverishly. He had brought a spade with him but took care not to damage any other artefacts the gravel might contain. We three stood close by, waiting in suspense.

Antonio uttered a sudden, smothered cry, flung the spade aside and, with trembling hands, scraped away the gravel from around a buried object. Before long, carefully cupping it in both hands like some fragile treasure, he extricated it from the ground in which it had lain for who knew how many millennia before being propelled to the surface by the earth stirring in its sleep.

"Well, tickle my arse with a feather!" Poldi exclaimed when she saw what it was.

"Bravo, Totti!" Uncle patted the dog contentedly.

Antonio was holding the upper part of a human skull. It was yellow and looked larger than a normal skull. Earth was still clinging to it and half the cranial vault was missing, but one thing could be clearly seen: the eye sockets were unusually close together — in fact, they almost merged above the bridge of the nose.

Parallel universe was all I thought.

Antonio was tenderly, reverently stroking the skull. He had tears in his eyes. "A Cyclops! Thank you, Martino."

"Beh!" Uncle said dismissively.

"Or a simple deformity," Poldi put in, thoroughly down-to-earth. "Either way, Don Antonio, it's not going to make your life any easier. On the contrary."

"I've never intended to publish anything," said Antonio, "but this is never going to be the site of a luxury hotel or anything of the kind, I swear." He looked at Poldi. "Would you take a photo of me?"

"Of course, Don Antonio."

He handed my aunt his mobile phone and posed, grinning, with his supposedly Cyclopean skull. Poldi took one picture, then another, and checked to see if they'd turned out all right. In so doing, she made a discovery of her own. She positively squeaked when she saw it. Antonio had generally confined himself to photographing the countryside and new dig sites. The miniaturised versions of his pictures all looked very similar, which was why this one had caught her eye. It was a selfie of Antonio and another man laughing at the camera like good friends. The other man was Thomas, and the photo had been taken the week before his death.

Antonio was dismayed to learn of Thomas's death. We were sitting around his kitchen table again, with the skull bedded down on a piece of paper towel. Its central eye seemed to be goggling at us.

"He was such a nice fellow," Antonio kept saying. "I met him in a bar in Enna, where I was having a quick coffee after doing my weekly shopping. This African man was standing there with his attaché case, drinking an almond milk and asking if anyone knew someone called Handsome Antonio. "That's me," I said jokingly, which was how we got into conversation. He was interested in Sicily and wanted to see where I lived, so I brought him back here. He was impressed, genuinely enchanted — he roamed the *macchia* for hours. That night he told me about his homeland. I think he was very lonely. Something seemed to be preying on his mind, possibly the contents of that attaché case, but he found a little peace here. A really nice fellow, Thomas."

"How long did he stay?" asked Poldi.

"Two days, then I drove him back to his car in Enna. He still had to find this other Antonio and do a deal with him. After that, he proposed to come back here, but I had a feeling he wouldn't make it."

Poldi looked at Uncle and me. "If Thomas failed to find Handsome Antonio, I suppose we might as well go home."

She had a point.

"He left something behind," said Antonio, breaking the silence.

He went over to a cupboard and returned carrying a red hoodie.

"Nothing else?" asked Poldi.

Antonio shook his head.

Poldi held up the hoodie with one hand and patted it with the other. Suddenly she frowned, felt in one of the side pockets and brought out two small pieces of paper and a key. One of the bits of paper was a return bus ticket from Catania to Palermo, the other a crumpled claim ticket from a laundry, the Lavanderia Graziella, no address. The key looked like a normal house key, but there was no indication of what door it belonged to.

Poldi handed me the claim ticket. "And what d'you think this means from our point of view?"

"Er, a minor change of route?"

"Full marks!"

Antonio provided us with a can of petrol and some food, and Poldi was urging us to leave when we heard Totti barking loudly outside. Looking through the window, we saw a black Toyota making its way slowly along the road towards the house.

"I've got a really nasty feeling about this,"

said Poldi, and her powers of intuition are, as we know, infallible.

"There's a path through the *macchia* behind the house," Antonio told us. "They won't spot you as long as you keep low. The path curves round and leads back to the road. I'll deal with the guys in the car."

"You mustn't put yourself in danger on our account, Don Antonio."

But Antonio merely grinned and pointed to the hook from which the tinfoil cap and the shotgun were hanging. "Don't you worry about that."

The narrow path through the scrub took us back towards the Maserati, just as Antonio had told us, and we hurried along it, bending low. We could hear him yelling and blazing away in the distance. I quickly refuelled the car and everyone piled in. Having folded the roof back, Poldi gave me a hard stare.

"Right, sonny-boy. Really step on the gas for once, OK?"

Only too happy to, I turned the car, tyres squealing, and sped off in the direction of Palermo.

10

Tells of double-yolked eggs, the Mafia, invaders, the secret of a happy life and a big hullabaloo. And also of men and sons. Poldi covers her tracks, gets changed and goes to pick up some laundry. While Uncle Martino and his nephew are having coffee, Poldi remembers the Crane and impresses Death.

Poldi told me to stop in the next village.

"Go on, pull over to the right."

"Why now?"

"Don't ask questions, just pull over."

The village, which made a bleak, unlovely impression, wound its way along the narrow street like a carelessly knotted string of beads. There was an *alimentari* and a rather uninviting bar. The few people to be seen were mostly old folks seated on folding chairs outside their houses, basking in the February sunshine. In such a place the

Maserati was about as inconspicuous as a battle tank in a swimming pool. Having parked behind a delivery van outside the *alimentari,* I saw Poldi crouch down and peer at the underside of the car. I gave Uncle Martino an inquiring look, but he just got out, strolled over to the old folks and engaged them in conversation. Totti farted again.

"Got you, you bugger!" Poldi tugged at something attached to the rear bumper and held it up proudly. "I might have guessed it."

A magnetically mounted GPS transmitter.

I was starting to worry again, unlike Poldi. In the highest of spirits, she told me to stand guard for a moment, then transferred the transmitter to the underside of the van in front of us and wiped her hands.

"That'll give us a bit of a start. Off we go!"

I pointed to Uncle, who was chatting with the old folks. He bade them a jovial farewell and sauntered back to the car.

"What were you asking them?" I wondered when we were back on the road.

"I asked them where one could buy eggs around here."

"What?"

"Eggs with two yolks. This district is

famous for hens that lay double-yolked eggs."

"I see."

"They'll remember that better than they'll remember the Maserati," he added contentedly, and Poldi gave him the thumbs-up.

I was feeling superfluous.

"What if our recent host is the Handsome Antonio we're looking for?" I asked.

"I thought of that," said Poldi. "But my gut instinct says no."

And my aunt knows a thing or two about gut instincts. Perhaps that was why she was looking so uneasy: because her gut instinct had just announced — ding-dong! — that she had recently overlooked something. It's just a detail, as a rule, but the kind that makes the crucial difference between reality and appearance, art and kitsch, plus and minus, life and death. The only trouble was, she couldn't think what it was. She knew that all she could do was keep calm and hope the penny would drop in good time.

We were taking detours again, believe it or not. Detour after detour after detour. We drove through Enna, which sits atop a table mountain and is built right up to its precipitous edges. We drove across Sicily at random, or so it seemed to me, but I didn't mind. On the contrary, we were driving with the top down through a mild, cloudless Sicilian February, and I could see that the island was getting ready to explode into bloom. Refusing to let Poldi hassle me any longer, I drove unhurriedly along the winding roads of this enchanted, vernal island, which seemed to give me a friendly wave like some distant relation on a flying visit.

Uncle held forth about bluefin tuna and the Phoenicians, but when we were driving through Corleone he switched to the Mafia. This surprised me, because like all Sicilians he was loath to use the M-word and talk about the Italian state's greatest foe, about speculative building, nepotism, corruption and the drug trade. About the intimidation of an entire nation by an organisation with links to the highest government circles. About atrocities and massacres, shootings and mutilations, about burying your enemies in concrete, dissolving them in acid or feeding them to pigs. Or about *lupara bianca,* the total disappearance of victims, which deprives their nearest and dearest of the chance to bury them and come to terms with their loss. Nobody likes to talk about such things when they happen on one's own doorstep. Or about *omertà,* the principle of unconditional silence that has become symbolic of the Sicilians' final surrender to the omnipotence of the *piovra* — the octopus — as the Mafia is also known. Sicily is so much more than the Mafia, of course, but they belong together, and no one who seeks to understand the former can avoid the latter. That's why it's lucky to have an Uncle Martino, who knows all about Sicily and can blithely fill any unimportant gaps in his knowledge with figments of his imagination.

I mean, Corleone! The very name gives me gooseflesh. Corleone, home of Cosa Nostra. Heaven knows what I'd been expecting — some kind of dark energy, at least — but Corleone disappointed me: just uniformity, one or two architectural eyesores, normal, everyday activity and the usual Sicilian taciturnity. The cemetery was too vast for such a small town, but that was all.

Uncle reported that the big estates owned by bosses now in custody had been converted into holiday resorts. I was underwhelmed by that.

"The historic Mafia is a romantic fiction," he said. "It doesn't become really interesting until 1860, after Garibaldi's unification of Italy. The capital was far away, and the Sicilians could never assimilate. The clocks here have always told a different time. The

Mafia found it all too easy to fill the vacuum with terms like honour, pride and betrayal. When the building boom started in the sixties, it went over to speculative construction, combining this in the seventies with the drug trade. It was also into protection rackets, but they aren't as lucrative these days. And the Mafia families have always been at each other's throats. Mind you, "family" no longer implies blood relationship but only describes a group with the same organisational structure. Things got very bad in the eighties, when the murders became more and more atrocious. There were shootings and bombings every day, and the Mafia took to attacking representatives of the state. Policemen, state attorneys, judges. It was a killing spree. Then some courageous prosecuting magistrates like Falcone and Borsellino had had enough and began to investigate. And, *ecco là,* there was a sudden emergence of renegades willing to spill the beans, because they'd become genuinely sick of murders and deaths and having their families wiped out. Since then, we've known that the Mafia is structured like a regular commercial firm and has a regular name."

"Cosa Nostra," I said smugly.

"Don't interrupt!" hissed Poldi.

"Beh," Uncle went on. "It's headed by the supreme boss and his advisers. Today we'd call him the CEO. Then come the under-bosses, or vice presidents, then the operational captains and soldiers, and finally, at the bottom, the ordinary members — the shareholders, so to speak. Falcone and Borsellino found that out and paid with their lives. After that, Sicilians had also had enough. People took to the streets en masse and demonstrated against the Mafia. The wall of silence crumbled, and that was how they caught Totò Riina, Bernardo Provenzano, Leoluca Bagarella and many others. Major Mafia trials were held. They even tried to nail ex-premier Giulio Andreotti, but he was one size too big, though there's a photo of him kissing a *capo dei capi* on both cheeks."

"And today?" I asked.

"Today? The Cosa Nostra still exists, of course — what do you expect? — but it has changed, modernised, altered its fields of business activity. They rob banks via computer, and the bosses are revered again like heroes. The current boss of bosses is Messina Denaro, who's supposed to have killed fifty people with his own hands. He's been living undercover for years, but he used to throw wild parties on the beach at Selinunte. These days he represents himself in letters to the press as an opponent of the system. Remind you of anyone? *Beh.*"

Most uncharacteristically, Uncle Martino directed me onto the motorway just before we reached Palermo. Beyond Monte Pellegrino he showed us the place near Capaci where the Mafia blew up Giovanni Falcone's car. Two obelisks commemorate the assassination that changed Sicily forever. Then we drove into Palermo. I had a very ominous feeling.

Palermo is different — different from basalt-black Catania and different from any other city in the world. There can be few places so often plagued and influenced, shaped and rejigged by invaders and armies of occupation. And all of them came there in the course of an odyssey, starting with the Phoenicians, who left almost nothing behind. Then came the Greeks with their temples and theatres, and after them the Saracens and Normans, who somehow contrived to live side by side for centuries and produced wonderful buildings like the Palazzo Reale and the Norman castle of La Zisa. These look thoroughly formidable and forbidding on the outside — almost Scandi in design — but the interiors boast magical

Arab opulence and ornamentation, coloured tiles and water features, rooms that seem airborne. The Normans live on in the blue eyes and Nordic features of many Sicilians, in the puppet theatres, the sentimental ballads, the painted donkey carts and Rosalia, Palermo's patron saint. The Byzantines were here, and so — naturally — were the Romans, the Hohenstaufens and Spaniards, Savoyards and Austrians, the Bourbons, Goethe and Wagner (from time to time), then the English, the Mafia, cheap flights and tourism.

Palermo was one of the first cities in Europe to be completely electrified. It's a light city in any case, with its pale sandstone masonry, broad boulevards, labyrinthine lanes and impoverished suburbs like Bagheria, within which enchanted palazzi still slumber. Anything but a quiet city, it is self-confident, generous and chaotic, and the name of its most famous market, Vucciria, really says it all: *vucciria* means "clamour."

And we were in the middle of it in the Maserati. It was late afternoon, and the rush-hour traffic was much worse than in Catania. I was also worried that, with the top down, we would be robbed at the next traffic light. Unlike me, however, Poldi and Martino looked as light-hearted as a pair of trippers on an outing — in fact, Poldi seemed to be enjoying the chaos. She waved graciously to young men on motor scooters, flirted with a gentleman in the car beside us and photographed an immaculately turned-out policeman on point duty. Performing pirouettes on a little podium in the motorised maelstrom, he created the illusion that he was actually managing to direct this telluric stream of traffic.

Since we were making only slow progress, Poldi and Martino leant out and asked sundry pedestrians and drivers the way to the Lavanderia Graziella. Most of them just shrugged, and the rest misdirected us, so we zigzagged all over Palermo. Uncle, lecturing me on cultural history the while, sent me the wrong way up one-way streets, along alleyways barely wide enough to admit the Maserati, and past Ucciardone Prison, where the great Mafia trials had been held in a specially constructed concrete bunker. I developed a headache. Even Totti quietened down and stopped farting. When I spotted a parking place outside a little pavement café, I pulled over and killed the engine.

"Hey, what's wrong now?"

"I've had it, Poldi. I'm not driving another metre. We're going to get out, have something to drink and ask around a bit."

To my surprise, she raised no objection. We sat down at a table outside, in the midst of a stream of passers-by, and ordered coffee and water, lots of water. I kept one eye on the Maserati, which was drawing a lot of interest.

"I need something suitable to wear, be back in a minute," Poldi announced abruptly. She got up and hurried off.

Uncle, already getting restless again, toddled off to ask for directions to the Lavanderia Graziella.

I remained behind with Totti, too wrung-out to protest, let alone go with Uncle. The waiters eyed me with suspicion — in fact, I felt convinced that everyone was staring at me, and that someone was about to steal the Maserati. But I was past caring by now. They were watching me? *Beh,* I watched them back. Coolly, out of the corner of my eye, like a genuine Sicilian.

It struck me that Sicilian hand gestures, of which there are many, were used far more intensively in Palermo than in Catania. Conquered by so many peoples over so many centuries, this island has developed a unique culture of nonverbal communication. I don't mean random gesticulations, but a genuine language capable of attracting someone's attention or warning them, affirming something or denying it, flattering, flirting or insulting — and all at a safe distance. There are age-old gestures that have become so ingrained in Sicilians as to be practically innate. Gestures also keep up with the times, and children's can often differ from those of their parents. The best known is, of course, the "little crown," in which the thumb and all the fingers are brought together and the hand or hands loosely or violently shaken in front of the body. This is a gesture of general activation with which to lend one's words emphasis or convey that the other person is talking utter poppycock. If you want to persuade someone or beg them to do something, you fold your hands loosely in front of your chest and shake them up and down. To signal to a friend that it's time to go or tell someone else to push off, you slap the back of one hand with the palm of the other. The sign for a hoodlum is a thumb drawn across the cheek like a knife. The gesture meaning "fear" is the little crown rapidly opening and closing. Thumb and index finger splayed and shaken signifies "Nothing to be done." Both index fingers extended close together and moving to and fro a little means "They're a couple, let's talk about them behind their back." If you quickly brush the underside of your chin with the back of your hand, it means "No, no way, never, forget it!" As children, my cousins and I had a gesture meaning "I'll kill you." This was two extended fingers rapidly applied to the lips. Nowadays children extend a hand and tap the clenched fist with the thumb as if operating a game controller. There are hundreds of gestures. They fill the whole of Palermo like a strange flock of birds excitedly fluttering along with its inhabitants and never coming to rest. And now I was fluttering along with them. I had seen a centaur and felt my *sicilianità* awaken.

After all of an hour, as if by prior agreement, Poldi and Uncle Martino reappeared from different directions.

"Hey," I said, "what's with the new get-up?"

Poldi was wearing a voluminous, old-fashioned black dress with a knitted waistcoat, black stockings and shoes reminiscent of my grandmother's. With a black shawl over her wig, she looked like a typical elderly Sicilian widow.

"Every operation needs special camouflage, remember that."

Uncle joined us and slid a slip of paper with an address on it across the table to her.

She took one look at it, then crumpled it up and put it in the ashtray. Me, she simply ignored.

"You two wait here till I get back," she decreed.

"He could drive you," said Uncle.

"Er, just a minute," I said.

"No, it's not far, and the Maserati would be far too conspicuous."

That was a new one.

In a flash, Agent Poldi was back in action and I was alone with Uncle Martino. Totti had started farting again.

"*Beh.* She won't be long, it's only around the corner. I need a coffee, how about you?"

"Why not. Go ahead."

The laundry was in the Via del Pallone, near the harborside botanical gardens. It was a shabby little street on one side of which dilapidated old town houses jostled architectural sins of the 1960s, while on the other side, behind garages with rusty iron gates, squat workshops, wasteland and ruins, things may have gone on that were better not known about. Battered runabouts were parked everywhere, guarded by hordes of patrolling cats. At the end of the street Poldi made out the remains of a Norman fortification, and in front of it a big mound of garbage — a typical Palermian sight that would have rejoiced any camera-toting tourist. There was, however, one blemish: parked outside the *lavanderia* was a Lamborghini Gallardo with violet mother-of-pearl paintwork.

Poldi waited for a moment in the shade of a balcony. Then a well-groomed middle-aged man emerged carrying a parcel of laundry, climbed into the Lamborghini and sped off with a full-throated roar from its ten cylinders.

"Buona sera!" Every inch the mistress of disguise, Poldi shuffled into the laundry with her back slightly bent and took a surreptitious look round. She couldn't manage the Palermian dialect with its strong Arabic twang, so she resorted to mumbling and hissing like someone with ill-fitting dentures.

The shop, which looked wholly unremarkable, smelt of chemical cleaning fluid and starch. Squeezed in behind the counter were two dry-cleaning machines, shelves laden with parcels of laundry, and racks of freshly washed and ironed suits and shirts in plastic sleeves.

Sicilians have a positively sensual relationship with plastic and polythene film. Everything imaginable is heat-welded, vacuum-packed or encased in plastic bags, preferably twice over. No barbecue or family picnic is complete without plastic plates and mugs, of which the latter are provided with little raffia coasters for stability. Then there are the omnipresent wobbly plastic chairs and the toys. As a child, I myself lusted after the plastic suits of armour and swords sold by the rubbishy stalls on the seafront. It sometimes defeats me how Sicilians managed to survive from ancient to modern times without plastic.

A young woman in the white smock glanced at Poldi's claim ticket, then gave an almost imperceptible start and eyed her suspiciously.

"One moment please, signora."

Without another word, she took the claim ticket and disappeared somewhere behind the scenes. Poldi heard voices speaking in Palermian dialect.

Soon afterwards a small woman of Poldi's age appeared. Dressed in widow's weeds like her, she had a strong, handsome face of Norman cast with bright, alert eyes and a healthy olive complexion. She had few wrinkles for her age, but there was a look of profound melancholy in her dark-ringed eyes and a hint of bitterness in the curve of her lips. She moved slowly and cautiously, like a cat on a narrow ledge, but the body beneath the black dress made a lithe and robust impression.

Holding the claim ticket in her hand, she likewise regarded Poldi with definite suspicion. "You aren't from around here, are you, signora?"

"I'm staying with my nephew. He left some washing with you some time ago and has only just remembered. He's rather scatterbrained, I'm afraid."

The other woman didn't reply. Without a word, she proceeded to compare the parcels of clean laundry on the shelves with the number on the ticket. Eventually she turned to Poldi with a small parcel in her hands. "It's been here since October."

"Yes, as I said, he's really very scatterbrained, my nephew. Thank you for hanging on to it."

All Poldi wanted to do was take the parcel and go, but an indefinable feeling made her hesitate. The sort of feeling one sometimes gets when something is badly out of kilter, but one doesn't know what.

When the widow held out the parcel her sleeve rode up a little, revealing a Rolex, set with diamonds. Poldi got the picture.

She walked out with the parcel, sat down in a bar on the corner with a view of the street, ordered a coffee and a grappa, and waited. She didn't have to wait long. After only a short time she saw Graziella emerge from the shop and hurry off in the direction of Via Nicolò Cervello.

Being an expert at undercover operations and tailing people, Poldi followed Graziella at a safe distance, cleverly switching from one side of the street to the other and using passers-by as cover or hugging the walls so as to be able, if necessary, to dive into a doorway or a shop. But Graziella never turned round once. Poldi followed her into Via Torremuzza and Via Butera, then left into Via Vittorio Emmanuele, and right, via the narrow Via Garraffello, into the heart of the Vucciria.

The Vucciria! Few places in Italy are more suffused with myth and legend, though the nearby Mercato Ballarò has acquired greater importance since the unsuccessful redevelopment of the old city some years ago. But La Vucciria, situated between Via Roma and the harbour, is and remains a legend, and not to be compared with the markets of mainland Italy. The Arab heritage lives on here. Just as in an oriental souk, whole streets are lined with serried rows of stalls and shops in the shade of awnings. Everything here is loud. The senses are overwhelmed by colours, smells, voices and people of dizzying diversity. The flagstones are slippery with squashed fruit and vegetables, fish blood, water, oil and heaven knows what else. Simply everything is for sale — too much of it and all jumbled together. Fresh pasta, fish and other seafood, sides of pork and rabbits, spices, grains, vegetables, sacks of beans, soap, toys, shirts, dried herbs, shoes, cigarettes, pistol-shaped lighters, grappa, wines, tinned anchovies, bread and cakes, candied fruit, CDs, kitschy coloured prints, exercise books, office equipment, plastic cans, figures of saints, salted capers, dried tomatoes, good-luck charms, scratch cards and cheap Asian tat. The air smells of wild fennel, cinnamon, lemons, herbs, moped exhaust fumes, charcoal and the mounds of garbage between the stalls. Haggling is taboo here, and one is lucky not to be ripped off. Scattered throughout the market are cookshops offering stewed *polipo* and fresh oysters, fried and breaded sardine rolls, *fritto misto,* little chickpea fritters called *panelle* and the Palermian classic *pasta con le sarde,* or pasta with sardines, pine kernels, raisins, wild fennel and saffron. And the whole place is dominated by raised voices, for still cultivated in the Palermian markets is the full-throated *ab-*

banniata, the cries of the stallholders and shopkeepers who advertise their wares in a mixture of oriental melody, Sicilian folk song and operatic aria. The air in the narrow streets vibrates to shouts and singing.

Poldi now had difficulty following her target. With the parcel of laundry under her arm, she zigzagged and squeezed her way through the crowd and between the stalls, lost sight of Graziella, spotted her again, was jostled, nearly ended up under the wheels of a moped, stumbled, swore and felt slightly dazed by all the shouts, smells, people and colours. By the time she got to Piazza Caracciolo, she had lost Graziella for good.

"Goddammit!"

Out of breath, she stood somewhat forlornly in the middle of the piazza but failed to spot the widow anywhere.

Frustrated and exhausted, she flopped down on a plastic chair outside the nearest bar and knocked back a grappa, hoping that Graziella would soon reappear.

But she didn't.

Having additionally refreshed herself with a small Prosecco, Poldi took a closer look at the piazza. It was dark by now, and the street lights bathed the square in a gentle glow. The fishmongers and butchers were packing up for the day. All at once, Poldi recognised this square in the middle of the Vucciria: it was where the manhunts in most of the Mafia TV series ended up. What was more, on one occasion many years ago she and Peppe had sat on the terrace of the restaurant immediately opposite. Called the Shanghai, it had for decades been a legendary Palermian institution. Not Asian at all, it had probably got its name from the orientally teeming crowds below the second-floor terrace and was really just a typical Sicilian restaurant. Poldi had eaten the best *pasta con le sarde* in her life there with Peppe, she recalled, and she had also apologised to him for a grave misdemeanour. The film crew of *The Godfather* had eaten there, and the restaurant had welcomed stars, politicians, Mafiosi and tourists without number, but it had now been closed for several years. The windows were boarded up, the terrace's rusty ironwork was protected by netting, and the walls were plastered with posters. It was a sad sight, and one that gave Poldi a faint pang. The sign was the only reminder of the ever-crowded restaurant with the bizarre Eurasian decor.

The longer Poldi stared at the Shanghai and devoted herself to sentimental memories, the more a thought took shape in her high-performance brain. It was one of those what-if thoughts that can take hold like a mountaineer clinging to a rock face. She felt in her handbag for the key from Thomas's hoodie and weighed it irresolutely in her hand. The thought worked its way a little farther up the rock face and Poldi decided to give it a try. Having bought a pistol-shaped cigarette lighter from one of the stalls selling tourist tat, she strolled over to the Shanghai's ill-lit entrance, which was in a side street. She waited until the coast was clear, her widow's weeds rendering her almost indistinguishable from the surrounding gloom. Then she tried the key in the lock, and . . . bingo!

Quickly pushing the door partway open, she slipped inside. Engulfed in darkness, all she could hear was the hustle and bustle of the market, which was now on the wane. She wondered whether to use her mobile phone as a torch, but decided against it. Laying the parcel of laundry aside, she crept up the stairs with ninja-like stealth, pistol lighter at the ready. There was no interior door; the stairs led straight into the restaurant itself. All was in darkness here too, but Poldi could vaguely make out the shapes of chairs and tables. She took a step forward, paused and listened. Not a sound. Nothing doing, she thought disappointedly, and felt for a light switch.

Then she became aware of a shadowy figure launching itself at her. She didn't see it, she simply *sensed* it with senses that had, I imagine, been fine-tuned over the years at secret-service boot camps. But perhaps it was only because she had turned to locate a light switch that she sensed it at all. She had no time to feel startled. Normal folk like me would have succumbed to the attack, but where highly trained professionals like my Auntie Poldi are concerned, their reflexes simply kick in. The body takes command and knows in nanoseconds what to do.

Poldi instinctively dodged and felt the figure brush past her, knocking the lighter out of her hand and bowling her over. Making the most of her momentum, she rolled aside, then sprang to her feet and assumed the stable stance known in kung fu as *deng shan bu,* both hands extended in the Crane fist.

"HOOOAAAH!"

The cry issuing from Poldi's throat was not of this world. It was a cry that released ancient reflexes, like a storm wind unearthing some precious object long buried in desert sand. Or so I imagine.

The figure also rolled aside, spun round and instantly resumed its onslaught. Moving with the agility and lightning speed of someone who was clearly an adept at martial arts like her, it went for Poldi two-handed. But Poldi, now in full ninja mode, parried the blows — *whoosh, whoosh, whoosh!* — with equal dexterity. At least this is how I picture the fight, based on her subsequent account of it. She ducked, changed her leading leg, absorbed her opponent's energy and boomeranged it back. Crane, Dragon, Monkey, Snake, Mantis — Poldi still had them at her fingertips. The series of movements had been slumbering within her for years and now came snarling back to life. Or so I imagine.

She spun round and — *thwack!* — delivered a side kick. To hell with her bad knee, she was agility personified. She was a fighting machine, but so, to be fair, was her opponent. The two of them pulled no punches. *Whoosh, smack, bang, wallop, hoooaaah!* Whirling around each other like ballet dancers, they flailed away and parried blows, eluded them and counterpunched. Pain they shook off like water off a duck's back. They exchanged kicks and flip kicks. Chairs got smashed — in fact, the two adversaries reduced much of the old restaurant furniture to matchwood. Poldi was hurled against the wall, panting, but her wig never budged. They grappled with each other, broke free, went head over heels and scrambled to their feet again. Jackie Chan or Bruce Lee could not have choreographed the fight more elegantly. The figure performed a forward somersault and swooped on Poldi like an eagle. Poldi simply dived beneath it and kicked its leg in passing. The figure uttered a cry as it fell. A shrill, high-pitched cry filled with rage, it puzzled Poldi for an instant. Her opponent promptly attacked once more, but was now breathless with exhaustion. Poldi herself was running out of steam, she realised, and it was time to bring matters to a conclusion. Making use of the entire room, she hurled some chairs at her opponent and proceeded to launch the decisive attack.

"HOOOAAAH!"

I can see her light-footedly running up the wall to the ceiling, pushing off with her feet, whirling through the air like a spindle, flying over a table, landing catlike, whirling around again and, while still flying through the air, dealing her adversary a full-blooded side kick. I wasn't there, of course, so I can only reproduce what Poldi told me later.

The figure crashed to the floor with a

groan and lay inert. Poldi, who was panting hard, took a moment to catch her breath and get her bearings. Then she hurried over to the light switch beside the entrance. The neon tubes on the ceiling clicked and crackled, bathing the wreckage of the restaurant in a flickering glare. Poldi saw the widow from the laundry sitting at one of the tables. She too was panting, and the gun she was pointing at Poldi was fitted with a silencer. It looked genuine.

Also seated at the table was Death. He gave Poldi a businesslike nod and then concentrated on his clipboard.

"You were pretty good, signora," said Graziella, still breathing hard. "But now it's over."

"Ah, Teresa!"

I'd had it with this family. Two hours we'd been waiting for Poldi outside that bar, binge-drinking coffee. It was getting chilly. Having stupidly forgotten to pack a sweater in the rush, I was wearing Thomas's hoodie. Not that it improved matters. By now I was in an overwrought state verging on hysteria — somewhere between freaking out and lapsing into a coma from lack of sleep.

For his part, Uncle Martino seemed totally impervious to caffeine. He was looking about as agitated as a Zen monk on a research trip to nowhere. His chain-smoking was all that testified to a certain rise in his metabolism.

"If she doesn't come soon, we must go and look for her," I repeated for the umpteenth time. "We . . . we'll have to call the police! Or phone Montana!"

"Take it easy," Uncle grunted. "You know the plan. Your aunt will manage all right." Then, rather vaguely, "She's coped with plenty of things before now."

"And what if she doesn't?" I almost screamed. "How can you be so calm? I just don't get it!"

Uncle Martino ordered another round of coffees and fondled the dog, which responded by farting in its sleep.

"Do you know the secret of a happy life?" he asked.

"What's that got to do with anything?"

"Keeping calm. And you know what your problem is?"

"Let me guess."

"*Ecco.* You don't keep calm. It was the same on your outings with me as a boy. You're always flying into a panic. As soon as something doesn't go as you expect, you're panic-stricken. Your expectations are always getting in your way. You never want to be where you actually are."

"So what? That's life."

Martino sighed. "Bullshit. You don't like yourself, that's all . . ."

"Sit down." Graziella was still holding the pistol, levelled at Poldi.

Poldi, who had an eye for such things, realised at once that, unlike Brigadiere Magnano, the woman was cold-blooded enough to use it. Cold-blooded, determined and very, very sad, as Poldi could tell from the look in her eyes. And Poldi knew a thing or two about sadness.

She sat down facing Graziella and cast an irritable glance at Death, who did his best to ignore her. That was not particularly re-assuring either.

"Let me see your hands," Graziella said.

Poldi laid her hands flat on the table. "You're not bad yourself," she said.

"It's a part of my way of life. So, signora, who are you and what are you after?"

"Call me Poldi. I'm looking for Handsome Antonio."

Poldi saw at once that the name meant something to Graziella. Her expression darkened — only for an instant, but Poldi felt quite sure of it.

"Never heard of him."

"I want a word with him, that's all. I'm looking for something, and he may be able to tell me where to find it."

"Where did you get the claim ticket?"

"I found it. The person it belonged to is dead."

Graziella seemed wholly unimpressed by this.

"Plenty of people are dead. We're all dead to a greater or lesser extent. Death has been my companion for a very long time. I sometimes get the feeling he's nearby — maybe even here at this table."

Death gave Poldi an apologetic shrug. She wondered briefly whether to risk a final attack but abandoned the idea. Graziella looked just too alert.

"Anything more to say before I shoot you, signora?"

Death cleared his throat.

Poldi sighed. She could have used a drink now.

"Give me a moment to think."

She looked at Graziella's beautiful, melancholy face and thought of Peppe. Of that night here at the Shanghai, of Montana and the many men who had crossed her path in the course of her hectic existence.

"I've always been unhappy," Poldi said. "All my life, even as a child. I always had the feeling something else was in store for me, but there never was. It was there already, only I failed to see it. That's because I didn't like myself. I was really pretty, you know, but I never liked myself. I needed admiration. I abandoned myself to love affairs and drink. I had my happiest time at the age of thirty. With Giuseppe, my husband. We were sitting right here. I confessed to having cheated on him yet again, and he forgave me as usual and went on trusting me. But then unhappiness overtook me once more. It made him fall sick and die. Love and unhappiness, the story of my life."

Poldi paused and looked at Graziella.

"Go on, signora."

"That and fear. Do I look frightened to you? Not very, do I? But fear has haunted me just like unhappiness. Fear of losing everything, yet I've lost everything so often and got to my feet again. I've risen from the ashes like a phoenix, because where there's a will, there's always a way. Strange, isn't it, that we so stubbornly refuse to accept that everything in life is only on loan. Sooner or later we have to give it back, that's why we should cherish it."

Death looked up at Poldi from his clipboard. "Cool! Can I quote that at the end of my next assignment?"

Graziella thumbed the safety catch on her gun and put it down on the table with the barrel pointing sideways.

"Antonio is my son," she said wearily. "He's in hiding. I hardly ever see him. The same goes for my husband. He was a *capo,* and he's been in prison for twenty-three years, like so many other men. But their businesses must go on, so we run them. We, the wives and mothers, and I'm getting tired of it. You won't find Antonio, signora, and even if you did, he would kill you. Because that's his profession: he kills people. He has already killed a lot of people. He sometimes comes here for a few days — that's why I always have clean clothes ready for him. But he never gets in touch, it's too risky."

She paused for a moment. Poldi didn't speak.

"The African man whose laundry you collected wanted to do a deal with Antonio. That's all I know. Deals of that kind are always done via the laundry, but the men never discuss the details with us. We just keep the books."

"That sounds vaguely familiar."

"Give me the key."

Poldi slid it across the table. Graziella took it, then felt in her pocket and put a black plastic card on the table. It resembled a credit card, but all it bore was an imprinted number and a combination of twelve numerals and letters.

"Do you know what that is?"

Poldi nodded, but she didn't touch the card. "I've seen something of the kind before."

"We don't want it." Graziella pocketed the pistol as if it were a packet of tissues. "I'm going now. Wait ten minutes, then you go too. Go home and forget the whole thing."

So saying, she rose and walked off without another word. Death rose likewise.

"You haven't heard the last of this, sonnyboy," Poldi hissed at him.

She stared at the black plastic card for a long time after Graziella and Death had left. Then she sighed, pocketed the card and the ridiculous pistol lighter, and scanned her surroundings. The restaurant looked like a battlefield. She eventually found what she was looking for in a side room: a narrow bed, a chest of drawers, and a wash basin against the wall — the sum total of the home comforts of a Mafia hit man in hiding. Hanging above the bed was a crucifix, a *pietà* and a holiday snap from happier days. The photo showed a younger Graziella with a youth, both of them smiling at the camera. A massive medieval building could be seen in the background. Poldi photographed the snap with her mobile. She now became aware of how exhausted she was. Every bone in her body ached. It was time to go, so she went back downstairs. Tucking the parcel of laundry under her arm again, she emerged into the Piazza Caracciolo.

Just as she was turning the corner into Via Pannieri, a big black Mercedes screeched to a halt beside her. Three brawny men in dark suits jumped out and hemmed her in fore and aft. The look on their faces was thoroughly unfunny.

"Would you mind coming with us, signora?"

11

Tells of Moorish pageboys, old men in masks, orgies and heavy metal. Poldi receives an invitation, powders her bosom, is asked what she wants and feels frightened. She makes a plan and gets someone to produce a photofit, and Uncle proves himself an effective satnav. Poldi makes the acquaintance of four young people on a sandy headland, and her nephew can't believe his eyes.

Poldi understood that this was not a request. It merely offered her a choice between getting into the car of her own free will and being manhandled into it. Having seated herself in the back with as much dignity as she could muster, she handed the parcel of laundry to the man beside her.

"Hold that, will you? And mind you don't crumple it, it's just been ironed."

The man said nothing, but his kind aren't

paid to chew the fat.

They drove through the centre of Palermo and out into the suburbs.

"Where are we going, guys?"

No answer, just a spasmodic tightening of the jaw muscles, because that's what their kind learn to do at their prevocational crash courses. The trio didn't utter a word throughout the trip.

Poldi kept wondering whether to try to escape at the next traffic light, but (a) she assumed that the car doors were locked, and (b) she was curious. Somehow she didn't get the impression that they were going to off her in the nearest cellar, so the evening promised to be informative.

They left the city and headed in the direction of Bagheria. The countryside became more rural. After a good half-hour they drove through a big wrought-iron gateway into some spacious grounds. The drive, which was flanked by flaming torches, led to an imposing floodlit palazzo.

Outside the entrance Poldi saw a queue of big limousines from which couples in festive attire were alighting. Getting offed in a cellar seemed a more and more unlikely prospect. On entering the house Poldi was greeted with an elegant bow by a young page in the livery of a Moorish catamite at the court of the Sun King. "May I have the honour of escorting you to your boudoir, madam?"

Poldi now saw that all the guests at this evening reception, or dinner, or whatever it was, were wearing seventeenth-century costume. She saw magnificent rococo ensembles, powdered wigs, extravagant head-dresses, white stockings, buckled shoes and tricorns. All the guests wore Venetian masks. The gentlemen looked mature or more than mature, whereas most of the ladies were very young. A chamber orchestra was playing somewhere in the distance.

Poldi allowed the young page to lead her through the palazzo. They climbed a wide marble staircase, then turned and went down a side passage. Poldi's Moorish escort eventually opened a door and showed her into a kind of dressing room, with adjoining bathroom, antique lacquered dressing table with big wing mirrors and a brocaded chaise longue on which a coral-coloured rococo gown and farthingale lay ready to wear. A stand on the dressing table held a powdered wig in the appropriate style and the evidently obligatory Venetian mask.

"Take as much time as you need, madam. I shall wait for you outside," said the page. He bowed and withdrew.

"Well, kiss my arse and hope to die!" Poldi exclaimed as soon as the door had closed behind him.

She stepped out onto the room's small balcony, which gave onto the rear of the palazzo. This side of the park was also lit by torches, and Poldi could make out costumed couples strolling along gravel paths.

She had abandoned all thought of escape, being far too intrigued by the whole charade. My aunt is a sensation seeker; she needs adventure just as a sailor needs to feel the swell of the sea beneath his feet. This did not mean that her alarm system had been completely switched off. Whoever was behind this bizarre invitation, he clearly meant to impress or possibly intimidate her. He little realised that he would meet his match.

Poldi lost no time changing into costume. She powdered her face and cleavage, put on the farthingale and slipped into the coral-coloured gown and a pair of high-heeled shoes in the same colour.

Everything fitted perfectly, another indication that her host knew plenty about her. The neckline was cut very low, which put her in mind of something.

Anyone who imagines that Poldi was worried about her less than youthful physique is very much mistaken. She regarded herself in the mirror with a certain degree of satisfaction as she adjusted her décolleté. Everything was in the right place — in fact, the tail feathers of her phoenix tattoo peeped out in a rather saucy manner. She dispensed with the powdered peruke, however, because her own wig was dramatic enough. Having donned the mask, she drew a *grain de beauté* on her bosom — the icing on the cake, so to speak.

As she inspected herself in the mirror, she was involuntarily reminded of her dream about the steel tower and Marie Antoinette's precarious climb. But she resolutely banished that image from her thoughts and squared her shoulders.

"Showtime, baby!" she told her reflection. Inserting the black plastic card beneath her garter, she called for the page.

He escorted her back downstairs to a mirrored reception room lit by hundreds of candles. The chamber orchestra was playing in the background, and some two hundred people were either trying to dance a sort of quadrille or enjoying themselves on couches disposed around the room. As Poldi had suspected, their forms of enjoyment were of a pretty unequivocal nature. The men, most of them elderly, were being caressed by very young and very undressed, not to say naked, girls. Insofar as the latter were wearing anything at all, the most they wore were miniature angels' wings. Liveried footmen served canapés and champagne while the occupants of the récamier couches and chaises longues smooched, groped and indulged in *it* with a variety of partners and in a variety of positions. One bald-headed signore, who had shed everything save his mask and shoes, was simply regarding their activities with interest, like a football fan watching a match on pay TV, and dreamily playing with himself as he did so. In short, Poldi had wound up at an orgy. An elegant orgy attended by people of the better sort, *benissimo,* but an orgy nonetheless. And although the ones she'd been to lay far in the past, my Auntie Poldi knew a thing or two about orgies and swingers' parties.

In my home town I've heard tell of a so-called burlesque club where such things take place every weekend. It really isn't any more iniquitous than a naturists' beach equipped with a dance floor and patronised by the local bourgeoisie. From a rational point of view, all that goes on there is *it* — in other words, the most natural thing in the world. It's got nothing to do with orgies. Despite my curiosity, however, I admit I'm too inhibited to sample the place.

"So what did you do?" I asked, rather warily, when Poldi described the whole occasion to me in minute detail.

"What would you have done in my place?"

"Er . . . looked for a way out? Or for the host, to discover what he actually wanted from me?"

"Heavens, what a yellowbelly you are, always running away from things. You'll never get anywhere with your novel if you don't allow time for detours, so bear that in mind. I was certain my host would make himself known in due course. It was a game — it was meant to intimidate me, but I said to myself, If you think I'm going to stand around playing gooseberry like some uptight would-be novelist, you've got another think coming. So I refused to be intimidated and did a bit of . . ." She harrumphed.

"Yes, I'm listening."

"Well . . . I went and did a bit of cruising."

"*What?*"

"Oh, you and your middle-class hang-ups! It didn't amount to anything. My life has always been a dance on the lip of a volcano. That's because I know everything could be over in an instant."

"You're . . . you're so shameless!"

"Wrong. I was on duty. I knew I was being watched the whole time."

Poldi grabbed a glass of champagne from a tray proffered by a well-built footman and knocked it back. She repeated this procedure at regular intervals on her brief tour of inspection. All the adjoining rooms presented the same picture: a display of groping and *it*. Poldi gave the so-called darkroom a miss. Another reception room did at least contain a lavish buffet, to which male guests in particular were applying themselves. As Poldi was taking a little refreshment on board, she spotted — for a change — some elderly ladies being pleasured by young men.

I've no wish to go into the details, of which she naturally gave me an unvarnished description, but I still can't rid my mind's eye of images of heads burrowing beneath billowing farthingales and sweaty faces sandwiched between buttocks, breasts and thighs.

Poldi surmised that the younger guests were the paid staff of this soirée and had probably been recruited from the sex workers' and porn industry, whereas all the rest had accepted an exclusive invitation to a networking event of a special kind, commonly known in Italy as *bunga bunga.*

From time to time Poldi paused to lift her elbow and eavesdrop on conversations. She picked up snippets like "voting rights," "stockholders," "share parcel," "senate," "takeover bid" and "win-win situation." The language employed was exclusively Italian. It was obvious where the land lay.

A handsome young male member of the staff, dressed only in a turban and endowed with an impressive *sicilianità,* put his hand on Poldi's behind and whispered, *"Buona sera, gioia,* your wish is my command."

Who wouldn't have welcomed such a declaration?

It was almost midnight before things got serious. Poldi, a trifle tipsy by now, was lying on a rococo sofa fondling the young man's head, which was pillowed on her lap, and listening to the story of his undeservedly problematic existence. His name — how could it have been anything else? — was Antonio. He was a sad, handsome Antonio such as Brancati might have devised in his day and age. As Poldi had surmised, he worked in the "adult entertainment" industry. A life on Viagra, he lamented — nothing but *it* for eight hours a day, but at home with his girlfriend

297

Ombretta, nothing doing. He reckoned it wouldn't be long before she walked out on him like all her predecessors. His relations with his family were also dire, absolutely dire. He dreamt of quitting and starting a new life, but somehow he never got around to it. Poldi was about to give him some motherly advice when she was accosted by the Moorish page.

"Madam? Someone requests a word with you."

Poldi was awake in a flash, of course. All her senses went to code red. "Who?"

"If you'd care to follow me."

The page led her back through the palazzo and into another wing. This time their destination was a kind of boardroom containing a big mahogany table and twelve massive chairs. The page gestured to her to sit down and withdrew.

Soon afterwards another door opened and a masked, thick-set, elderly signore in a black dinner jacket sat down across the table from her. Poldi shivered; it was as if his entrance had lowered the temperature by ten degrees. Looking at his hands, she estimated that he was all of eighty years old.

"Signora Poldi," the masked man began after a moment's mutual inspection. His voice was soft and slightly husky, but razor-edged. "Thank you for accepting my invitation. You enjoyed yourself, I saw, though the young man could have been of far greater service to you than you allowed him to be."

Poldi hesitated before replying, possibly because she was feeling rather dizzy after the hectic events of the previous day and night, and she might have done better to give those last two glasses of champagne a miss. Then again, perhaps it was because Death had reappeared. He was now seated at the head of the table, feverishly leafing through the papers on his clipboard. Poldi gave the man facing her an undaunted stare.

"No problem," she said as firmly as she could. "It's just that I have certain principles."

The masked man did not speak for a moment, almost as if he had to ponder the meaning of a foreign word. Then he asked quietly, "Where is it?"

"Where is what?"

"Oh, come now, Donna Poldina! Do we really want to play that game?"

"Who are you, anyway?"

A dismissive gesture. "Let's say I'm someone for whom the welfare of this country is very close to his heart."

"Not forgetting your own."

"My welfare and that of the country are

bound up together. I endeavour to maintain a balance of power. People trust me. I'm someone who tips many a scale."

"And you're so incredibly modest, too — not conceited in the least."

The man cleared his throat. His tone of voice sharpened. "I'm also someone accustomed to getting answers, not giving them. All right, where is it?"

Poldi could already guess what this was about, and she knew at once the sort of person she was dealing with. A very powerful man with a very big ego. Someone who had always got what he wanted, except that it was never enough. Someone incapable of love who had never been loved. A shadow of a man. The most dangerous kind of man in existence. She decided to bluff.

"What would I get in return?"

The masked man shrugged. "Your life?"

Meanwhile, Death was sending Poldi surreptitious signals. He shook his head and tapped his list in a meaningful way.

Poldi ignored his efforts.

"If you really know so much about me, you ought to know how little I care about it."

The man put something on the table that she instantly recognised.

Her stolen address book.

She could have grabbed it, but she didn't. "Thanks for wrecking my house. I hope it was worth it, at least."

Her host gave another shrug. "Your address book proved worthless. I was already familiar with most of the phone numbers. I'll ask you again: where is it?"

"Know something? Even if I did know, you can go and jump in the lake."

"Then I'll have to be more explicit, Signora Oberreiter. I want that attaché case. I want it at all costs, understand? I'll give you four days." He slid a slip of paper across the table. "My phone number. As soon as you have the case in your possession, call me. Don't imagine your 'firm' can help you. No one can. My people will find you wherever you go."

"What if I don't find the attaché case within four days?"

"One member of your family will die for every day you are overdue, starting with that nephew of yours."

Death threw up his hands as if apologising for his inability to do anything, and Poldi felt suddenly sick. Her breathing quickened, and it was all she could do not to tremble.

"I can offer you ten million dollars. At once. Here and now."

301

The masked man brushed this aside. "Money doesn't interest me." He got up without replacing the address book in his pocket. "I want that attaché case. Four days. Don't waste them."

Poldi didn't confess the bit about the death threat until much later, when it was almost too late. It was past midnight by the time she returned to the little café, which was shut by then. I had settled down in the back seat of the Maserati with Totti and was vainly trying to sleep. Not so Uncle Martino, who was stoically sitting there smoking. I sat up with a start, alerted by Totti's barking, to see Poldi returning in her black widow's outfit, the parcel of laundry under her arm. She was looking exhausted and in a hurry. The sight of her made me feel boundlessly relieved and then angry in quick succession.

"Where the devil have you been?" I may have shouted the words at her. "Have you any idea how worried we've been? You could at least have given us a quick call. Hello?"

"Shut up," she snapped, thrusting the parcel into my hands. "Stick that in the boot, then we'll get cracking. Martino?"

Uncle came toddling over to the car.

"Get cracking?" I said in despair. "What

about some sleep? Ever heard of it? I know it sounds uncool, but there are actually supposed to be people who need some."

Poldi ignored this. Instead of answering, she made a phone call.

"Hello, signora. Poldi Oberreiter here. You recently introduced me to your son . . . Yes, I know what time it is, but this is important. Please could you wake him for me? It really is urgent."

A minute went by. "Antonino? Hello, Poldi here. The one with the wig, remember? Sorry to wake you, but I need a favour. If I email you a photo of a man, could you imagine what he'd look like in twenty-five years' time and draw a picture of him, a photofit of sorts? You could? Excellent! Tomorrow morning will do. I'll owe you one." Having rung off, Poldi showed Martino a photo on her mobile. "Recognise the building in the background? Know where it is?"

Uncle fished a pair of reading glasses out of his gilet and examined the photo. "That's the Santuario di San Vito lo Capo. It's not far from here."

"Let's go, then."

"I've had it, guys!" I protested.

"Don't be a drag, just drive."

Poldi was silent on the way. Something

303

was preying on her mind, it seemed. To keep myself awake, I tried to pump her about what had happened, but she clearly wasn't in a chatty mood. She merely handed me a black plastic card.

"Put that in your pocket and take good care of it."

"What is it?"

"Ten million dollars."

"*What?*" I nearly drove us off the road.

"And I'd appreciate it if you didn't kill us all."

"What is it, a credit card?"

"*Bah,* it's hard cash, or as good as. The money's in a fiduciary account in Panama. The depositor no longer has access to it. The only person who can access it is someone who calls the phone number stamped on the card and recites the code. They can then withdraw the money in cash, less a ten percent service charge, or transfer it to another account. Very practical."

"Where did you get it from?"

Poldi looked at me for the first time since she had reappeared. I couldn't see much of her face in the darkness, but I think it wore an expression of mild regret.

"I'll tell you everything tomorrow, my boy, OK? Take it from me, I've had enough for one day."

Thereafter she brooded in silence.

In retrospect, I imagine it was during this drive that she came to a decision.

A good hour later we drove into San Vito lo Capo, a little town of five thousand inhabitants situated on a sandy headland west of Palermo. Miraculously enough, Uncle Martino's directions and Poldi's obstinacy found us a modest hotel whose night porter reluctantly let us have two rooms, one for Poldi and the other for Uncle, Totti and me. I couldn't have cared less. I slumped down on the bed fully dressed and sank at once into a comatose sleep.

Difficult investigations sometimes — not always, but sometimes — entail the participation of a not particularly popular but often indispensable colleague: Inspector Chance.

You know, the lazy slob at the end of the passage, the one with the stable work-life balance who prefers a quiet existence and can create havoc if he's hassled. But when he's right off the radar, he can suddenly emerge from his cubbyhole, chip in uninvited and profit from his colleagues' careful spadework. Then he steps back and does as little as possible. Inspector Chance is modest. He doesn't need much in the way of praise and plaudits, but simply does his thing and is good at it. Yet he knows his worth and appreciates other people's hard work, devotion to duty and perseverance. He also demands a lot of intuition and readiness to improvise on the part of his colleagues, which isn't everyone's bag either.

Poldi once told me that it was the same with writing. No idea how she knew such a thing, but she did have some understanding of chance, intuition and improvisation.

Poldi had a pleasant dream, but as so often happens, her memory of it faded soon after she awoke. The dream did, however, leave a slight imprint on her mind that filled her with cheerfulness and confidence. She needed that after the events of the previous night. She had four days, and she had a plan. The sun was just rising outside.

She checked her mobile and was delighted to find that little Antonino from Sant'Alfio had indeed sent her a kind of photofit. It was another of his masterly drawings, highly detailed and very lifelike. Poldi realised on seeing the picture that she had seen the man before. Yesterday, in fact. Outside the laundry, when he had got into a violet Lamborghini and driven off.

"Well, I'll be buggered!"

This meant she was hot on his heels, so she hurriedly completed her morning toilette and then went for a walk through the town.

San Vito lo Capo appealed to her. Although it looked desolate, this was not unusual for a holiday resort in February. She liked the name, too. The Vito part reminded her of Montana and made her feel a little sad. She didn't find a violet Lamborghini, but she did come across the small, foursquare *santuario,* which was built in the Middle Ages to protect fishermen from pirates and contained a small chapel.

Inside the chapel, because she somehow found it appropriate, Poldi lit a candle for Peppe and said a prayer. Then she folded her hands on her bosom and said, *"Namaste."* And, as ever, "Poldi *contra mundum!"*

Because she knew a thing or two about the right way to communicate with the universe.

There was a small esplanade and some benches beside the sea, and Poldi found she wasn't the only early bird in town.

It feels weird having ten million dollars in your trouser pocket. I found on waking that I'd spent the whole night sleeping with my hand in there. The edges of the black plastic card had left painful dents in my fingers. It felt curiously heavy, like a stone trying to drag me down into depths of some kind.

Needless to say, I was on my own again. It was already light outside, and the cloudless sky portended another mild, sunny day in early spring. I presumed that Uncle Martino and Totti had gone off on a recce. I could hear nothing of Poldi in the room next door, nor was there any response when I knocked. Still, a glance out the window told me that they hadn't driven off without me. The Maserati was still parked in the side street that flanked the hotel.

I was feeling rested and more lucid. Lucid enough to realise that this whole trip must be terminated soonest, before we got into serious difficulties. In other words, got rubbed out.

So I showered and got dressed. Having forgotten nearly everything of importance in our rush to leave, I had no alternative but to open Thomas's parcel of laundry. In it I found some shirts, underpants and a couple of printed T-shirts. In memory of my performance of "Valerie" with Poldi, I chose a black one with a stylised Amy Winehouse motif. The T-shirt somehow felt like a suit of armour — and that was something I could have done with.

San Vito lo Capo was deserted because it depended on the holiday trade and there were few fishermen left, but I didn't grasp the full extent of the exodus until I ordered a cappuccino and a *cornetto* in the only bar open. The town was practically uninhabited. Dead. I was the only customer.

"Where is everyone?" I asked the barista.

"In Thailand. They all go there out of season. Then they all come back just before Easter. Like birds of passage."

"The whole town?"

He merely shrugged.

So as not to intrude on his solitude any further, I finished my *cornetto* in a hurry and went searching for the family.

I liked the look of San Vito lo Capo. An agglomeration of dazzlingly whitewashed houses, it displayed the signs of dilapidation so typical of Sicilian towns: that special kind of neglect, born of poverty, ignorance and botched work, which lends itself to picturesque photos. Electric cables winding their way up walls like aerial roots, crumbling mildewed plaster, splintered shutters in the last stages of disintegration, rusty ironwork, graffiti like *Ti amo* or *Buongiorno vita mia*, tattered posters and obituary notices, garbage, palm trees in cracked terracotta tubs.

Somehow I found this soothing. The entire place seemed to be whispering, "The people who live here have something better to do than present a superficially smart appearance." San Vito lo Capo might have seemed remote from the world, but it looked authentic and wholly at ease with itself.

I found Uncle and Totti in the ruins of an old *tonnara,* a former tuna factory. Clinging to a rock on the beach, the crumbling brick building already looked like part of the rock itself. There wasn't much left to see, but Uncle was inspecting every nook and cranny like an archaeologist.

"Have you seen Poldi?" I asked him.

"She went for a walk along the beach. What do you say to a coffee?"

I declined with thanks. My stomach churned at the very thought of another caffeine binge with Uncle. Besides, I was on a mission. A mission that would cost me the last of my aunt's goodwill, but I had to go through with it.

I failed to spot Poldi right away as I walked along the shore, because the bay claimed my full attention. I'd never seen such a gloriously beautiful beach. The sand was as white and fine as powdery snow, and it glittered in the morning sunlight. The whole bay, enclosed by that compact headland, formed a gentle curve, as if embracing the luminous turquoise of the sea. I took my time, shuffling along through the sand and digging furrows in it with my heels. I tested the water: far too cold, but I'm not too fond of water anyway. I only like looking at it.

I eventually spotted Poldi sitting on a bench on a small esplanade a little way inland. She was wearing red stretch pants and a blue-and-white-striped fisherman's sweater. What with her wig and the way she held herself, she looked like a French film star of the fifties — a regular eyeful. The only incongruous feature of this scene was the quartet of metalheads on the bench beside her.

Edging closer, I saw that Poldi's four companions really were members of a heavy metal band, because I made out some guitar cases behind the bench. Three men and a woman, they were holding beer cans, and more cans littered the ground around them. The men looked young and sinister, the way metalheads are supposed to look. The heavy one on the far right had long black curls. The other two guys were tall and clearly twins, judging by their identical ash-blond manes of hair. Heavily tattooed, all three wore black leather trousers, black T-shirts adorned with Satanist motifs or the band's logo, and black leather waistcoats and hoodies.

But what really fazed me was the girl seated between the twins. She was also tattooed, but her skin looked as pale and luminous in the morning sunlight as the beach itself. A dainty, almost fragile-looking figure with long black hair, she had to be younger than me. I estimated that she was in her mid-twenties, but everything about her made an unearthly impression. She might have been a species of elf, not human at all. I was looking at the living embodiment of Ilaria, the preternaturally beautiful Cyclops of my novel.

"Good morning," said Poldi. "May I?"

The four metalheads just stared at her.

She repeated the question in English.

The heavy one shuffled sideways a little to make room for her. Without ado, he handed her the last can of beer.

"Kippis!"

That told Poldi they were from Finland. They clinked cans, drank, stared at the sea.

"How long have you been sitting here?"

The answer took a while to come. It was as if her question had had to circle the equator before being carefully processed.

"Two days," said one of the twins.

"Oh. Why?"

"Van broke down. Then Pekka disappeared."

"Our manager."

"Really? Where to?"

The other twin pointed to the sea. Then, after another brief delay, "Saw an apparition."

"A mermaid or something."

"Went in after her."

"Into the sea?"

A quadruple nod.

"Hm," Poldi said. "He probably won't come back, then."

This seemed to give the quartet food for thought.

"Where are you from?"

"The Arctic Circle."

Poldi nodded. "Cold there."

A quadruple nod.

"And dark, man," the fatso added with surprising vivacity. "Dark as this!" He spread his arms as though defining the size of a tuna. Then he relapsed into brooding silence.

"It's nice here, though," said the girl. "Very nice."

More silent beer-drinking and staring at the sea.

"Where are you headed, my dears?"

"Gibellina," said the girl. "Got a gig there tonight, but it's a no-go without Pekka."

Poldi saw the problem. It gradually transpired that the four of them were stars in the heavy metal firmament. Their band's name was Goblinhammer, and they performed their special blend of doom and Viking metal all over the world. Considering their concerts filled whole stadiums and that they'd been getting sozzled for two days, Poldi found them quite modest and sensible. It touched her that they missed their manager.

The girl, whose name was Olga, pointed to a figure at the end of the esplanade. "He's been watching us the whole time."

"Oh, that's only my nephew," Poldi explained. "He's a bit shy, that's all." She got out her mobile phone and brought up the picture little Antonino had sent her. "If you've been sitting here for two days, maybe you've seen this man. He drives a violet Lamborghini."

The four of them looked at the drawing and nodded.

"I've got a Lamborghini too," said one of the twins. "Mine's matte black."

"He was here last night," said the heavy one. "Sat just where you're sitting. And sad, man. Sad like this!" He spread his arms again to indicate the extent of Antonio's sadness.

"He was here?" said Poldi, galvanised. "Just here? Why was he sad?"

He shrugged. "He said he just wanted to look at the sea and think of something nice."

"He offered us the Lambo, but the four of us couldn't fit into it," said one of the twins.

"Anything else?" asked Poldi.

"He said he was looking for someone."

"Did he by any chance say who?"

The three boys put their heads back and thought hard. Poldi could empathise with this. She knew what it was like to try to recall something after a long night.

"I've got it!" one of the twins said eventually. The others stared at him expectantly. "He was looking for someone called Poldi."

12

Tells of beauty and decay, Sirens and broken hearts. And — this time — only a little of men. Poldi receives some information, her nephew shows some guts, and Uncle Martino refrains from saying all he knows. Poldi loses her temper and has to improvise. Which leads all three to a town encased in concrete and a kind of Sicilian Disneyland, where Poldi does what she has to.

I was about to saunter casually over to the bench (Poldi had beckoned me over) when my aunt bore down on me, looking agitated.

"Are they a band?" I asked rather idiotically.

"Where's Martino?" was all she snapped.

"Er . . . somewhere over there."

"Fetch him. After that, a briefing session at the hotel."

She strode on.

I hurried after her, feeling perplexed. "What's happened?"

"Don't ask. Go and get Martino."

She made to hurry on, but I didn't feel like being ordered around again. The fact is, I can be quite stubborn when I want to be. Having debated how to question her about the four metalheads in the most skilful and innocuous-sounding way, I blurted out, "That girl was quite pretty."

That's how skilful and innocuous-sounding an interrogator I am.

Poldi came to a halt and looked at me. "So you noticed that. Why didn't you come over, then?"

"I didn't want to intrude."

She cast her eyes up to heaven and strode on.

"May I ask you something, Poldi?"

She sighed. "What?"

I drew a deep breath. "How do you manage it?"

"How do I manage what?"

"To like yourself so much?"

"Do I? Well, I'm at least trying to. It's a work in progress, and I'm not always successful."

"I mean, hey, don't get me wrong, but . . . well, you're sixty, but even so . . . I mean, that girl on the bench was pretty. All right, she looked absolutely stunning, I admit."

"Hear, hear."

"But you, sitting beside her — you did too. How do you manage it?"

She paused again and looked at me as if she'd just discovered something that wasn't there before. Obviously wondering how to phrase what she wanted to say, she pointed to a balcony on the other side of the street. Like most of them, it was dilapidated. Plaster and mortar were crumbling away, the wrought-iron railings had rusted, patches of black mildew were burgeoning all over the place, and the succulent plants sprouting from the cracks were so prolific they resembled luminous green fur. With a limpid blue February sky in the background, the balcony looked extremely picturesque.

"How do you like that?"

I shrugged. "It's beautiful."

"Why do you think so? It's falling to pieces."

"Maybe that's why?"

She smiled at me. "You see? Life means change, and decay is a part of that. That's the whole secret. I'm well aware I'm nearing my sell-by date, but I've still got good skin, a firm arse and an impressive bosom. What's more, I'm fun."

I couldn't help grinning. "Looked at from

that angle . . ."

"You can't do anything about decay," she went on, "but you can view it differently. That's to say, as a source of beauty."

An hour later, being unable to find Uncle Martino and Totti anywhere, I went back to the hotel. I wasn't worried — Uncle could find his own way out of a jungle — and besides, I guessed his disappearance was due to his usual eccentricities.

Poldi received me cheerfully in her hotel room, brought me up to date and finally recounted the events of the previous evening.

"Awesome!" I said when she described her fight with Graziella. And again: "Awesome!" when she came to the orgy and the masked man.

"So what happens if you don't produce the attaché case within four days?"

"Why, he threatens to kill me, that's quite clear," she said airily. "But he's barking up the wrong tree, his lordship is, because he doesn't know how little life means to me these days."

"Oh? Lately I've been getting a different impression, but OK."

"Don't go wetting your pants, we've now got a lead!"

She went on to tell me about the photofit picture and her morning encounter with Goblinhammer.

"This isn't good news, Poldi. Not good at all."

"Why not? We needn't go looking for him any longer, just make ourselves a bit more visible. With the Maserati, that shouldn't be hard. He'll find us all right."

"Yes, and kill us all!"

I think I was getting a bit hysterical again.

"Steady, my lad. We're well prepared — we set Handsome Antonio a trap a long time ago. We've got him just where we want him."

"A trap? What sort of trap? Are you crazy? He's a Mafia killer — you don't set traps for guys like that! Remember that black Toyota? We've probably been followed the whole time by an international gang of hit men."

"And we've managed to shake them off, so no panic on the *Titanic*."

I didn't like the sound of this at all.

"We badly need police protection, Poldi," I groaned.

"Get along with you," she scoffed. "Pros like that would smell a rat ten miles upwind. Besides, you really think the police would believe anything we said?"

She had a point, but I felt more than ever convinced that this insanity had to be stopped as soon as possible. I urgently needed to discuss an exit strategy with Uncle.

"I'm going to look for Martino," I said wearily.

"Fine, but be quick. We must be off. I've got a plan."

"Yes, yes, that's clear."

I went to look for Uncle feeling rather rattled and despairing, but he seemed to have vanished from the face of the earth.

Instead, I came across Olga.

She was standing on the beach by herself, staring out to sea, her slim black figure and dark hair sharply silhouetted against the white sand. There was no sign of her three bandmates. I hesitated to approach her, but she suddenly turned to me as if she had sensed my presence. She beckoned me closer, so I plucked up my courage.

"Hi," she said.

"Hi."

"You're the nephew, aren't you?"

Sure, the nephew. The eternal nephew.

"Uh-huh."

"What happened to your nose?"

"I bumped into a glass door."

321

She laughed. "Your aunt is awesome."

I made no comment, just stared at her, I think. She looked even prettier at close quarters. She was wearing a sleeveless black T-shirt two sizes too big for her and adorned with Goblinhammer's logo and tour dates. Up close she looked far from fragile. On the contrary, she had muscular arms and a swimmer's well-developed shoulders. I noticed something else about her too: her eyes were different colours, one pale blue and the other brown.

She pointed to my own T-shirt. "Cool T-shirt."

I was surprised. "You dig Amy Winehouse?"

"Sure. She was one of the greatest."

"Er, yes."

"Shall we swap?"

I nodded, so she pulled off her shirt and tossed it to me. I gulped involuntarily. Her arms, back and legs were tattooed with images of angels and demons, but the rest of her skin was as white as the sand. Almost translucent, it had a rosy sheen in many places and her arms were covered with the finest down. She displayed no embarrassment, just looked at me intently. Rather than stand there stupidly staring at her, I pulled off my own T-shirt, feeling shy, and

we swapped shirts like a couple of foot-
ballers. Hers only just fitted me.

"Coming for a swim?"

"What?"

"Come on, I'm sure it'll be lovely."

Without more ado, she stripped naked,
sprinted straight into the sea and dived in
head-first.

"Come on!"

It was almost noon and the day was warm,
but by my standards not warm enough for
sea bathing. Olga's powerful crawl had
already propelled her some distance from
the shore. Hesitantly, I approached the
water's edge. When I stuck one foot in the
sea, I thought I'd die of shock, so I abandoned the idea of going in.

Olga was shivering when she emerged
from the sea soon afterwards and came up
to me. On impulse, I took her in my arms,
intending to chafe some warmth into her.
She not only hugged me back but suddenly
kissed me. Not for the first time, all I
thought was *Parallel universe, it's just a
dream.*

I don't have too clear a recollection of all
that followed, it happened so quickly. I only
remember the peaceful sensation that overcame me a little later, when we were sitting
on the bench in our swapped T-shirts and

she began to sing. A song in Finnish or something, she sang it with a delicacy and intensity that shook me, but also, in the upper register, with a piercing melodious clarity that almost splintered like the thinnest of ice. I couldn't help thinking of the mythical Sirens of the Aeolian Islands, who drove seamen to distraction with their beguiling songs. That was how I myself felt, like a demented, infatuated Odysseus lashed to his foremast, and it dawned on me that in Sicily, any myth can really come true.

"What was that?" I asked softly when her voice died away.

"A Karelian folk song. It's about a troll who falls in love with a beautiful shepherdess."

I found that appropriate somehow.

"It's so lovely here," she said. "I'd like to stay here forever."

"Then let's."

"I can't. We need to get to Gibellina — got this gig tonight — but we won't get away from here without a car."

That was when I saw the light. The exit strategy, I mean. I felt in my trouser pocket and handed her the keys to the Maserati.

"It'll be a bit of a squeeze, but you'll manage."

She beamed at me. "You could come too.

You could be our new manager."

Nice thought.

But I shook my head. "The car's too small for five people plus guitars. And anyway, I . . . well, I can't, because . . ."

She put a finger on my lips. "Because you're a band too."

Miraculously enough, Uncle was already there and looking for his glasses by the time I got back to the hotel.

"Good God, where have you been?" was Poldi's impatient greeting. "Having a quickie or something?"

I braced myself. "Poldi, we need to talk."

"We can do that on the way. The bags are already in the boot."

At that moment the Maserati started up outside.

Transfixed by the roar of its engine, Poldi stared at me for an instant. "What the . . . ?"

She stormed out before I had a chance to explain. I dashed after her, as did Uncle and Totti, but we emerged from the hotel in time to see the Maserati speed off, laden with the four jam-packed Goblins and their guitars. Our bags had been deposited on the pavement. Olga gave us a parting wave.

"Hey!" Poldi yelled after them. "Come back, you shitheads!" Then she had a light-bulb moment and glared at me. "Was this your doing?"

"I had no choice," I said firmly. "One of us had to apply the emergency brake."

She showered me with Bavarian oaths and expletives, cursed me by God and all the saints, and hoped I would suffer from plague, impotence, failure and sundry other afflictions.

I had expected this, however, and was feeling vaguely liberated. When I snatched a moment to glance at Uncle, I saw him wink at me.

"This is the bitter end!" Poldi fumed. "What if Handsome Antonio blows the Finns and the Maserati to kingdom come? Did that occur to you?"

No, it hadn't. Sudden terror seemed to sear my limbs. I gave an involuntary sneeze.

"See what I mean? It was a bloody stupid thing to do!"

She was about to continue her tirade, but she stopped short. Approaching us from the end of the street was a carabinieri patrol car. Pulling herself together, Poldi adjusted her wig.

The patrol car pulled up beside us and two carabinieri got out. Not the most attractive of young men, and their faces were set, as usual, in a grimly official expression that might conceivably have impressed a child of five.

"Good afternoon, signori. Is there a problem?"

Poldi drew a deep breath. "No, Brigadiere, not at all. Everything's fine."

"No, it isn't," I heard myself say. "There *is* a problem, actually. Our Maserati has been stolen."

"Stolen? When? Where?"

The carabinieri promptly stared at me, gimlet-eyed. Poldi's jaw dropped.

"Here, just now," I said. "It's funny, because we'd already stolen the Maserati ourselves."

Poldi stared at me as if I were mad. Uncle grinned. I was feeling great. All would be well again. There would be a certain amount of trouble, for sure, but no Mafia hit man was going to off us.

The carabinieri finally made the transition from siesta mode to condition yellow. Squaring their shoulders, they tried to keep tabs on all four of us at the same time. One of them very casually allowed his hand to hover over the butt of his service automatic.

"Who are you? Name?"

I was about to give him my personal particulars when I saw, out of the corner of my eye, Poldi rummaging in her handbag.

"Freeze!" In an instant she was covering the carabinieri with her pistol lighter. "Move a muscle and I'll drill you both!"

She really said that, I swear.

I mean, the pistol lighter was quite impressive, but at a second glance any pro would have noticed that it was not a real gun. But then, they were carabinieri, after all, and not the brightest candles on the table. The policemen's tough demeanour collapsed like a punctured soufflé. They turned pale and raised their hands at once.

"Careful with that gun!"

"Take it easy, signora, we've both got families."

Poldi brandished the lighter at them. "Up against the wall. Move!"

They complied.

Me, I couldn't believe my eyes. Uncle Martino was looking quite imperturbable, and all Totti did was prick up his ears.

Poldi herded the frightened carabinieri over to the wall, disarmed them like a TV cop and forced them to their knees.

They both had tears in their eyes, I swear.

Then she handcuffed them to each other.

That done, she pointed to our bags. "Put those in the boot. We've got to get out of here, but this time I'll drive. My lack of a licence doesn't matter any more."

"Are you completely nuts?" I cried. "In a stolen patrol car?"

"Precisely. Come on, get in."

I was about to protest some more when my next sneezing fit almost incapacitated me. I must have caught something on the beach. I saw Uncle Martino calmly load our bags into the Alfa's boot and get in the back with Totti. Impatiently, Poldi pushed me into the front passenger seat and slammed the door, then got behind the wheel. I was sneezing again.

"Serves you right, you miserable traitor!" Poldi hissed. "It's karma!"

She started the patrol car and stepped on the gas. On the outskirts of San Vito lo Capo the black Toyota passed us coming the other way, but we were already going too fast for me to make out the faces of the two men inside.

"That was them again!" I cried.

But Poldi simply floored the accelerator and careened around the next bend. I was now sneezing incessantly.

We did look a trifle conspicuous in a police car, so Poldi followed the minor roads that Uncle recommended to her in a whisper from the back seat. I had my doubts as to whether he was always sure of the way, but

I was far too busy sneezing to worry about that. Besides, Poldi had stopped speaking to me. She was looking as grimly determined as a crusader knight on a tomb, but at least she seemed to enjoy giving the Alfa a thorough workout. She had turned off the annoying police radio and was taking every bend at full throttle. She adhered to the perfect racing line, drifted a bit and braked only when absolutely necessary. Uncle Martino didn't seem to turn a hair. I, on the other hand, wondered whether to pray. Besides, I imagined we were being pursued by every police unit in Sicily. My mind's eye pictured helicopters, roadblocks and snipers, plus Handsome Antonio and the killers in the Toyota. Strangely enough, we were not stopped, nor did we see any police or choppers, the Toyota or the violet Lamborghini.

And the longer we drove, the less the situation bugged me somehow. Like a Zen monk able to detach his mind from the ordure of this world by means of meditation, I concentrated on what I would bequeath to posterity if I were spared and time permitted: my novel.

I had a vivid picture of Barnaba in middle age, sometimes strolling down Via Etnea in an immaculate white linen suit, sometimes in khaki fatigues and a solar topi on Kilimanjaro, and sometimes in a Gestapo-esque black leather coat and broad-brimmed felt hat in the pouring rain in forties Berlin. By his side, the mysterious and capricious Pasqualina, with whom he has recently discovered the remains of Atlantis on the seabed off San Vito lo Capo, where he heard the singing of a preternaturally beautiful Siren with eyes of different colours and fell head over heels in love with her. However, various occult organisations pursue him and Pasqualina to the ends of the earth. The end was inevitable. Lured to Gibellina by a mysterious object in an attaché case (marginal note: ???), Barnaba and Pasqualina fall into a trap set by the Templars and Vitus Tanner, who sees the day of vengeance dawning at last. The outcome is a battle of the giants, which I planned to describe in a stirring and adjectivally potent manner. The odds are simply too great. Although Barnaba manages to save Pasqualina by pushing her over the edge of a precipice strapped to a parachute, he himself dies a heroic death under a hail of bullets. Tanner is maddened by this. He begs Pasqualina for forgiveness on his knees, but she brusquely and majestically spurns him. After a long odyssey she returns to Munich to inform Federico and Walter of their father's heroic death and advise them on business matters. By this time, however, with Mussolini's downfall Italians have fallen into disfavour in Munich. Federico and Walter are compelled to give up their market stall and, after Federico has been badly beaten several times by Barnaba's former business partners, their various commercial sidelines as well. Then the war ended and a new era dawned, and I was ready to open my eyes again.

Poldi seemed to have simmered down a little. She took her foot off the accelerator, desisted from driving like a lunatic and gave me a sidelong glance. "Scared, were you?"

I sniffed. "May I ask you something?"

"Aha!"

"Why did you never have any children?"

She looked at me.

"Who says I haven't?"

"Er . . . what?"

She sighed. "Change of subject. Was it nice on the beach with Olga?"

"Mm."

"I get it. You did something totally irrational for once, bravo. And you came to a decision. An utterly daft decision, but it took some guts. Congratulations."

I stared at her. "You mean that?"

She drew back her hand and cuffed me hard on the back of the head.

"Ouch, that really hurt!"

"I'm proud of you. Make the most of it."

And we did. Uncle Martino started blathering and smoking again, Totti farted happily to himself, Poldi put on an Italo-pop CD she found in the glove compartment (yes, the carabinieris' patrol car did boast a CD player), we sang along with *Nel blu, dipinto di blu,*" and I began to suppress the thought of what sort of vehicle we were in.

Nel blu, dipinto di blu! Felice di stare lassù!

I had experienced miracles in recent days and was in a kind of serene limbo, a curious condition probably akin to nirvana. Whatever happened, I was ready for it.

Or so I mistakenly believed.

Poldi looked at me again. "All right, let's have it."

"Er, what is it this time?"

"Why, the truth about your broken nose, of course. Did you really think I'd let you get away with that currant bun story?"

I'd been afraid of this. I drew a deep breath, like someone preparing to dive off the ten-metre board. And then, all in one go, I came out with the full story of the disastrous episode that had begun last

November and left me with a broken heart and nose at the beginning of February. I recounted it as if it were something that had happened to someone else a long time ago, and it surprised me how many details I remembered. Poldi listened attentively, neither rolling her eyes nor interrupting. She didn't speak for a while after I had finished.

"Well, well," she said eventually, "you poisoned your heart good and proper."

One way of putting it.

"How was she in bed?"

"Fantastic."

"At least you've got some pleasant memories."

"What if I want her back?"

Poldi sighed. "Where there's a will, there's always a way, but life can only give you back what you've really and truly let go of. And the first things to relinquish are your expectations."

I was going to say something, but she ploughed on.

"You simply met someone who doesn't like herself. Strangely enough, that's often true of the most attractive and talented people. They feel perpetually ill at ease and incomplete in themselves, so they need a constant supply of admiration and adulation. They need to lie to themselves and everyone else, but that's never enough for them — it's like an addiction. In time, not that they notice it, the lie enters their flesh, their bloodstream. If you ask me, she was in love with an illusion, not with you at all, get it? In love with the idea of being in love — at most, in love with your *pesciolino*. And when the rose-tinted spectacles came off, there was a hard landing. That's what it looks like to me. Mind you, *you* cherished all kinds of illusions too, didn't you? That's because you still believe in soulmates."

"What's so wrong with that?"

"You know what I always say . . ."

"Yes," I said with a sigh, "happiness equals reality minus expectation."

"Go to the top of the class! Get this: a good relationship isn't one with a perfect soulmate, but with someone you learn to live with, paying special attention to all their flaws, quirks and shortcomings. Unless you do that, you'll someday regret having lost them. And that, let me tell you, can really hurt. Maybe people like you and me need the pain of a lost love to make us feel truly alive. Chin up, be thankful and breathe. Every cloud has a silver lining. I know what I'm talking about. Nothing is so bad it's beyond repair. You want to be happy? Then live that way, for God's sake. Take note of the good people around you, because you're one of them. Always be yourself. Because," she added, lowering her voice a little after a momentary pause, "you're an artist, after all. You can always make a silk purse out of a sow's ear."

I stared at her. "Did you just say 'artist'?"

She shrugged. "An artist with a driving licence."

I sat back with a sigh. Something was flowing out of me like pus from a lanced abscess.

"I love you, Poldi."

We got to Gibellina that afternoon. Our first sight of the town was the low hill bearing the concrete-encased ruins of Gibellina Vecchia, which resembled a gigantic turtle dozing in the sun. In the late 1960s a violent earthquake had completely destroyed the medieval town and its neighbouring towns of Salaparuta and Poggioreale. Nearly four hundred people lost their lives and over four thousand were rendered homeless. The latter were compelled to put up with lousy emergency accommodations for ten years, until the government had conjured up a brand-new town for them: Gibellina Nuova, dashed off on an architect's drawing board, nice and near the motorway and the railway, with little squares, front gardens and garages, and utterly soulless. International sympathy at the time was immense. Celebrated architects and sculptors donated works of art to the new town. Today Gibellina boasts the highest density of modern art in all Italy, but the surviving residents have never felt really at home in their new surroundings, and many have moved away. In commemoration of the murderous earthquake, the artist Alberto Burri created a monument by burying the ruins under a thick layer of white concrete criss-crossed with incisions recording the layout of the original streets. Weather-worn and covered with moss, it now resembles a monstrous scab in the midst of the countryside. Elderly survivors of the earthquake sometimes visit the place as though the ghost of Gibellina has yet to find peace and is calling them.

Soon afterwards we drove under the Star of Gibellina, a five-pointed concrete sculpture that spans the access road and resembles a sloppy mandala. Surmounting it was a big banner advertising something. I was sneezing violently again, and Poldi was driving too fast for me to read it properly. That didn't matter, though, because our drive abruptly ended just beyond it.

When Poldi spotted the roadblock around the bend, she braked so hard, I would have gone through the windscreen but for my seat belt. The road ahead was sealed off by a barrier, I saw. Behind it were men in yellow hi-vis vests and two carabinieri patrol cars. I couldn't tell if we'd been seen, but at least the carabinieri didn't jump out of their Alfas, guns at the ready. Not yet, anyway.

"What now?"

Poldi, still clutching the steering wheel, was scrutinising the roadblock.

"They aren't waiting for us," she said eventually.

"No?"

"Take a good look. Only two police cars, which means only four carabinieri, but a dozen . . . What are they? Law enforcement personnel of some other kind? Security men? Why the barrier if they're only waiting for us?"

That had occurred to me too. We saw a van drive up to the barrier. One security man checked the driver's ID, another waved a metal detector around beneath the vehicle, and a third made his German shepherd take a sniff at it. Then the barrier was raised. The next vehicle to appear was not allowed through and had to do a U-turn.

"What was on that banner?" I asked.

"No idea," said Poldi.

"Tech Summit," Uncle Martino said placidly from behind us. "A big affair — it was all over the papers. Today and tomorrow, one of those tech giants from Silicon Valley is throwing a huge shindig, with conferences, workshops, full board and parties. But all without the local inhabitants — they've been moved out for two days. Take it from me, the whole of Silicon Valley is an invention of the Templars. Over the next two days they'll probably be forging a whole new world order in Gibellina."

Poldi and I stared at him in amazement.

"And you never thought to tell us?!"

Martino lit his next cigarette. "*Beh!* If I'm your special satnav, you should turn me on."

"You do realise we're all in the same boat," Poldi snapped.

"Yes," I said, sniffing, "a goddam stolen police boat!"

"Know what you need to be?" said Martino.

"Don't tell me."

"Calmer."

At that moment the violet Lamborghini roared past. We didn't have time to take cover anywhere, as Handsome Antonio was travelling fast, but luckily he didn't appear to have spotted us in our new form of transportation. I saw the squat missile's brake lights flash just before it reached the barrier. The Lamborghini was checked — and allowed to proceed. I was gobsmacked.

"How come?" I exclaimed. "He's a wanted man."

"Beh!" said Uncle, as though that said everything about Italian law enforcement.

"This is a fine mess," Poldi groaned, glaring at me.

We needed a plan, that much was obvious. Our patrol car had been parked on the verge for far too long. Sooner or later our "colleagues" over there would notice — that is, if they hadn't already tried to call us on the radio — and as soon as we three jokers plus dog got out, the game would be up. It didn't look as if it would be so easy-peasy to gain access to the town and recover our Maserati.

"We need a plan."

Poldi felt in her handbag and produced her old address book. "Just give me a moment." She turned the pages until she found the phone number she was looking for and dialled it.

"Who are you calling?" I asked warily.

"Mark. If he's organised this shindig and he's paying for it, he'll probably be here himself, won't he?"

"Er, you don't mean *the* Mark, do you?"

At that moment someone at the other end picked up, and Poldi silenced me with an upraised hand.

"Mark? Hi, it's me, Poldi," she trilled in English. "That's right, Poldi Oberreiter. Fine, thanks . . . Yes, I should have called you ages ago, but you know how it is, always up to my eyes. So glad my idea for that online platform found favour, it obviously paid off . . . Mark, listen, you won't believe it, but I'm stuck here on the outskirts of Gibellina with my nephew and my brother-in-law, and they're very keen to hear that Finnish pop group. You couldn't by any chance . . . ? Oh! That'd be great!"

Less than fifteen minutes later a black van with tinted windows drove slowly past and parked on the verge just ahead of us, obscuring our view of the carabinieri and vice versa. The sliding door opened, a hand beckoned to us, and we got in. Waiting for us inside was a young Asian woman in a breathtaking Suzi Wong gown, who handed each of us an all-access pass to hang round our neck.

"Mark is very busy right now," she said, "but he looks forward to catching up with you later."

We got past the barrier without any problem and drove into Gibellina.

Into my next parallel universe.

The sight of it stunned me. I couldn't absorb it all in such a short time, nor did I ever get to meet Mark. His people had completely transformed the town. All the buildings had been draped in illuminated banners displaying the medieval façades of Gibellina Vecchia, interspersed with those of famous Italian palazzi. Thousands of people wearing passes of different colours, some in manga costumes, were strolling through the town or gliding around on Segways like extraterrestrial invaders after terraforming. Small autonomous electric vehicles were transporting people to and fro. I saw no normal cars, all of them having been diverted to a car park on the outskirts, so I didn't spot the violet Lamborghini — not that this reassured me. Erected in the squares were some futuristic-looking beehives in which workshops were being held or lectures delivered, and parked all over the place were food trucks from which attendees could obtain snacks upon producing their passes. Most of them were sucking straws immersed in plastic mugs as if they were life-support systems. Gibellina Nuova resembled a Sicilian Disneyland, but without Sicilians. The latter had been moved out so the internet elite could network and preen undisturbed in this iridescent bubble. I had never seen anything more depressing.

The metallic rock music howling and chain-sawing away in the distance grew steadily louder, like an unwelcome truth that refuses to be suppressed. The van drove us right up to the rear of the stage, and there was our Maserati with the key in the ignition. Theft in this remote artistic location did not appear to be an issue.

"In an hour's time I'll come and fetch you for a meet-and-greet with Mark," said our guide, and she left us to ourselves. Rather bemused by the 130-decibel music and the atmosphere in this Gibellina space station, I stood beside the Maserati feeling thoroughly odd and at a loss. I may have been expecting to be killed at any moment, or perhaps I was expecting something else, I don't know. Poldi and Uncle Martino seemed to be in a similar state. Even Totti was looking bemused.

"Go on!" Poldi eventually bellowed above the din, prodding me in the ribs. "Go and take a look at her!"

Which reminded me what I was really after.

Accompanied by Uncle Martino and Totti, I made my way round to the front of the stage. And saw Olga. She was up there with the rest of the group, still wearing my Amy Winehouse T-shirt. Decibels abraded my ears, bass notes punched me in the guts. The three friendly Finnish guys were whirling around the stage like raging demons. Pyrotechnics exploded rhythmically in the wings, bathing everything in a spasmodic, nightmarish glare. The thousands of people in front of the stage were wagging their heads to Goblinhammer's apocalyptic beat, waving their horned hands in the air and singing along to the lyrics. I had eyes only for Olga. She was singing again, not in the bell tones of the beach, but hoarsely, loudly and very, very angrily, like Signor Satan himself. With the microphone clamped to her mouth, she strutted defiantly up and down in convulsions and showered us with all the salivary fury of an extinct civilisation.

At some point she must have caught sight of me, because all at once she pranced towards me like a goblin, glared at me with the eyes of a troll and bellowed her despair in my face. I think she meant it in a nice way, as a sort of fond farewell. Then she spun round and went whirling off across the stage again.

I sometimes think it's possible that the

universe lent her to me for the bat of an eyelash. At that moment, though, she belonged to no one but herself and a world of pain and darkness. It was nice all the same.

I turned to Uncle Martino, who was watching the hellish spectacle attentively and with interest. Even Totti had pricked up his ears. Martino was saying something.

"What?" I yelled above the din.

"It's Templar music!" he shouted back. "I like it. Do you know Adriano Celentano? He was a rocker too. A rocker and a Templar!"

"I'm fond of you too, Martino."

Just then I noticed that Poldi wasn't with us any more. Feverishly, I turned round in search of her and elbowed my way through the crowd, but I couldn't see her anywhere. Instead, I caught sight of Handsome Antonio, whom I recognised at once from the photofit. Seemingly also in search of someone, he was prowling around like a predator. Panic-stricken, I wondered whether to get in touch with security, but feared it would only waste time — even if they took me seriously, which was doubtful.

So I followed Handsome Antonio at a safe distance. Suddenly he seemed to have spotted something, because he set off at a run. I dashed in pursuit, just in time to see him collide with a woman on a Segway and send them both flying. Instantly, four paramedics appeared out of nowhere and attended to him. Mark and our guide had certainly organised everything to a T. Handsome Antonio tried to free himself, but he was powerless against the resolute solicitude of the paramedics, who swarmed over the two prostrate figures like ants over grains of sugar. Prostrate figures were frowned upon here, it seemed. They were considered embarrassing and uncool.

And then I saw the Maserati. It drove straight past me, almost close enough to touch, with Poldi at the wheel. Flabbergasted, I watched her cruise by.

"Bloody hell, Poldi, I thought we were a team!"

She turned, saw me and blew me a kiss. Then, casually honking the horn and zigzagging between food trucks and knots of people, she headed for the outskirts of town and disappeared from view.

13

Tells of men. Young men, old men, inebriated men, dangerous men, men in love, powerful men, handsome men, resolute men and armed men. Poldi concocts a final plan and, soon after that, makes a date. She gets her act together, sits on the beach with vodka and goes on a jaunt to the temples. Handsome Antonio has a question to ask, and the Maserati has transmission problems.

Nothing mystified my Auntie Poldi more than this one enigma: men. She simply didn't understand them. Or, to put it another way, she had grasped that men don't understand themselves, and that this torments them deep inside like an ingrowing toenail. They suffered from themselves like an autoimmune disease, that much was certain. But as for what really motivated men — all the subsurface currents and ed-

347

dies that turned them into notorious liars, unreliable lovers, devoted fathers, heroes, murderers, prigs, slackers, detective inspectors, priests, gurus, know-alls, fantasists, punters, sympathetic companions and, quite often, all of them together — that remained a mystery to Poldi. No other creature on earth seemed more paradoxical to her. Men seemed to her to consist solely of contradictions sketchily held together by suits, three-quarter trousers, uniforms and steaks. Even the most self-assured of them, the greatest egoists, the most dependable, sincere and faithful — even they, who seemed genuinely at ease with themselves, were secretly at odds with their own shortcomings. At best, they accepted this, as if the whole of life were just an entrance examination for something greater at which they could only fail. Men liked to roam in packs, yet Poldi had never met one who didn't regard himself as a lone wolf. Every man seemed to feel certain that he had to confront the whole world on his own, but why? Poldi couldn't fathom this, and women seemed incapable of helping them.

Poldi had long suspected that it had to do with the penis, which steered a man sometimes in one direction, sometimes in another, like a faulty compass needle, and caused him to zigzag through life without ever coming to rest. Poldi liked penises, it must be said. She had always been able to delight in a shapely, erect, pulsating *membrum virile,* and had always had a great deal of fun playing with that mutable force of nature, which — often to the man's great surprise — obeyed its own very individual rules. But the penis, Poldi had realised, was not the problem at all; ultimately, it was just the twitching indicator of a man's profound and disturbing inner confusion.

There were exceptions, though. Pathological exceptions. There were very rare men without internal contradictions, singletons who didn't have to fight internal battles but, once on track, coasted through life without any scruples or self-doubt. In Poldi's experience, those men were the most dangerous — more dangerous even than the worst narcissists with vast egos and undersized willies. For men without inherent contradictions — this much Poldi *had* grasped — were just empty and evil. And the masked old man in the palazzo was precisely one such.

Whoever he was, she had no doubt that he would cold-bloodedly carry out his threat unless she handed over the attaché case within four days. She couldn't escape that realisation. The man wouldn't hesitate to wipe out her entire family, one by one, in order to get what he wanted. That was because he had always got what he wanted. Apart from love, of course, but men like him were totally indifferent to that.

And now the quandary: Poldi hadn't the foggiest idea where the attaché case was, let alone how to lay hands on it. Her whole plan had hitherto been based on the assumption that Handsome Antonio had killed Thomas and appropriated the attaché case. The trouble was, since Handsome Antonio was pursuing her, he clearly didn't have it and appeared to think that *she* did.

The next three days would go by and the masked man would have her family killed one by one, starting with her untalented nephew. Calling in Montana or the police in general would achieve nothing, she knew that. Poldi didn't know the identity of the masked man, and even if she did, he was a very powerful and unscrupulous figure. Someone who didn't give a fig for the law. Someone who regarded the state and its organs as his property, like everything else, and could do with them as he pleased. And did. Someone who always got away with it.

Poldi could see only one way out of this dilemma: she had to remove the central problem in the whole of this screwed-up affair. Namely, herself. Her original plan when she moved to Italy, which had been to drink herself to death with a nice view of the sea, had not really worked, so she had to devise an alternative. It wasn't that she'd been particularly unhappy in the past few months. After all, she had solved two murder cases, got to know Vito Montana (in the biblical sense as well) and made new friends and a new home. She had rediscovered some of her joie de vivre — quite a lot of her joie de vivre, come to think of it. But the way things stood, these had only been short-term loans from the universe, and she now had to relinquish and repay them. For to claim that all will always be well, that nothing bad exists, that we live in the here and now without any expectations, is one thing; believing it oneself is another.

Poldi's plan matured as she drove out of Gibellina and back along the motorway towards Castellammare del Golfo. No longer "whether or not," the question was "how." Although still undecided, she had faith in her talent for improvisation. The Maserati had already provided a certain amount of inspiration, and she could always, if necessary, get herself offed by Handsome Antonio. It was never wrong to leave a difficult job to a pro. On the other hand, Poldi was a self-made woman who had never liked having things taken out of her hands, least of all by men. She preferred to run her own life, with all its mistakes and bloopers, so she had no intention of weakening now, when it came to her own suicide. True to her motto "Moderation is weakness," she proposed to go out with a bang, and she still had three days left in which to do so.

She hung her head out into the cool breeze, feeling simultaneously sad and light-hearted, pumped up and even jaunty. The air itself seemed to taste of adventure.

At Alcamo she turned west towards Trapani. She had no definite idea of where she wanted to go; she simply obeyed her instinct, the wind, the moon and the stars. Eventually, late that night, they guided her to Erice, where she took a room at a small hotel in the centre of town, intending to devote the following day to planning her own demise in a calm and rested condition.

An enchanting medieval town near Trapani, Erice sits perched on the top of Monte Erice and consists entirely of quaint, tortuous alleyways, flights of steps, chiaroscuro and cobblestones. A serpentine road winds its way up to the well-restored town, which commands spectacular views of

Trapani, the sea, and the windmills and salt pans far inland. Erice has a town wall, a campanile, a Norman castle and the famous Pasticceria Grammatico, which purveys the most delicious *cannoli, paste di mandorla, cassate siciliane, genovesi al cuore di crema, crostate alla marmellata, bocconcini, amaretti* and *buccellati di fico* obtainable west of Etna. Although nothing, absolutely nothing, beats the confectionery of the province of Catania (a little personal remark of my own), a trip to Erice without a detour to Maria Grammatico's would be as incomplete as a pilgrimage to Rome without a visit to St Peter's.

So Poldi fortified herself there the next morning, first with an espresso plus grappa and then with a grappa sans espresso. And then another of the same. She was wearing her favourite dress, the red one with the white polka dots, and a white, broad-brimmed sun hat. Feeling fine and ready for a spot of breakfast, she partook of a fresh *cornetto alla crema di ricotta* and a cappuccino whose foam the young barista had imprinted with a little swan. Or a phoenix, depending on the beholder's powers of imagination.

"If this is meant to tell me something, universe," Poldi murmured, shaking her head and blowing on her foaming phoenix, "you could have saved yourself the trouble. I've risen from the ashes for the last time, got that? *Namaste.* Poldi *contra mundum,* et cetera."

"Excuse me, signora, are you German?"

Turning, she experienced a minor shock. A pleasant sort of shock, though — one of the "Wow!" variety. The kind that makes your heart give a jump and, in the case of Poldi's finely calibrated pleasure centre, occasioned an instant transition from a state of repose to high alert. Why? Because standing over her was a *vigile urbano,* or traffic cop. Somewhat shorter and a trifle older than Poldi, he wore an immaculately pressed uniform and had a firm little tummy. The white hair under his cap was luxuriant, his beard and moustache were neatly trimmed. No wedding ring — Poldi clocked that at once. His amiable, open face was weather-beaten but made a youthful impression, largely because of his bright, watchful eyes. And his laughter lines. Poldi had seldom seen a man with so many laughter lines around his eyes and the corners of his mouth. In short, she was looking at her kind of guy.

"Well, *hello,*" Poldi said softly. Then, a bit louder, "Yes, I'm German."

"May I sit down for a moment? I'd like to ask you something — a question concerning grammar. But only if I'm not disturbing you."

Poldi graciously indicated the seat beside her. "This *is* the Pasticceria Grammatico, after all."

The *vigile* smiled broadly at her and sat down.

Poldi put out her hand. "Poldi."

He took the proffered hand and brushed the back of it with his lips. "My name is —"

"Let me guess," she cut in. "Antonio?"

He stared at her wide-eyed. "How did you . . . ?"

Poldi flapped her hand at him. "It's a long story, and you'd never believe it anyway. Well, Antonio, how can I be of help?"

"The thing is," he began, "I'm just learning German and I'm not quite clear about the use of the subjunctive and the conditional."

Poldi looked at him attentively. "Why do you want to learn German?"

"Oh, I simply enjoy learning languages. I've learnt several in my life. Spanish, Arabic, Hungarian, Greek, Swahili."

"Swahili? Really?"

The *vigile* made a deprecating gesture. "Oh, I'm not fluent."

355

He appealed to Poldi more and more.

"But why German in particular?"

Handsome Antonio gave an embarrassed laugh. "Well," he prevaricated, "first because it's a difficult language, and second — please don't be offended — because it's useless."

He went on to tell Poldi that he had no use for the many foreign languages he'd learned in the course of his life. He learned them purely for his own amusement. He had spent the whole of his life in Erice, directing traffic, writing parking tickets, escorting drunks home, nabbing pickpockets and keeping logs. Hardly a stimulating or intellectually demanding life, hence his adoption of languages as a hobby. The criteria governing his selection of which languages to learn were always the same: difficult and useless.

"I like that, Antonio," said Poldi. "You've no idea how much."

Antonio ordered himself a coffee, and Poldi discovered that he was a widower. His wife had died ten years ago, after a long illness, and their two married daughters lived in Brescia and Naples with their husbands and families. A long way off.

"But the German language isn't as useless as all that," Poldi protested. "You can read the German Romantic poets."

"You're right," the *vigile* said enthusiastically. "Eichendorff, for example." Having collected his thoughts for a moment, he proceeded to declaim in a strong Sicilian accent: "If, in each ever-dreaming thing, / A song sleeps on and on unheard, / The world would surely start to sing, / Were you to say the magic word."

"That was wonderful!" Poldi whispered, laying her hand on his.

He did not withdraw it.

"I'm afraid I have to go on duty now, Signora Poldi. However, perhaps we could have a chat about the subjunctive or the conditional this evening?"

"Both, perhaps?" Poldi trilled a trifle equivocally. In her head she sent the universe a brief inquiry as to how to proceed — she had decided to kill herself, after all, but then she couldn't help herself and made a date with this man. And, because this put her in mind of the photo album containing her collection of snaps of policemen, she added, "But only, Antonio, if you let me take a photo of you outside."

Poldi had briefly considered adhering to her original life-terminating plan and carrying it out that night after stocking up on booze

357

at the nearest supermarket. For one thing, though, the alcoholic solution struck her as too uncertain, and for another, she was looking forward to her date that evening. Besides, she still had two days left, so she decided as usual to take one thing at a time.

After a short walk through the town, she identified a tight hairpin bend in the switch-back approach road, where there was a gap in the wall just above a sufficiently sheer drop. A perfect spot for a spectacular demise in the Maserati, she told herself.

She spent the rest of the day in her room with a bottle of Prosecco, writing farewell letters to Montana, the family and one or two other people she was fond of. It wasn't too easy to find the right words, but by that evening a dozen neatly addressed envelopes lay on the desk in her hotel room. Poldi felt satisfied.

Antonio took her to a little trattoria with rickety chairs and checked tablecloths on the outskirts of town. It offered mountains of couscous and seafood accompanied by white *catarratto* from the slopes of Monte Erice, which flowed like water, as did the *spumante* and, to end with, the sweet *passito.* The hump-backed proprietress with the enormous breasts cuddled Poldi like an old friend and called her *gioia.* Antonio was now wearing jeans and sneakers, a white shirt and a blue sweater. A bit too conservative for Poldi's taste, but she liked this typical Italian get-up all the same. In her opinion, men of mature years who wore it always presented a *bellissima figura.* Antonio chatted informally about his life, his late wife, whom he had loved dearly, and his daughters. He didn't take himself too seriously and laughed heartily at Poldi's anecdotes — in the right places, too. Although his life hadn't always been easy, he seemed thoroughly at ease with himself. Poldi found him one of the few examples of the male species who could be taken seriously. He was a keeper, if a keeper was what one wanted.

There was no more talk of grammar. At some point Antonio took her hand, and when she didn't pull it away he asked for the bill. The further course of the evening and night may be left to the imagination. Poldi would have preferred to spend her last night of love with Montana, for Montana, she realised more and more clearly, was her sexual open sesame. She hoped he would at least preserve some pleasant memories of her. Surprisingly, the handsome *vigile* from Erice proved to be a tender and passionate sexual explorer with skilful and remarkably gentle hands. He found planet Poldi's secret places and magical treasures, took his time surveying it, thoroughly savoured all the abundant natural amenities it had to offer, delighted in the gifts he received and was an unflagging, unerring wielder of his *sicilianità*. Antonio was a gentleman who gallantly yielded right of way to Poldi, even on entering the Temple of Dionysus. But on reaching the ecstatic holy of holies himself, he metamorphosed into a frenzied, rapacious, all-devouring satyr. Poldi, crying aloud for joy, willingly allowed herself to be borne off and devoured by this unleashed force of nature (who was, of course, both Sicilian and a policeman). And all this, as I am sure the reader can imagine, went on time after insatiable time until far into the night.

Slightly dishevelled and more than a little tipsy, but in excellent spirits, Poldi tottered back to her hotel in the small hours and spread out the farewell letters neatly in a prominent position on the desk in her room. Then she went back downstairs and started the Maserati. It would be nice, she had thought, to be found at dawn. After a short drive she sighted her chosen spot in the switchback and pulled up a little way short of it. The road curved gently downhill for about a hundred metres before reaching the hairpin. Poldi estimated precisely how to send the Maserati hurtling through the gap in the wall, and it occurred to her that she would be airborne just before she entered the Great Light. Perhaps she would find Peppe waiting for her on the other side.

"*Namaste,* life," she said with quiet determination. "The rest of the world can kiss my arse."

And she gunned the engine.

The six-cylinder engine roared, the Maserati gave a lurch and leapt forward. Poldi grasped the wheel tightly, her eyes firmly focused on the gap. Everything looked good — she would make it. The precipice came nearer.

But Sicily is complicated. Something always intervenes, and this time it was Death. Suddenly materialising in the passenger seat, he hauled on the handbrake and made a grab for the wheel.

"Hey!" yelled Poldi, but before she could react, the Maserati swerved and skidded.

No wonder, in view of its rear-wheel drive and front-mounted engine. With a hideous sound of metal on stone, the car crashed into the wall, bounced off it like a rubber ball, rotated once on its own axis, crashed into the wall on the opposite side of the road and careened onwards, out of control. It was a miracle it didn't overturn. Then Poldi's reflexes, honed at rallies in the old days, kicked in. She took her foot off the gas, spun the steering wheel and pumped the brake pedal to avoid locking the wheels. Once learned, never forgotten. Somehow she made it around the bend and came to a stop just beyond it, sideways-on.

"Good God, are you crazy?" she yelled. "You could have killed us both!"

Death merely looked at her, shaking his head and sighing. Then, without a word, he got out of the car and started walking back into town.

"Stay here, you stupid idiot!" Poldi shouted after him. "This is *my* life, get it? *I* decide when and how the lights go out!"

Still feeling rather tipsy and traumatised, Poldi refrained from making a second attempt. She drove the battered Maserati back to the hotel, stowed the farewell letters in her handbag and wrote the handsome *vigile* a card.

Stay the way you are!
NAMASTE! POLDI

With two days still to go, Poldi adhered to

her original plan: she would show Death how to go out with a bang. She left Erice before sunup, heading south. The Maserati was making such suspicious rattling noises, Poldi guessed that it had suffered from its recent contretemps and would soon give up the ghost. By then, however, she hoped all would be over.

But, as already mentioned, Sicily is complicated.

Poldi drove past Marsala and Mazara del Vallo, bought a bottle of vodka at a motorway service station and then went looking for a nice, lonely beach. She eventually found one in a delightful nature reserve near Selinunte. The beach was not only long and deserted but largely hidden from view by a row of sand dunes.

There Poldi spread out the batik cotton towel she always packed when travelling, planted the vodka bottle in front of her and watched the sun rise above the sea on her left. The morning air was cool, and she suspected that drowning herself would require a certain amount of willpower, if only because of the sea temperature. Hence the vodka. She tested the water with the tips of her toes. Drowning wasn't the smartest idea, perhaps, but still.

At that moment she saw she wasn't entirely alone. A familiar figure in a hoodie was holding a clipboard in one hand and derisively tapping his forehead with the other. Poldi tried to ignore him. She was about to turn and drink away the last of her inhibitions when she noticed another figure.

A naked corpulent man was sitting on the sand some two hundred metres away, staring out to sea. His long fair hair fluttered in the morning breeze, and Poldi could see that his body was tattooed nearly all over. She guessed who he was.

"Well, I'm damned," she said with a sigh, giving Death a glare.

She picked up the vodka bottle, went over to the naked man and sat down beside him on the sand.

"You must be Pekka," she said in English, handing him the bottle. "Halfway around Sicily, eh? Quite a swim."

The Finn turned to her and nodded, displaying absolutely no surprise. He didn't seem to be cold, either. Then he noticed the bottle in her hand and his eyes lit up. Taking it from her, he glugged down half the contents.

"How did you get here?" Poldi asked.

The Finn thought hard. "No idea, man." Then, "I think I was in the sea. Saw a mermaid."

"Yes, so I heard. Was she worth it?"

Pekka stared at her. "I had the best sex of my life, man. At least, I think I did." He lapsed into another reverie, then shook his head and took another swig.

"I think you should lay off the drugs in future."

Pekka considered this and nodded. "I'm going to wait for her, man. Next year, when the currents are favourable, she's bound to swim past again."

Poldi sighed. "Sure, but first let's find you something to wear."

Hanging on to the vodka bottle, Pekka followed Poldi across the sand dunes to the spot where she had parked the Maserati. Just as they reached it, Poldi heard a distant *boomdy-boom* and saw a brass band coming towards them along the deserted road. It was blaring out a discordant funeral march, and as it drew nearer Poldi saw that the musicians were all dressed in black. Behind them came four men pulling a handcart with a plain, varnished coffin on it, and they were followed by a small group of mourners. Rather moved, Poldi and Pekka stood and watched the little funeral procession file past. Pekka, who seemed unembarrassed by his nudity, did at least hold a hand over his genitals.

The brass band now struck up a somewhat livelier tune from a Puccini opera, though the rhythm and tempo were so far adrift that Puccini would have rotated in his grave. It was as if the piece were just a rough guide for a collective improvisation. Each of the bandsmen tooted away as he pleased, not that this detracted from the mood of the funeral procession. Everyone looked solemn but contented, children and ancient mourners alike.

Poldi guessed that they were all looking forward to a lavish *pranzo* after the burial, possibly provided by the family or neighbours of the deceased, whose framed photograph a man was carrying behind the coffin. She also spotted Death among the mourners. He put two fingers to his hoodie in a casual salute and then ignored her. Poldi resolved to give him a piece of her mind on the Other Side. He didn't know what he was in for, she told herself.

Needless to say, some surreptitious or overtly inquisitive glances were cast at the naked Finn and the strange-looking woman in the black beehive wig standing beside the Maserati, but no one seemed really surprised by them.

Until a very old woman peeled off the

funeral procession and came over. She was tiny and wrinkled and had a humped back. Despite her obviously biblical age, her dark, boot-button eyes shone with curiosity. She turned to Pekka. "Why aren't you wearing any clothes, young man?"

"He saw a Siren," Poldi told her.

The old woman seemed to find this a sufficient explanation. "You should put something on all the same, young man, it's chilly."

"He's a Finn," said Poldi, "but we're going to get him something."

The old woman indicated the Maserati. "Nice car. Did you have an accident?"

"Oh, it still goes," Poldi said dismissively. She pointed to the procession, which was shuffling on regardless, though one or two of the mourners were glancing back at the old woman irresolutely. "You'll miss the bus, signora."

The old woman shrugged. "This ridiculous procession was Angelo's dying wish. He always had a thing for parades, but my feet aren't too good today. If you offered me a lift, I could give your friend a few of my late husband's things."

Poldi beamed at her and opened the car door. "It would be an honour."

Poldi and her two passengers puttered

along after the cortege. The old woman's name was Rosaria. She heaved a sigh of relief as she got into the back seat. Rosaria was a hundred and two years old.

"I don't believe it," Poldi said. "You look eighty years younger than that!"

Rosaria giggled. "Oh, stop it! Still, Angelo made it to a hundred and three. Eighty years we were married."

"Incredible! So he was the love of your life?"

The old woman shook her head. "Oh, no. That was Graziano Scrudato, but he was snapped up by that whore Maria Bonaccorsi. If I ever see her again I'll scratch her eyes out. Angelo was a good husband, but a terrible bore."

Poldi regarded Rosaria in the rear-view mirror. "What kept you together?"

"We owned a small shop. Then there were the children, grandchildren, great-grandchildren. And the sex, of course, though nothing happened in bed for the last ten years. Zero. That was a bit hard."

Poldi stared at the old woman for a moment, then burst out laughing. "Donna Rosaria, you're my kind of woman!"

Pekka, who had been drinking throughout the drive, was looking fresher and pinker with every swig.

Up ahead, the brass band was belting out Abba's "Mamma Mia."

"What were you doing down on the beach so early?" Rosaria asked abruptly.

Poldi shrugged. "I was planning to end myself."

Rosaria considered this awhile, then said, "Well, everyone should be able to decide when to go, but in your case that surprises me."

"Why?"

"Because you aren't finished here, Donna Poldina. I think you're just trying to duck out of something."

This made Poldi think. She also remembered having carelessly overlooked a vital part of the whole case. But she didn't have much time to mull it over, because, as I've said before, Sicily is complicated. Something always intervenes.

As the mourners reached the outskirts of Selinunte and were turning off towards the cemetery, Poldi spotted an old man beside the road, sitting patiently on the bench in a bus shelter. As old as Rosaria in appearance, he wore a baseball cap, a pair of blue workmen's trousers and a football shirt in the Italian national colours. The most striking thing about him was not his clothing, but the rabbit he was cuddling on his lap. A large rabbit — or it could have been a hare, Poldi was no expert. It was very big, anyway. In the sense of huge. Gigantic. The old man was holding a hare the size of a chubby twelve-year-old child in his arms. The huge hare had fluffy white fur and was sniffing the air with its ears pricked up and its gigantic paws at full stretch. Both the man and the hare looked perfectly satisfied with themselves and with the world in general; waiting for a bus seemed to be their sole preoccupation. Poldi pulled up beside the bus shelter and stared at the curious pair as if they were a mirage that might dissolve at any moment.

"Good morning, signore," she called from the car.

"What a beautiful hare," Rosaria said affably. "And so . . . so big."

Pekka said nothing, just stared at the hare and drank.

"Cesare is a German Giant," said the old man. "That's the name of the breed. He's already won several competitions."

Poldi seemed relieved that the hare's name wasn't Antonio.

"Where are you taking him?"

"Agrigento. I was only here on a visit, to show Cesare to my great-grandchildren, but the bus is late." The old man tickled his

German Giant behind the ears. "Still, we aren't in a hurry, are we, Cesare?"

Rosaria leaned forward. "Tell me something, Donna Poldina," she said over Poldi's shoulder. "Do you have anywhere definite in mind — I mean, for your . . . *project*?"

Poldi caught on. "No. The 'where' doesn't matter, actually."

"Well, I wouldn't mind seeing the temples of Agrigento again," said Rosaria. "They're really majestic, and who knows how much longer I've got?"

Poldi rolled her eyes. The flirtatious looks Rosaria had been giving the old man on the bench hadn't escaped her. She could almost hear violins playing.

"Don't you ever give up? What about Angelo's funeral?"

Rosaria brushed this aside. "I've buried my parents, my children, several grandchildren, nearly all my family and all my friends. That's enough. I can't stand funerals. Angelo knows that, he'll manage without me. Anyway, we'll be seeing each other again soon enough."

So Poldi called to the man on the bench. "It just so happens we're on our way to Agrigento ourselves. We'll give you a lift if you like."

371

■ ■ ■ ■

Five minutes later, old Gaetano was sitting beside Rosaria in the back. He was ninety-six — a mere youngster, as Rosaria put it, giggling, and the two of them billed and cooed like a couple of teenagers. "Where are you from?" — "Why haven't we bumped into each other before?" — "Oh yes, I know her, how funny." — "You don't say! How exciting! You must tell me more about it." — "I used to have a rabbit as a child." — "Size isn't everything."

Poldi tried not to keep looking in the rearview mirror and to concentrate on driving. Pekka, beside her in the front, was now holding the German Giant in his arms. Pensive and fairly drunk, he spent the whole time whispering to Cesare in Finnish. Just before they got to Agrigento, Poldi saw Gaetano give Rosaria a kiss. Rosaria chuckled.

"You should be mindful of your reputation, Donna Rosaria," she called reprovingly.

"At my age, Donna Poldina, one doesn't have anything left to lose, time least of all."

Poldi could see her point. She left the pair in the back to hold hands and canoodle to their hearts' content and now looked forward to visiting the temples of Agrigento. Perhaps they would provide her with a nice mise-en-scène in which to stage a dramatic demise.

I sometimes picture this strange quartet: Poldi in her wig and red dress, a naked, inebriated Finn with a huge hare on his lap and two centenarians necking in the back of a battered Maserati. I see them as being happy at that moment — happy and reconciled to the life that had brought them ebb and flow, given them children, lovers and material possessions, and taken them away again. I see them as being grateful to fate for bringing them together that day in an old Maserati, ready to watch my Auntie Poldi picturesquely throw herself off the roof of the Temple of Concordia.

But — you've guessed it — Sicily is complicated; something always intervenes. This time it was the violet Lamborghini, which appeared from out of nowhere, so fast and squat and sinister that all Poldi saw was a violet shape flash past like a metallic god of vengeance. Then the Lamborghini's brake lights flashed and it skidded to a halt across the road. Poldi saw at once that she hadn't a hope of getting past.

"Hold tight!"

She slammed on the brakes and crashed the gearstick into reverse. Unfortunately, it now became clear that the sensitive sports car had suffered from its recent rough treatment, because apart from an ugly crunching noise and a smell of burnt oil, nothing happened. The Maserati refused to budge.

They were stuck.

Trapped.

"What's wrong?" asked Rosaria.

"End of the line," said Poldi.

Ahead of them, she saw Handsome Antonio get out. He really was very good-looking, she had to admit. Jeans, white shirt, shades. His outfit was as casual as the way he strolled towards her, cocking the .44 Magnum as he came and levelling it at her.

"Where is it?" he called.

"Where is what?" asked Gaetano.

"It doesn't matter," Poldi said in a low voice. "I don't have a clue where it is."

Handsome Antonio was quite close now.

"Where. Is. It?"

Then Poldi had another light-bulb moment and everything became quite clear to her. The context. Handsome Antonio. The photo. She heard a door close at the end of a passage and, all of a sudden, she knew.

What she had overlooked.

Who had killed Thomas.

Where the attaché case was.

She sighed when she realised how obtuse and self-satisfied she must have been, but none of that mattered any more. She had thoroughly messed up. She deserved no better. Abandoning all hope, she shut her eyes.

"*Namaste,* life. The rest of the world can kiss my arse."

14

Tells of reality and magic, honey traps, seeking and finding, sacks of rice and miracles. And of men again, of course — seven men, to be precise. Poldi changes her method of transport, has to improvise again and loses her temper. Her nephew makes coffee, and Handsome Antonio gets sick of messing around.

The mechanism of the human brain is genuinely odd. It can rattle, click and purr along in a well-lubricated and uncomplaining fashion for a lifetime, cracking difficult problems; it can give a sudden squeak and seize up for good like a defective gear train; it can get stuck and have hiccups, cure itself and storm the supreme heights of knowledge. But one never knows when it will do any of these things. If well maintained it can reliably perform its function to the end, but it can't be forced. It goes its own convoluted way, and it sometimes, belatedly or too belatedly, spits out the answer to a problem, like a fortune-teller machine ejecting a little ticket with a prediction on it.

Click! Poldi's inner eye saw Inspector Chance shut his office door after work and toddle off, just as she herself was bidding farewell to life.

She had read somewhere that you don't hear the sound of the shot that kills you, because a bullet travels much faster than the sound of gunfire. So she simply waited a little before opening her eyes again, ready to enter the Great Light. To her astonishment, she found that events had got snarled up in some way. She was still sitting in the car with Pekka, Rosaria, Gaetano and Cesare, and Handsome Antonio was still standing there, gun in hand. Because something had intervened — namely, Cesare.

Any animal in the world enlarged to twenty times its normal size would look weird and spooky, genuinely nightmarish. With one exception. Rabbits can grow as big as they like, but they always remain what they are: cute. The very look of them beguiles and soothes us. Now multiply that effect by twenty.

Handsome Antonio just couldn't open fire. The sight of Cesare had pierced his heart and reminded him of Ludi, an Angora rabbit his father had brought him as a child. One glimpse of the enormous, peacefully nibbling hare beside Poldi and his soul underwent a sort of sugar rush. His killer instinct disengaged and knocked off for the day. Although he continued to point his gun at Poldi, he couldn't pull the trigger. He simply couldn't.

"Where is it?" was all he growled with an effort.

It took a moment for Poldi to catch on. Then her brain went into overdrive again. With a crash, she put the car into first and floored the accelerator. She drove onto the verge and past the Lamborghini without wasting another look on Handsome Antonio, who had been paralysed by an overdose of cuteness. The Maserati howled like a whipped cur, but Poldi now had to ask the utmost of it. It wouldn't be long before Handsome Antonio pulled himself together, so she turned off down the nearest side road, Martino fashion, and flogged the Maserati on along dusty farm tracks and bumpy secondary roads, hoping the car would hold out long enough.

Her passengers endured all this with remarkable equanimity. Perhaps it wasn't so surprising that two centenarians and a naked, inebriated Finn who had spent four days submerged in the Mediterranean — not to mention a giant hare — were not so easily fazed, even by a Mafia killer and a hell-for-leather drive across country. All that seemed in a bad way was the Maserati, which whimpered for mercy and rattled pitifully, and Poldi had a hard job changing gears.

Not until she felt relatively safe did she pull up beside the road and check her mobile phone. More precisely, the photos she had taken in recent days. As her light-bulb moment had disclosed, that was where the solution lay. It was so obvious, she groaned aloud.

"Aren't you feeling well, Donna Poldina?" asked Rosaria.

"On the contrary, Donna Rosaria. I'm a blithering idiot with a screw loose, but all's well in other respects."

"Believe me, Donna Poldina, I've known a lot of idiots in my life, and you don't qualify."

Poldi wondered what to do next. She realised she couldn't call Montana, because even if he arrested the murderer at once and secured the attaché case, she couldn't hand it over to the masked man. In other words, he would ruthlessly carry out his threat to kill her family one by one. So it was no use, she would have to clean up her own mess single-handed, go all the way and solve the case on her own.

She dropped the two ancient turtledoves and the giant hare at the entrance to Agrigento's temple precincts. The car park was deserted, the ticket window still shut.

"Not to worry, I know a secret path," said Gaetano, winking at Rosaria.

Cesare was already hopping busily around in the bushes.

Not far away Poldi could make out the Doric columns of the rebuilt corner of the Temple of the Dioscuri and those of the Temple of Hercules. She would sooner have gone for a walk there with her new friends than apprehend a murderer. She would have liked to sit for a while on one of the toppled columns and stroll through the Kolymbetra Garden, nor would she have said no to a nap in the shade of one of its two-thousand-year-old olive trees. As things were, though, she was bound elsewhere.

"How about you, Pekka?" she asked. "I could drop you in Agrigento."

Pekka shook his head. "I'm going to stay a bit longer. It's nice here. I may never leave."

I can visualise Poldi in that car park. I see her changing into an outfit appropriate to the occasion, slipping into her camouflage-pattern trouser suit. I see her looking a trifle sad as she drives off and sees her strange new friends waving goodbye in the rear-view mirror. I see her now in full hunting mode, devoid of a definite plan but determined to head for Thomas's murderer, because she now has barely a day in which to call the masked man's number and hand over the attaché case. I see her flogging the wheezing Maserati onwards and entreating it to hold out a bit longer. I see her driving along roads powdered with cement dust, through the sulphurous smoke from the factories flanking them, past pathetic little roadside fruit stalls and a deserted, garishly decorated Luna Park. Past rubbish dumps bathed in an unreal February light replete with contrasts, and through desolate towns where fat men wearing fanny packs leer at her and lick their lips. But I visualise lots of things when I'm bored, so I may be wrong.

What I do know is that Poldi didn't get far. Only as far as Palma di Montechiaro, or less than thirty kilometres. Russo's Maserati was groaning in agony, so she turned off perforce to Palma, to rustle up some new form of transport. Not far from the baroque Chiesa Madre in the Piazza Duomo, with a loud bang and an oily farewell from the gearbox, the Maserati finally gave up the ghost. It did so immediately opposite the Madonna del Castello bar, where I was sitting in the warm February sunlight with my third espresso and my second cigarette.

Palma di Montechiaro is a small town situated on a hill between Agrigento and Gela. It has an historic old quarter, the baroque church and the usual architectural eyesores round about. Lampedusa described the place in his novel *The Leopard,* and some scenes from Visconti's film of the book were shot there. Little of this Bourbon romanticism remains, however. The old quarter is in a dilapidated condi, its signs of decay universal but not picturesque. Although Palma is filled with light, it makes a more forbidding impression than any other Sicilian town I know.

Very, very bad vibes, I felt. I had taken a few photos and been promptly bawled at by an irate old man in a peaked cap. The dark energy I had failed to sense in Corleone seemed all the more oppressive here. Not a good place, so I was planning to leave Palma di Montechiaro behind as soon as possible. But then, thanks to my Auntie Poldi, everything turned out differently again.

I admit it: my aunt's expression, when she

caught sight of me, chilled me like a glass of ice-cold almond milk on an August afternoon. She stared at me as if I were a ghost or a hallucination. Then she pulled herself together, adjusted her wig in the rear-view mirror, got out of the car and sat down beside me.

"You've got some explaining to do," she said.

Fortified by my new-found sang-froid, I took my time. I sipped my espresso and mashed out my cigarette before replying.

"I took a leaf out of your book," I said. "Intuition and improvisation."

"Pure chance, in other words."

I sighed. "I was really worried about you, Poldi — shit-scared, in fact — but fortunately you left a bit of a trail. I asked about ten million people if they'd seen a red Maserati. I've hardly slept for the past two days, just been driving around looking for you. I was in Erice, and before that I came across those mourners in Selinunte. They told me that the old signora you abducted got to know her husband Angelo in Palma di Montechiaro and might want to go back there. Where did you leave her, actually?"

Poldi shrugged. "Long story." She beckoned the waiter and ordered a double grappa. "Where did you leave Martino?"

"He wanted to stay in Gibellina. He liked it there."

"And how did *you* get here?"

I pointed to a brightly painted Ape, or "bee," one of those typically Italian three-wheeled delivery vans with a two-stroke engine. I had swapped Olga's T-shirt for it with a Goblinhammer fan in Gibellina.

Poldi gave it an admiring nod, then turned to me. "You're looking smart."

This was an allusion to my new outfit. Having left my bag behind in Gibellina in the rush to get away, I'd hurriedly kitted myself out in Trapani. For obvious reasons, I had adapted my style to the mission. I was wearing a dark suit, a black shirt and black sneakers. I was also wearing shades. Combined with the plaster on my nose, they made me look incredibly sinister.

"Thanks," I said. "Your turn now."

"I know who the murderer is and who's got the attaché case."

"Cool. Who?"

"I can't tell you that for certain reasons. Just give me the key to the Ape. I need to move on fast."

"Forget it, Poldi. Start talking or you're out."

She snorted indignantly. "You realise you're impeding a murder investigation, don't you?"

But she wasn't going to get off so lightly, not after all that had happened.

"Why did you run out on us in Gibellina?" I demanded. "Because we were too much of a nuisance? Two useless appendages? Because you wanted to solve the case in glorious isolation?"

I may have been a little bit too caustic. At all events, my Auntie Poldi's expression when she looked at me was a blend of anger and melancholy.

"No," she hissed. "Because I wanted to be alone when I killed myself."

And then she told me the whole awful truth. I listened to her aghast while she sank a second double grappa, and a third. She eyed me oddly when she'd finished, almost as if she expected me to burst into tears or something. Instead, I came out with what had been bottled up inside me for the past couple of days.

"Are you out of your mind?" I yelled at her. "What is all this shit!"

"Hey, calm down."

"No, I won't calm down, I'm just beginning to get worked up. You're damn well going to listen to me for once. Maybe you *are* entitled to piss off out of *your* life. But not out of *ours.* You've no right to kill yourself without reference to other people!"

"But I was doing it for your sake!"

"Bullshit, Poldi! You didn't consult us. I thought we were a team. I genuinely believed that, but when it comes down to it, you're no better than all the males you're always complaining about. You always do *your* thing."

"He was going to kill you all. I had no choice."

"I don't care, haven't you got that? My God, I'd need a change of underwear if it were all true, but the threat itself makes me very angry. I've had the time of my life this past week, and I want to see it through to the end, don't you understand? Besides," I added, swallowing hard, "I don't want to lose you." It's possible my eyes watered a little just then, but luckily I was wearing the shades. My voice went a trifle husky, however. "Even though you're an egotistical cow's arse!" I managed to add.

There was nothing more to say. I fumbled another cigarette out of the packet.

Poldi chuckled. "Cow's arse. I like that."

"Bully for you."

She looked at me again, and this time there was something akin to genuine admiration in her expression. "Well, well," she said softly, "seems our Sancho Panza has turned into a Don Quixote."

I made no comment.

I did have a question, though. "Why didn't you manage to . . . ? You know."

She turned her face to the sun. "Well, you know. Sicily is complicated."

I nodded. "Something always intervenes."

She smiled at me. "Friends again?"

I rolled my eyes. And before I knew what was happening, Poldi had hugged me so tightly and planted such a smacking kiss on my cheek that I couldn't breathe and my ears rang. I guess that meant we were a team again.

"What do you plan to do now?"

"I need to get hold of that attaché case, there's no alternative. Do you still have the card?"

I fished it out of my pocket and handed it to her.

"Hang on to it for now. We'll use it to create a honey trap. And then — snap! — we'll spring it."

"Er . . . is that all your plan consists of?"

"You think it's silly?"

I refrained from commenting.

"But first," Poldi went on regardless, "there's something else we must do."

She paid, rose and strode resolutely up the steps of the Chiesa Madre, which, like

387

the church in Torre Archirafi, is dedicated to Santa Maria del Rosario. There she lit a candle, thanked the Lord that she was still alive and asked Peppe to forgive her for keeping him waiting a bit longer.

"*Namaste,*" she said in conclusion, bowing with her hands clasped together.

"Kiss my arse and hope to die," I said, and promptly earned myself a cuff on the head.

"Quiet! This is a church!"

We returned to the bar, where the defunct Maserati and my bargain Ape were parked.

"What are we going to do with poor old Rosinante?"

"We'll worry about that later. We need to lock it, that's all."

We closed the Maserati's doors and Poldi locked them securely. We are Germans, after all.

We had only just turned away and taken a few steps towards my colourful Ape when all hell broke loose.

The Maserati exploded behind us with a thunderous roar. Simultaneously, the blast wave knocked us off our feet. I think I even became briefly airborne, because I came down hard on the cobbles. I saw Poldi land flat-out on the ground in front of me and go rolling over and over like tumbleweed.

Curiously, what puzzled me most was that her wig continued to cling to her head like a limpet. Deafened by the explosion, I rolled over on my side and saw that it was powerful enough to have hurled the Maserati across the street. Flames and smoke were rising from its shattered remains.

I crawled over to Poldi and shouted something. She shouted something back, but I couldn't understand a word. All I could hear was a shrill ringing in my ears.

Her trouser suit was torn, her forehead was scratched, and her wig looked like storm-tossed black candy-floss, but she seemed otherwise unscathed. She pointed down the street.

When I turned to look, I saw Handsome Antonio coming towards us. He was holding an automatic rifle, which he cocked. I helped Poldi to her feet and we ran like hares. I don't know if Antonio fired at us because I couldn't hear a thing. Miraculously, the Ape was undamaged. The blast wave had only propelled it a little way up the street. I opened the side door and squeezed into the tiny cabin. Poldi thrust me aside, took the wheel and started the engine. The Ape swerved around like an inebriated duck. A very, very slow inebriated duck. I could see Handsome Antonio sprinting after us in the rear-view mirror. As bad luck would have it, our escape route ran uphill. Poldi screwed away at the throttle like mad, but our pursuer drew ever nearer. Eventually he took a chance and lunged. The Ape gave a lurch. Antonio had managed to grab the flatbed but failed to haul himself aboard. We were virtually towing him along.

"Poldi!" I heard myself bellow above the ringing in my ears.

Instead of replying, she swung the wheel this way and that. This made the Ape swerve even more violently, but I got the point of it: she was trying to unload our unwanted ballast. Give the devil his due, Handsome Antonio was tenacious. But when we reached a black dumpster a little farther on, *finita la commedia.* With a hilarious *boing* sound, Handsome Antonio collided with the dumpster and finally let go. The Ape gave a relieved lurch and puttered on up the street.

I raised my hand in preparation for a high five, but Poldi merely shook her head at me and said something. Judging by the movement of her lips, it might have been either "Wait!" or "Wanker!" Both would have been equally right, because a professional killer doesn't give up, especially when he's feeling sore. Before we knew it, the Lamborghini was on our tail. It came racing up behind us, rammed us and shoved us uphill. Then it slowed down briefly and rammed us again. The Ape started to corkscrew. It was only a matter of time before we were tipped over.

"Poldi!" I shouted, panic-stricken.

I could hear quite well again by now.

"You're repeating yourself!" she shouted back. Then she did what she did best: she improvised. "Take over for a moment!"

I took the wheel. For her part, Poldi put her head out of the side window and whipped off her wig. I couldn't see, I swear, I was too busy driving. I may have caught a glimpse of something out of the corner of my eye, but I'm not quite sure.

The surprise coup worked. Clearly flummoxed by the sight of Poldi without her wig, Handsome Antonio took his foot off the gas and the Lamborghini fell back. Poldi didn't hesitate for an instant. She clapped her wig back on, grabbed the wheel and turned left down the nearest alleyway, which was too narrow to admit the Lambo. We raced along it, bore right, then made a 90-degree turn. It was like riding one of those retro Wild Mouse rollercoasters. I saw a descending flight of steps ahead of us, but instead of pulling up, Poldi pressed on and sent the

Ape juddering down them. We were shaken around like dice and I hit my head on the roof. Once at the bottom, Poldi swung the wheel round and rattled off at full speed down another alleyway.

"We must dump the Ape!" I yelled.

"We wouldn't stand a chance on foot!" Poldi yelled back. "No, we need a bolthole!"

She sent our gallant little flatbed zigzagging along the narrowest possible side streets and out of town. The buildings became sparser, and fields and hills overgrown with wild *macchia* came into view. Poldi took a farm track leading upwards, but it eventually ended in an old stone wall. All that lay beyond this was more *macchia,* but farther up the hill, amid thorn bushes and wild cacti, stood a house. A small, decrepit, pink-washed farmhouse, it stood all by itself on a little knoll. The windows were boarded up.

"That'll do," cried Poldi.

We pushed the Ape behind the stone wall, where it would at least be invisible from the road, and set off up the hill. It was quite a strenuous climb, I must say. The *macchia* was as dense as Sleeping Beauty's bramble hedge. We scratched our hands, tore our clothes and made slow progress. At some stage Poldi decided it would be wiser to crawl, because we would do better beneath the bushes than above them. Her theory was a new one on me, but we really did go a bit faster. The only thing was, I ripped my pants and scratched my face and hands more often. No matter, we got to the farmhouse and, guess what, it was locked. Boarded up, bolted and barred. The chunky padlock on the only door seemed to sneer at us. I gave the door handle a rather half-hearted shake.

"OK," I said, ever practical. "Being a secret agent and a pro, you're bound to be carrying some cool gizmo from the special equipment lab."

"Uh-uh," said Poldi.

"Wire? Hairpin? Plastic explosive?"

She shook her head.

I sighed.

Poldi stared grimly at the door. "I do have one thing," she growled. "I've got a temper. A foul, stinking, God-awful temper."

Before I could say "Er . . ." she took two steps back, gathered her strength and launched herself at the door. As though fired from a cannon, she shot towards it with all the momentum born of her naturally opulent figure and elemental Bavarian rage. She was virtually antimatter condensed into unadulterated fury.

"HOOOAAAHHH!"

She leapt into the air, turned once on her own axis and struck the door's solar plexus with such a well-aimed kung-fu kick that the ground shook. Momentum is mass times speed times rage, and my Auntie Poldi combined all three. She positively detonated — to be honest, she frightened me. Anyone seeing her in that state would have had to include her in disarmament talks. Smitten by her apocalyptic, Poldian momentum, the door gave way with a crash.

"Er . . ." I said.

Poldi pushed the door wide open and peered into the little house. Its single room was sparsely furnished with a crude wooden table, four chairs, a washstand, a gas cooker, some crockery and an unmade camp bed. Clearly, it had once been a billet for seasonal field hands. The only thing that puzzled me was the faint smell of coffee, but I gave it no further thought.

Poldi found the house a perfect bolthole. She operated the number-withholding function on her mobile phone and sent the murderer a text message:

We know everything All we want is the case
$10 million

Deal must be clinched today
or you bite the dust
FOR HANDOVER SEE LOCATION

Having sent the message together with the GPS coordinates of our location, she gave me a contented smile.

"All we have to do now is wait."

"You do realise we're unarmed, don't you?"

"Poor baby," she said.

So much for her plan. However, and it goes against the grain to repeat this, Sicily is complicated. Something always intervenes. In Poldi's case, a statistically significant cluster of handsome Antonios.

I'd found half a packet of coffee and some stale almond biscuits in a tin. I had just got some out for us when the door burst open and Handsome Antonio charged in with his assault rifle at the ready. And that was finally that. We were caught in our own trap.

Which brought us back to my nightmare, or rather, to the original outline of the dream which, in a slightly dramatised and heavily filtered version, wakes me up with a start every night. For reality — need I say this? — is always far more sordid, colourless and commonplace than any dream or memory or novel. Reality smells of sweat and has coffee stains on its vest. Reality means pleas for mercy, stammering attempts to alter a course of events that has long been decreed by fate. Reality means too many words and too little influence. Reality means an absence of magic. I don't like reality, least of all one in which I'm menaced with an assault rifle while sitting beside my aunt secured to a chair with duct tape. I don't like reality when it means that someone brandishes a huge fish cleaver under my nose and yells at me. But I had no choice.

Handsome Antonio was sick of messing around. Poldi had given him the slip again and again for nearly a week, but now he'd caught her. He'd caught both of us. He had taken off his nice white shirt for fear of blood spatter and was wearing only his fine-rib tank top with the coffee stain on it. The little farmhouse was one of his numerous boltholes, it seemed.

Great, I thought, and cursed myself for not having followed up my strange feeling about the smell of coffee. But of course, one is always wiser after the event.

Handsome Antonio had been grilling us for hours. The unproductive quiz between him and Poldi had bred irascibility on both sides and led to a shouting match in Bavarian and Sicilian. I was so scared I nearly wet myself, but then I saw Poldi giving Handsome Antonio the eye, and that was when I, too, had had enough.

"Shut up!" I yelled. "*Basta!* Cut it out! Calm down, the pair of you!"

I felt incredibly cool, what with my tattered man-in-black outfit, the plaster on my broken nose and my sudden brainwave, which was to act as the voice of reason. *You're a cool dude,* I told myself, *an expert at empathetic negotiation.*

Handsome Antonio didn't share my opinion.

"Balls," he said wearily. "You're just stringing me along. You really don't have a clue where it is, either of you." Then he pointed the cleaver at my aunt. "All right, shut your eyes."

He drew back his arm and brought the blade whistling down.

Did I already mention that Sicily is complicated and that something always intervenes? In this case it was beauty. The beauty of Sicily and the magic of this remarkable island, with which I've often been at odds. Handsome Antonio had too, perhaps, but he had just become infected with the beauty of Sicily and recognised himself as part of it. He drew back his arm and the cleaver came whistling down, but it missed.

Handsome Antonio eyed us wearily with the fish cleaver hanging loose at his side. "I can't," he said dully. "I can't kill any more."

Poldi gazed at him, oozing with compassion. "You don't have to, Antonio," she said in Italian.

"Yes, I do. It's my profession, but I just can't do it any more. This morning, when I saw that hare, I still thought it was just a phase. A kind of hay fever that would pass. But I simply can't kill, not any longer."

"What happened?"

He subsided onto a chair. It didn't occur to him to release us, though.

"I was supposed to hand that case over to Thomas. A simple job. The most important rule in a job like that is never to look at the goods. But I opened the case and it changed me. It changed Thomas, too. We suddenly saw this island with different eyes. It's so beautiful. So . . ." He struggled to find the words.

"Magical," Poldi whispered softly.

"Yes, magical. Exactly. I've driven around a lot these past few months. Nobody stopped me, the police took no interest in me. I've seen miraculous things. The latest was that great big hare this morning."

Poldi nodded. She knew a thing or two

about magic and miracles.

"All I wanted was to get that case back and keep it. But Thomas was killed and the case disappeared."

He lapsed into a gloomy silence.

"What happens now?" Poldi asked quietly.

Handsome Antonio shrugged his shoulders. "I can't let you go." He picked up his assault rifle and eyed it sadly. "I must straighten myself out."

Bang! At that moment the splintered wooden door flew open and the next handsome Antonio burst in. He was holding a Walther P99 in one hand and a black leather attaché case in the other.

"Freeze!"

This handsome Antonio was wearing a peculiar outfit: colourful hiker's gear. It made him look like a bit of a nerd.

He had clearly counted on something else when he burst in with his gun, because he stopped short and looked mystified on seeing Poldi and me taped to chairs, not to mention the other handsome Antonio, who leapt to his feet at once and pointed the rifle at him.

"Good God, what are you doing here, Poldi?"

"Who are you?" yelled the first Antonio.

The two handsome Antonios menaced

each other with their guns over our heads. My short-lived sense of relief at the favourable turn of events evaporated like a bead of moisture on a hotplate.

"May I do the honours?" Poldi asked serenely. "Antonio, Mafioso and killer, meet Antonio, brigadiere and ditto. How nice of you to come, Antonio, and bring the case with you."

The two men glared at each other.

"What's he doing here?" demanded Mafia Antonio.

"He's brought the case," said Poldi. "He killed Thomas and hung on to it."

"Let's see!" cried Mafia Antonio.

The policeman held it up, then slowly put it down on the table. Tightening his grip on the pistol, he continued to level it at the first Antonio.

"How did you find out?" he asked Poldi, never taking his eyes off the Mafioso.

"I almost missed it," Poldi said calmly. "I had secretly taken a picture of you in Sant'Alfio. In it you were wearing a flashy silver ring with a flat blue stone. Thomas was wearing the same ring in a selfie which another very nice Antonio took recently."

The handsome policeman frowned. "I should have thought of that."

Poldi stared at him. "Why, Antonio? Why

did Thomas have to die?"

He spoke without looking at her. "I caught him burying the case under the old chestnut tree. I was going to arrest him, but he begged me to forget the whole thing. He showed me what was in the case and offered to go halves. And, well . . . I liked him. I took him home with me. He told me so much about himself, about Tanzania and his dreams. And then . . . then he kissed me." The handsome brigadiere paused. "He spent three days with me. I took some time off and we never left the house. I fell in love with him."

"But then he wanted to leave, didn't he?"

"I caught him trying to make off with the case. So I snapped."

"And because you learned how to gut fish in your parents' shop, and because Thomas had told you about Kigumbe and *muti,* you tried to make it look like a ritual murder. But it preyed on your mind, didn't it?"

The policeman nodded wearily.

"You used me, Antonio," Poldi said in a low voice. "You're a dirty dog, you know that?"

"That's enough!" cried Mafia Antonio. "Hand over that case!"

The handsome brigadiere shook his head. "Drop your gun or I'll shoot you," he said.

The situation was becoming messy, I thought, but it became positively Byzantine when, a moment later, three men burst in brandishing Uzis and yelling in English. Two beefy young toughs and a somewhat older black man, they all wore dark suits.

"Freeze! Drop your guns at once! Over against the wall!"

The two Antonios spun round and levelled their weapons at the intruders. Five men were now confronting one another, jaw muscles twitching.

I shut my eyes.

"What a surprise," I heard Poldi say. "But I'd be lying if I called it a pleasure, Mr. Kigumbe."

That promptly piqued my curiosity. I opened my eyes and stared at the oldest of the three newcomers. I couldn't help thinking of all the horror stories Poldi had told me about him.

"I merely want my property back, Mamma Poldi," he said in a voice to rival Paul Robeson's. "No one need die today if I get that case."

"The case belongs to me!"

"No, to me."

What a mess, I thought in despair. What an unutterable mess. We're up shit creek. It's hopeless.

And that was when the next participants in this drama arrived on the scene. *Bang!* As though on cue, another two men burst into the house brandishing guns. Poldi knew them only too well.

"Hands up! You're surrounded, so drop your weapons and freeze!"

"Vito!" Poldi said. "John!"

Vito Montana and John Owenya made an incongruous but thoroughly cinematic pair of cops. Grasping their guns two-handed, they each covered a segment of the room.

This meant that the two handsome Antonios, a Tanzanian crime boss and his two bodyguards, plus two detective inspectors were all menacing each other with single- or double-action semi- or fully automatic weapons. All being pros, they knew that the slightest false move — even a twitch or the bat of an eyelid — could unleash an inferno of gunfire, but none of them wanted to be the first to lower his weapon. A chaos-theory researcher might laconically have labelled the situation "highly unstable" and delivered a lecture on the causal relationship of Amazonian butterflies to Indian thunderstorms, or toppling Chinese rice sacks to worldwide economic crises. And in the middle of the whole shemozzle: an attaché case, my Auntie Poldi and me.

In such situations the brain takes in curious details, possibly to distract itself from the imminent prospect of being riddled with bullets. I, for example, noticed that the house was pervaded by a pungent smell suggestive of a dead rat somewhere under the floorboards.

"What are *you* doing here, Vito?" Poldi demanded.

"*Madonna,* Poldi!" Montana said. "Did you honestly think you could get away with swanning around Sicily in a stolen Maserati and a stolen patrol car, just like that?"

"Vito and I have been tailing you for days," said John. "Ever since Russo reported that the Maserati had been stolen."

"Oh," said Poldi. "So it was *you* in the black Toyota?"

Montana did not reply. He was entirely focused on the current stand-off. "Now, we're all going to lower our weapons, very slowly"

Sadly, no one complied.

Instead, a sack of rice fell over. Metaphorically speaking, I mean.

To recap: When Handsome Antonio burst into the house, I had just put some coffee on to percolate. I had filled the old aluminium *caffettiera* with a generous measure of coffee, tamped it down good and hard, and put the pot on the gas. In chaos-theory terms, I had thereby rendered the situation even more unstable. Why? Because an overly tamped-down filter holder and a clogged safety valve are a disastrous combination.

When the *caffettiera* exploded with a loud report, everyone let fly. All seven men fired wildly at each other, creating a diabolical din more ear-splitting than the preceding explosion. Within seconds the room was filled with a cloud of gun smoke so dense that no one could see a thing. It smelt as if an entire city were celebrating on New Year's Eve. Coughing violently, I shut my eyes. The seven men continued to blaze away, with Poldi and me still pinned down in no-man's-land.

But silence fell at last — apart, of course, from a loud ringing in the ears. The first thing I saw when I opened my eyes was Poldi looking at me thunderstruck and saying something. Then I saw the cloud of dense grey gun smoke drifting sluggishly out the doorway. Visible in that cloud were seven figures, still on their feet with their empty weapons at the ready, staring at one another in amazement.

In amazement, because we were all still alive.

15

Tells of the relativity of the laws of nature, of buddies, transposed digits, Orpheus, men and the Aeolian Islands. Poldi appropriates something and grasps the surrounding circumstances. Her nephew reads himself to a standstill and relieves himself of a burden. Poldi goes on holiday, but before doing so she takes her nephew on a short trip to return something to an old friend.

I must correct what I said earlier about the relationship of reality to magic. Reality is full of magic. One has to want to see it, that's all.

The seven men didn't move. They simply couldn't believe the unbelievable. They had emptied their magazines at each other and were still alive. The floor was littered with cartridge cases. Still drifting sluggishly out the door, the gun smoke had now cleared sufficiently to disclose that the walls were riddled with bullets. By rights, according to the laws of nature and the dictates of common sense, we should also have been perforated with bullets and dead as mutton. But we weren't. We were still alive.

The handsome brigadiere was the first to drop his gun and leave the premises without a word, like a schoolboy sent home after a severe reprimand. Mafia Antonio did likewise, and Kigumbe and his two bodyguards also left this scene of a miracle in silence. John followed them out.

But Montana hurried over to us. He freed first Poldi and then me from our duct tape restraints. Poldi flung her arms around his neck and smothered him in kisses.

"You came!" she cried. "You found the steel tower!"

I hadn't a clue what she was talking about, so I tactfully turned to go.

When I emerged from the house I saw a helicopter, or rather, two helicopters. No, three. Two of them were hovering just above the ground outside the house, and the third was circling not far above it. I supposed they belonged to the Italian military. What looked like the rest of the Italian army was working its way up the hill towards the house, together with Sicily's entire complement of policemen. I saw them arrest the two Antonios and the three Tanzanians. Unsurprisingly, since they were now unarmed, they offered no resistance.

I watched the whole proceedings like a movie as I filled my lungs with fresh air, delighted with my rebirth and the fact that the ringing in my ears was gradually subsiding. I hadn't gone deaf after all.

John caught sight of me. Grinning broadly, he came over and shook my hand. "You must be the untalented nephew," he said in English. "Only joking," he added when he saw my expression. "Hi, I'm John Owenya. What happened to your nose?"

Montana and Poldi came out of the house a moment later, Poldi carrying the attaché case as if it were the most natural thing in the world. Just as naturally, Montana and John bumped fists.

It transpired that they had taken up the chase after Russo informed Montana that Poldi had stolen the Maserati. Montana and John had been working together far more closely than Poldi had suspected, but in the course of the trip they had become genuine buddies. Poldi merely rolled her eyes when they told her what a good time they'd had together and what man-to-man talks they'd had about guess who.

"But how did you two comedians always manage to find me again when I kept giving you the slip?"

The two policemen exchanged a look that said they weren't sure they ought to tell her. Then, bravely but gently taking hold of her wig, John dug around in it and withdrew something that looked like a small button with a whisker of wire protruding from it.

"You discovered the GPS tracker," he explained, "but not this miniature tracking device. It doesn't have much of a range, but we always managed to pick up a signal after a bit of toing and froing."

I didn't really take all this in. John loaded me into one of the choppers, which dropped me at Catania Airport, where Uncle Martino and Totti were expecting me and drove me to my cousin Ciro's. I heard nothing from Poldi for three days, but I didn't mind. I had plenty on my mind, and to be honest, I'd had my fill of her and her dramatics. On the morning of the third day, however, she called me.

"Everything OK?"

"So-so."

"Like to drop in? I've got something to show you."

"To be honest, Poldi, I —"

"God Almighty! Borrow Ciro's car and

get over here or I'll put a firecracker under you!"

Poldi had also done a lot of thinking in the previous three days. Mainly about the attaché case, which was lying on the coffee table in her living room like some artefact from an extraterrestrial civilisation. Montana had initially wanted to take it away from her, since it was a piece of evidence. But after his new buddy John had taken him aside for a moment, he frowned and let her keep it without inquiring further.

Vito had changed, Poldi thought. Somehow he made a less uptight impression on her. He made no mention of the miracle in the little farmhouse, almost as if all concerned would instantly drop dead if he did. It was as if that miracle were a Pandora's box to be locked and buried forevermore.

Poldi's handcuffing of the two carabinieri in San Vito lo Capo and her theft of their patrol car had naturally caused some feathers to fly, but since it was a pretty embarrassing business and the results spoke for themselves, Montana had succeeded in getting it swept under the carpet.

Poldi's remaining problem was the attaché case. No member of her family had hitherto died under suspicious circumstances, but every time she looked at the slip of paper bearing the masked man's number, it seemed to whisper, "I'm not waiting much longer."

She now knew the contents of the case, so she also knew its value and, above all, its importance. She was uninterested in its financial value, but in the wrong hands its contents could seriously harm an old friend. And as Poldi saw it, no hands could be more wrong than the masked man's. In short, she was in a cleft stick. She knew she should act but could see no solution.

On the evening of the second day, when she went to the kitchen to get a bottle of beer from the fridge, Death was running himself a glass of water at the sink. His clipboard with the list attached was lying upside down on the counter.

"Make yourself at home, why don't you?" said Poldi.

"No probs," Death said in his nasal voice, holding a finger under the tap. "Not cold enough yet. I like it cold as the grave."

"Who'd have thought it?"

He refused to be ruffled. "I know you're mad at me, Poldi, but it just wasn't your turn."

"It's all right."

Death filled his glass at last, took a sip

and turned back to her. "Can't we be friends again?"

Poldi cast her eyes up to heaven. "If you insist."

He beamed at her. "Something silly happened to me recently."

"Oh?"

"I made a boo-boo. Got some numbers the wrong way round. It doesn't happen to me often, but I'm afraid it's a done deal now — can't be changed."

"What are you getting at?"

"Well, somebody had to depart this life before his time." He took the latest edition of *La Sicilia* from the kitchen table and tapped the front page.

It carried a full-page black-and-white photo of a very well-known politician who had helped to govern the destiny of Italy for decades, founded political parties and driven them into the ground, and owned numerous companies. Sicilian by birth, he had twice been premier of Italy but had retired from politics years ago in order to avoid prosecution for corruption and links with the Mafia. Poldi had never liked him, and now he was dead. She hadn't taken any notice of this news report throughout the day, but now, as she studied the photograph more closely, the scales fell from her eyes. It was the masked man!

She gave Death a searching stare. "I see. A mix-up, was it?"

He shrugged apologetically, making a supreme effort to look remorseful. "A slip of the pencil. Silly of me, but what's done is done."

"I hope you didn't get into trouble."

He shook his head. "Not to worry. We have a, er . . . subsection in the firm. They'd long been expecting him."

Before Death knew it, Poldi had clasped him to her bosom in an almost suffocating embrace. *"Namaste,"* she said softly.

All the time she'd been telling me this, I had been staring at the case that had caused the whole shemozzle.

The house was hushed and smelt rather strongly of . . . dead mouse.

"Where's John?" I asked, breaking the silence.

"Back in Arusha, making out charges against Kigumbe. But first the crime boss is facing a serious charge here in Sicily." Poldi sipped her Prosecco.

I noticed that she had cut down on her drinking again.

"John gave me back his cheque, by the way, but I've already put the money into a trust fund. As soon as little Antonino from Sant'Alfio reaches the age of eighteen, it should be enough to help him study art in Florence or Paris."

"Apropos of money," I said, and tossed the black plastic card on the table like a stolen nuclear fuel cell to be disposed of before it irradiates everyone.

"No, hang on to it," Poldi decreed. "We'll worry about it later."

Reluctantly, I put it back in my pocket. "What about the other two Antonios?"

"They'll probably get life," Poldi said happily. "It happened the way the brigadiere said: he fell for Thomas and killed him when he tried to vamoose. The head, the hands, the heart and the . . . well, you know — they were in a plastic bag in the deep freezer in his parents' seafood shop. He couldn't do much with the attaché case, which was why he reacted at once when I offered him a deal."

"Why did Thomas come looking for you?"

She threw up her hands. "I don't know. Maybe he simply meant to ask for my help. You know, to return the case to its owner. When he failed to find me, he tried to park it somewhere for a while, and then — well, everything went wrong."

I nodded. "What did Russo say about the

Maserati?"

"He wasn't very happy, as you can imagine, but he didn't make a big fuss in the end because he'd used me too. Little Toni Amato had spilt the beans and told him I wanted to steal a car, and Russo thought to himself, Let her, then she'll lead me to this valuable attaché case everyone's after. That was why he had me watched for weeks, the dirty dog. Those new neighbours, remember? They were his people, but he'd only just withdrawn them when the masked man organised a break-in and the theft of my address book. Russo was really bugged by that."

From the look of it, we had been the unwitting quarry of any number of people. Nevertheless, we had experienced one miracle after another, so I now asked the question that had kept me awake for the past three nights.

"How did we survive that gunfight, Poldi?"

"You mean you still haven't caught on?"

"Er, no. By rights we should be dead."

"Smell that attaché case."

I bent forward, sniffed the leather case and promptly recoiled.

"Ugh! So that's why it reeks in here!"

"I told you some of the *muti* medicines stink to high heaven. Yes, you see now, don't you? This was Kigumbe's case, and he had it protected with a *muti* spell."

"And you think . . ."

"Well, the case was lying right in the middle of the room during that gunfight. If you've got a better explanation, I'm listening."

I shook my head in bewilderment. "I still don't believe it."

She shrugged. "Then don't."

"And what did he put in the —"

"Believe me, you don't want to know."

I went on staring at the case.

Poldi looked at me expectantly.

"God Almighty," she sighed eventually. "Go on, or do you need a special invitation?"

No, I did not. I turned the case to face me, snapped the combo locks and opened it.

My immediate reaction was one of disappointment. Heaven knows what I'd expected to see. Something mysterious, a prehistoric relic, a magical amulet, a mini–nuclear reactor, a laser gun, a four-dimensional object, a huge diamond or at least the Holy Grail.

What the case did in fact contain, embedded in polystyrene foam, was a thick wad of printed, spiral-bound paper. A manuscript. There was no author's name. All that appeared on the uppermost page, printed in 12-point Courier, the commonest of all typefaces, was the title: BECOMING ITAL-IAN.

It meant nothing to me.

"Well, take it out," Poldi told me.

I removed the manuscript from its plastic foam surround and riffled through it. It consisted of almost five hundred pages, in English, neatly printed with one-point-five-line spacing, paginated and adorned with occasional handwritten corrections.

"Is this all?" I asked.

Poldi smiled at me. "Read it by tomorrow, then we'll take it back."

I read the manuscript in one sitting, all through that day and night. In spite of its being in English, I positively devoured it. It told the story of a kind of Orpheus in the underworld, a singer named Anthony who was so handsome and talented that everyone loved him. Everyone came to hear him sing and succumbed to his charms, even animals, the sea and the rocks. The only person who failed to love him was himself. He dreaded getting older and losing his voice, so he fled from the world to a mythical land named Sicily, where he witnessed miracles and rediscovered beauty, his own true beauty included. In that mythical land he found what he was seeking: peace and quiet, pistachio ice cream and love.

I wept when I finished it. I had never read such a beautiful book — so beautiful, it hurt. I also wept with envy, I admit, because that manuscript had everything my own novel lacked: thrills, suspense, sensuality, believable characters, realism, lightness of touch, drama. I kept coming across ironic allusions to prominent contemporaries and satirical revelations involving uncomfortable truths about the entertainment industry, politics and the state of the world. The book told of seeking and finding, relinquishing and acquiring, eternal beauty and fleeting evanescence. It was filled with tenderness and sincerity, warmth and surprising twists and turns. It made all that I had experienced on my travels with Poldi seem meaningful and perfectly real. The book opened my eyes to Sicily, portraying the island as a living creature full of contradictions, passion and grace. No wonder it had charmed and changed Thomas and Handsome Antonio. Whoever had written it, I was amazed by the paucity of adjectives employed. The whole island buzzed and hummed like an insect, the October clouds clanged like discordant church bells. I might as well have chucked my half-baked family saga in the bin. I wound up feeling very small, but also fulfilled and happy to have been privileged to read the book. I was also eager to make the acquaintance of the author or authoress.

Early the next morning Poldi and I puttered off in Ciro's Fiat Panda, first towards Messina, then on to Milazzo. The manuscript reposed in a padded envelope bag on Poldi's lap; the attaché case we had burnt on the beach at Praiola.

Poldi wouldn't tell me our destination, but when we boarded the ferry at Milazzo I guessed we were bound for one of the Aeolian Islands. We sailed past Vulcano, which stank of sulphur, then past Lipari and Salina. The weather was fine and the dark-blue sea as calm as a soul at peace with itself. Poldi and I stood leaning on the rail in the bow, not speaking, just breathing in the salt air and catching a bit of a tan in the February sunlight.

"I've been thinking," I said after a while. "I may decide to write up your cases after all."

"You don't say!"

"But not till I'm through with my novel."

"Of course not. If you do, though, don't lay it on too thick. Make it nice and understated and believable, right? I want to come across as the authentic me. In other words, modest, level-headed and grounded, not a drama queen."

"Check."

"And don't leave out the sexy bits."

"How could I?"

She regarded me with amusement. "Got that black card with you?"

Of course I had. I could feel it weighing down my wallet all the time.

I took it out and handed it to her. "Here, take it."

"I don't want it."

"So what now?"

She shrugged her shoulders. "The fact is, the depositor has no access to the money and has long ago written it off as transfer charges, so you can do what you like with it. It belongs to you."

"Seriously?"

Poldi nodded. I looked at the card. Ten million dollars. Not exactly peanuts. Ten million units of purely negative energy. I drew back my arm and threw the card overboard. Poldi grinned at me.

I sometimes imagine that the card will be swallowed by a tuna and found by a fisherman smart enough to call the phone number and reel off the code. I hope it'll make him happy.

Poldi felt in her handbag for something to throw into the sea likewise. It was a bunch of envelopes with names on them, one of them mine. She tore them up one by one and allowed the breeze to carry them away.

I had assumed we were going all the way to Stromboli, with its small, still-active volcano, but after three hours we put in at Panarea, and Poldi said, "This is where we get off."

Panarea is regarded as the fancy-schmancy pearl of the Aeolian Islands because it's so popular with celebs and boasts some upmarket hotels and restaurants, though it looks as plain and simple as one of the Greek Cyclades. The only three centres of habitation on the eastern side of the island, Ditella, San Pietro and Drauto, look like a collection of big white building bricks. They seem to consist purely of light and shade and potted plants. The houses have blue doors and window frames, shady terraces and friendly inhabitants. There are hardly any cars because everything can easily be reached on foot or by bus.

Nevertheless, Poldi and I went ashore in Ciro's Panda. Poldi seemed to know her way around. She directed me from the harbour through San Pietro and then along a dirt road into a nature reserve in the middle of the island. We had to stop at a barrier with a guard's hut beside it. Poldi had a word with the guard, who made a brief phone call, and the barrier was raised to let us through. Soon we came to a long, densely overgrown ridge on the western side of the island. I had to drive with the utmost care because the narrow track led right along the top of the ridge, and the ground fell away sheer to the sea. We came to another guard's hut as we neared a house in the Aeolian style — it punctuated the end of the coastal cliffs like a white dot — but that guard also looked relaxed and merely gave us a casual salute. We were clearly expected.

As we neared the property I saw a woman with short, dark hair standing on the terrace, waving to us. She wasn't much older than me but looked more mature and relaxed than I am ever likely to be. Typically Sicilian in appearance, she wore a simple summer dress and was heavily tanned. She had put on a little weight, and it suited her the way life suits you when you've accepted it. I'd seen too many strange things in recent days to be surprised — in fact, I should have expected it.

When we reached the terrace, the woman flung her arms around Poldi and hugged her.

"Poldi! At last!"

"I'm so sorry I couldn't make it before, Amy darling," Poldi said in English.

"How do you do, Miss Winehouse," I said when our hostess finally bade me welcome too. "I've read your book."

"I'm now known as Arianna Rizzello," she said in perfect Italian. "But here you can call me Amy. What did you think of it?"

"It's brilliant," I told her, striving to sound as casual as possible.

I might have guessed that my Auntie Poldi and her "firm" had helped Amy to fake her own death and go to ground.

Looking wholly relaxed and unassuming, Amy laughed a lot and treated us to glasses of home-made lemonade from the lemons in her garden.

"How did you find out, Poldi?" she asked.

"I didn't catch on for ages," said Poldi, "but once I'd read the book, all became clear. That was why the masked man stole my address book too. They were all just after you, not the book."

Amy chuckled. "Thank you for saving

me." She turned to me. "She's great, isn't she?"

"Mm." I nodded and just kept staring at her.

She seemed so unreal to me, yet there she sat: a little older, it was true, but as relaxed and easy-going as any next-door neighbour. Like a real person, in fact. I don't know if I would have recognised her in a Sicilian street market despite her numerous tattoos.

Cheerful and light-hearted, she told us that the islanders left her in peace. People sometimes stared at her and spoke to her because of the tattoos, but then she would tell them a touching story: that she had been Amy Winehouse's greatest fan, had wanted to look like her, and had been devastated by Amy's death. Everyone had believed her till now, because without her make-up and wig she passed for a typical Sicilian woman — for Arianna Rizzello from Lentini, in other words.

"It's far less unusual than you think," Poldi whispered to me. "A lot of really famous celebs are often mistaken for look-alikes rather than themselves. Haven't I ever told you about the time I was with Madonna and our car broke down?"

I ignored this and asked Amy for more details of her new life. After holding back for a long time, she told me, she had actually met someone, a chef from San Pietro named Andrea. She could imagine a future with him, possibly even children.

"We'll see," she said quietly, as if loath to awaken a slumbering demon.

She also said that for the first two years after her apparent death, the "firm" had sent her from place to place around the world, more or less at random, so as not to endanger her incognito. But nowhere had appealed to her until her old friend Poldi had suggested Sicily. Hard though it was to believe, Amy had spent a year travelling around the island, unrecognised, before eventually settling in Panarea, to embark on the novel she had for so long dreamt of writing.

"In the end," she said rather sheepishly, "it turned out quite unlike what I originally planned."

"Will you ever publish it?" I asked.

Amy shook her head. "It's just too personal. Even if I published it under a pseudonym, it might blow my cover. I realised that too late, unfortunately."

That saddened me, I must confess. The thought of not publishing a masterpiece! But thanks to my Auntie Poldi, I also realised that publication doesn't always matter. Although only a handful of people had read Amy's book, it would remain a masterpiece forever.

I still had one question, though.

"How did Kigumbe get hold of the manuscript?"

Amy and Poldi exchanged a look.

"Well . . ." said Amy, lingering on the word. "When I heard that Poldi was in certain difficulties in Tanzania, I offered Kigumbe a deal via a middleman. And because Kigumbe is a great fan of mine, he accepted."

"If only I'd known, Amy!" Poldi said, sounding moved to tears and hugging her tight. "You shouldn't have had to do that for me."

On this touching scene, we fade out. Why? Because for reasons of discretion I must refrain from recounting all the wonderful reminiscences, stories and anecdotes Amy told us over lunch, not to mention all the dark sides of show business she had seen. For reasons of discretion, too, the island's name isn't Panarea. It's lovely there all the same, though.

One other thing: Amy's natural modesty and words of encouragement had such an inspirational effect on me, I began to conceive of writing my novel after all.

426

Poldi made me perform my "Valerie" number, and for the first time in my life I didn't find it embarrassing to do such a thing. After the first few bars, Amy and Poldi joined in beside me, and all I thought in my state of euphoria was *parallel universe.*

We intended to catch the afternoon ferry back to Milazzo, so time was running short. Poldi promised to pay Amy a longer visit in the near future. When saying goodbye, she surprised me by asking Amy for a dated autograph.

"Not for me, of course," she said when she saw the look on my face. "It's for Russo, because he's a great Amy fan and I had to promise him one to get him to forget about the Maserati and the whole affair. That's so Arianna can continue to enjoy her peace and quiet."

Shortly after our return, Poldi went off on a kind of honeymoon tour of Italy with Vito Montana. I don't imagine they saw much more of Italy than various darkened bedrooms in romantic hotels or cosy B&Bs, but what do I know? Anyway, I preferred not to picture their jaunt in too much detail. I was simply happy to be able to spend a couple of undisturbed weeks in the Via Baronessa, working on my novel.

"Could you do me a favour?" Poldi asked me just before leaving. "I left a few things at Valérie's in Femminamorta. They need picking up. Would you be a dear?"

Unable to believe my ears, I drove there that same afternoon.

Oscar, the little mongrel, barked a welcome, but no one else seemed to be home. After strolling across the garden, I eventually discovered Valérie in the vegetable plot behind the house. She was crouching down planting tomatoes.

From what Poldi had told me, I had always pictured her as a preternaturally lovely, incredibly ethereal, utterly sexy French beauty of the cinematic type. You know: slender, dainty, pale-faced, pageboy coiffure, Breton shirt, chain-smokes, drinks red wine, reads Sartre. But the real Valérie looked different. Taller than I had imagined, and slim but not fragile — robust, in fact, with muscular arms and long, firmly grounded legs, a physique more than capable of planting tomato seedlings. Her mid-brown hair was loosely gathered into a ponytail, and strands kept falling into her eyes. I felt ever so slightly disappointed.

Just as I cautiously came up behind her, she swore because she'd cut herself on the trowel.

"Can I help?"

She gave a start, then turned and got to her feet.

My disappointment swiftly evaporated, because I now saw how lovely she really was. Everything about her was lovely. Lovely and entirely real. Confronting me was no fantasy figure from my half-baked novel, but a real person. "*Mon dieu,* you startled me!" She brushed a strand of hair out of her eyes — it promptly fell over them again — and stepped out of the tomato bed, holding her gashed right hand.

"Do you, er . . . need a plaster?"

"It's all right."

"I'm the nephew," I said.

I couldn't think of anything smarter to say.

"I thought as much." She paused in front of me, still holding her right hand, then tilted her head to one side and looked at me as if she still had to make up her mind what to think of me.

She had brown eyes with faint shadows of fatigue beneath them. Her nose was a trifle crooked, and I detected some tiny spots on her forehead. I found her quite enchanting.

"How was your trip?"

I thought for a moment.

"I saw a centaur," I said eventually, "and

429

a Cyclops's skull. The dog kept farting, my uncle turned me into a coffee addict, the Maserati blew up, Poldi tried to kill herself, we were shot at and threatened with a cleaver, and I was shit-scared the whole time. It was the best trip I ever went on in my life."

She gave me a broad smile. "I always pictured you as a horn-rimmed tree-hugger, but you actually look quite normal."

Normal. That's always nice to hear.

I shrugged. "Sorry. Is that bad?"

She laughed. "*Mon dieu,* no." She pointed to the vegetable bed. "Can you help me plant the rest of these tomatoes?"

Of course I could. I would have liked nothing better.

We squatted down side by side, planting tomatoes while Etna loomed over us like a strict *padrone* supervising our activities. I dug little holes, and Valérie handed me seedlings and checked whether I'd planted and filled them in properly. I could smell her fragrance — ripe figs and a soupçon of sweat — and sense the warmth she gave off.

After we had planted all the seedlings, she asked if I had a cigarette. When I nonchalantly tried to shake one out of my packet, most of the contents spilled out onto the ground. She laughed again, but heartily, as if it were a good joke, not maliciously, as I hastily scrabbled in the dirt. Her laugh enchanted me too.

When we each had a cigarette at last, I found I'd lost my lighter.

I patted my pockets feverishly. "Sorry."

"I've got one," she said.

Holding the lighter in her left hand and shielding it from the breeze with her cut right hand, she gave me a light. I took the sheltering hand in mine to hold it steady, and that was when it happened. I know how mawkish this sounds, but it really was a *coup de foudre.* I had never experienced anything like it. When our hands met, something seemed to flow from her to me and back again. Something akin to electricity, it created an instant connection, permeated the whole of my body and rendered the sight of Valérie more vivid than ever. It was as if a person you've been missing for ages suddenly materialises right in front of you and whispers, "I am life. Real life. Reality. The here and now. Complicated, to be sure, but magical."

I think I simply stared at Valérie, amazed and bewildered, but I could tell it was the same for her.

"Mon dieu," she said softly.

ABOUT THE AUTHORS

Mario Giordano, the son of Italian immigrants, was born in Munich. *Auntie Poldi and the Sicilian Lions,* his first novel translated into English, was an IndieNext Pick, a B&N Discover Selection, an Amazon Top Ten Best Book of the Month, and a Costco Staff Pick. He lives in Berlin.

John Brownjohn lives in Dorset in the UK. His work has won him critical acclaim and numerous awards on both sides of the Atlantic, including the Schlegel-Tieck Prize (three times), the PEN American Center's Goethe House Prize, and the Helen and Kurt Wolff Prize for Marcel Beyer's *The Karnau Tapes* and Thomas Brussig's *Heroes Like Us.*